YESTERDAY
TODAY
ALWAYS

Melanie Robertson-King

King Park Press

Published by King Park Press
70 Park Street
Brockville, ON
Canada K6V 2G5

ISBN: 978-1-9994257-6-0

DEDICATION

To the men and women who have lost their lives in the pursuit of North Sea oil and gas.

ACKNOWLEDGMENTS

Thanks to everyone who put up with my daft questions during the research of this novel. Without your help, the book would not have come to fruition.

Chris Longmuir, you've been an angel. I've bent your ear more than once asking for help, and sometimes it's been the same questions repeatedly. You've always taken the time to answer them graciously, and offer support.

Huge thanks to my fantastic team of beta-readers, Dorothy Bush and Julie Jordan. Sadly, Julie didn't live to see the book published. You helped with fuzzy logic, when I was at a loss how to rephrase something to eliminate unnecessary repetition. If I've missed any member of my team by name, I apologize.

I'd especially like to thank my husband, Don, who continues to support and encourage me, and provides a shoulder to cry on when things don't go well. He redesigned my website making it mobile-friendly and taken charge on the domestic front giving me time to write.

Prologue

1st December, 2010

The ScotRail service to Aberdeen pulled away from the platform at Stonehaven. The next stop would be his destination. As the train accelerated, the carriage swayed from side to side. The action reminded him of his mum rocking him after a bad dream. He drifted into a light slumber. When the compartment he was in crossed through a switch, it lurched waking him.

Less than thirty minutes to go. He settled back but was too excited to relax. When the Girdle Ness Lighthouse came into view, he knew he was almost back to the place he was born.

New, to him, construction dotted the landscape. Fresh graffiti adorned the stone parapets of the bridge over the River Dee. The Mitchell Tower at Marischal College, the clock tower of the Aberdeen Town House and the Salvation Army Citadel, vied for attention over the tops of the cluster of newer buildings.

He fooled the medical staff at the secure forensic unit in the south of England. After feigning rehabilitation, they released him into the community but he didn't stay there long. He did a runner. He had unfinished business in the north east of Scotland.

Adrenalin coursed through him. Giddy with excitement, it was hard for him to remain calm. He shook his hands to try to stem some of the fidgetiness. Now, he was back in Aberdeen where it all began. How much of the city would he recognize? What changed since his departure?

Were the authorities looking for him yet? He would have to act normal so as not to attract attention. Stepping off, he adjusted his Fedora and strode across the concourse to the exit. Diesel fumes hung in the air and caught in the back of his throat. He coughed.

With the exception of the Union Square shopping complex adjacent to the railway station, Guild Street stayed more or less unchanged. Some of the storefronts in the granite buildings transformed, but overall, not a huge difference since he left.

The pavement ended at Market Street forcing him to cross over the road. He continued eastward. The location he sought should be nearby. He stopped for a breather – pressed his back against the building. The ships that supplied and supported the offshore oil industry occupied the available berths on this side of the harbour. Through a gap, the ferry to Lerwick and the terminal were visible on the far side.

The familiar Maritime Museum dominated the head of Shore Brae. Beyond that, the artery curved and became Shiprow. The cobbled road surface and pavement were difficult to traverse. Even the larger stones nearer the buildings were uneven. When he rounded the corner at Provost Ross's House, another well-known building peeked out. He had come so far now, he couldn't go back. He strode with purpose up the hill.

The Aberdeen Town House clock tower stretched above the roofline but that was the place he sought. Nestled between Henry's Bar and the pedestrianized portion of Shiprow stood the *As the Pages Turn* bookshop.

When a customer exited holding a carrier bag emblazoned with the same signage as over the door, his heart skipped a beat. He hoped the establishment's ownership hadn't changed. That would defeat the purpose of his returning to Aberdeen.

The voices in his head only told him to come back. He had unfinished business with the woman with ginger hair – the one with no soul – who ran the retail outlet in front of him.

Now, to find a suitable place to wait and watch and bide his time until the moment was right.

~ 1 ~

31st December, 2010

He stepped out from the entrance of the Vue Cinemas. One day she would be his. But not today. Now was not the right time. He was not ready. No instructions came from within his brain. The voices hadn't spoken to him yet. Only when they did, would the time be right.

In the month since his arrival, he spent hours at the Central Library searching through the city directories to confirm ownership of *As the Pages Turn*. The business had not changed hands. In addition to those, he perused back issues of The Press and Journal on microfilm for more information about the shop and its owners.

The streets were busy tonight. A group of giggling young women, their skirts too short, and their heels too high, wearing far too much makeup, walked past his hiding place forcing him to retreat further into the shadows. Any one of these girls could be his, but his heart was set on the one with the fiery red tresses. The owner of the bookstore.

Captivated by her beauty, he emerged from the darkness and started across the street, careful not to be seen by the CCTV camera. He crept to the corner of the casino building giving the video surveillance a wide berth.

Back garden fireworks popped and banged. The occasional starbursts of red, green, blue and white rose above the buildings. One, louder than the others made him jump – so nearby it could have been set off beside him. Aberdeen's official display wouldn't start until midnight. The clock, barely visible over the rooftops read fifteen minutes to six.

His threadbare overcoat was useless in this cold, damp night air. He rubbed his hands up and down his upper arms in an attempt to warm himself but the action only provided temporary relief.

He pressed himself against the back wall under the shelter of the roof. He could see her clearer. No one could notice his interest in her.

Oblivious to his presence, she carried on as usual. Just the way he wanted. She couldn't be aware of him. Not now. Not yet. He was the invisible man, skulking in the gloom a short distance from her store. Just beyond her vision. He didn't exist to her, as it had to be for now. But the day would come and she would be the first to know when he was ready to reveal himself.

The loud, drunken, off-key strains of *Auld Lang Syne* echoed through the quiet outlet. Six blokes, in their mid to late twenties judging by their clothing, staggered down Exchequer Row jostling one another as they went. After receiving a shove, one of the early Hogmanay revellers toppled into the large, metal wheelie bin on the pavement sending the object crashing into the granite wall. The impact rattled the shop's windows. The jocular mood changed to anger – singing replaced with shouting.

Katherine Murphy stood primed to pick up the telephone handset and dial nine-nine-nine if things got out of hand. A man in an ill-fitting, worn topcoat and a Fedora pulled down over his face lurked in the shadows of the cinema entryway. Her sightings of him on previous occasions had been on the busier thoroughfares of the city.

Darkness fell around four o'clock that afternoon. Custom had been slow since midday. At five, she dispatched her part-time employee, Melissa Nicholas, to the post office, and to retrieve the chalkboard sign from the tourist information outlet at the intersection of Union and the pedestrianized section of Shiprow.

The mahogany grandfather clock chimed six o'clock. The young woman should have been back by now. Even if the

Royal Mail centre on Castle Street was busy, it did not take that long to walk there, collect the A-frame and come back.

The raucous group scarpered down the cobbles towards the harbour, perhaps scared off by uniformed constables on foot patrol. There would be plenty of cops out tonight because of the parties at the pubs and the fireworks display.

Katherine shrugged on her wine-coloured mac and situated the closed placard in the bookshop's window. All she needed now was her employee and the sign.

When the door opened, jingling the Victorian shopkeeper's bell above, a blast of damp, icy air followed.

Melissa, excitable at little things, piped up, "This new chalkboard advert is heavy, Miss K. I could barely carry the thing."

"Perhaps that will deter thieves from nicking it."

"You think? Lucky for me this nice bloke offered to help me."

"Where do you want me to put it?" he asked.

That voice. Although it had been years, she knew it as well as her own. It burned through her. Was her mind going? She stopped digging in her handbag for her keys. "J-Jared?"

"Kat?"

She nodded. It had been so long since she saw him and even then, long after their romance. Her body flooded with those familiar tingling sensations she got when she was with him.

"You two know each other?" Melissa asked, her bright, blue eyes widening behind her tortoiseshell, cat's eye glasses under her blonde fringe. "Cool. Well if nothing else, I'm off now. Meeting some friends for a drink."

"You go on ahead. I'll see you after the Bank Holiday."

The young girl turned to the door, revealing the neon pink and orange streaks in her hair beneath her ponytail. "That creepazoid is out there again. I seen him when we came down Shiprow. He's hiding over the road."

There in the shadows, skulked the man Melissa mentioned. A chill ran down Kat's spine. "He must have just moved there. He was in front of the cinema earlier."

"You want me to move him on?" Jared asked.

"No. He's harmless. Just a homeless person. He usually hangs out on Union Street or near the Bon Accord and St Nicholas shopping complex. Not lucrative enough up there so my best guess is he decided to try another location. Mind you, I would have thought closer to the casino would be better than down at this end."

"I don't want to leave by myself," the teenaged girl said. "That guy scares me."

"Which way you goin'?"

"The Illicit Still."

"I'll walk you back up Shiprow to Union then you're on your own." He turned to Kat. "Bolt up behind me."

"And be on time," she called after her employee even though that part of their conversation had long since ended.

She locked the door. Melissa's imagination running riot frightened her, too. While she awaited his return, the unfortunate man went back to his spot at the movie theatre.

When Katherine opened the door to let her friend from the past in, he asked, "Your admirer gone?"

"Back to the cinema. That was the last place I saw him ... and what do you mean my admirer?" If that man was one of them, seeking her attention to get to know her, he was going about it all wrong.

Jared raked his hand through his dark brown hair. "A drink isn't a bad idea. Come on, let me buy you one. I saw a pub next door."

"B-but, I have to go to the bank with today's takings," Katherine hesitated. "Such as they are." She hoped he didn't hear.

"Take them in the morning and deposit them through the hole in the wall."

"Could do." Back in the day, he could be persuasive and still possessed the ability. She removed the envelope containing the paper notes from her bag and locked them in the vault in the office.

When she re-entered, she took a cursory glance around the retail space before she switched off the lights and turned on the night ones. At the door, she punched the code into the alarm then hastened him out ahead of her.

While Katherine fumbled with her key, the handsome man's steely blue eyes bored through her. A bead of sweat formed at the base of her skull and slowly trickled down her back. She became cotton-mouthed. No longer a silly teenager, why did he still have this effect on her after all this time?

When she finally managed to keep her hand steady enough to insert the key and turn it, he spun her around and mashed his mouth on hers. His tongue teased her lips open and he pulled her to him. Her pulse quickened and she let herself melt into his strong arms, those years apart, non-existent.

"If we don't soon go for that drink, I won't be responsible for my actions." His voice was husky.

At that particular moment, Katherine wanted time to stand still. Pressed against him was a place she could spend the rest of her life. She nuzzled her head into the hollow at the crook of his neck and hugged him tighter. He caressed her forehead before disentangling himself from her grip and wrapped his arm around her.

The tang of the salty North Sea and fumes from the ships in the harbour lingered in the heavy air. Those smells, while powerful, couldn't mask the seductive aroma of men's cologne. When they dated before, he wore Hugo. Was he wearing that now? Held next to his muscular body and inhaling his scent, Katherine lost her balance and toppled into him when one of her stiletto heels slipped into a crack between the cobbles. Despite the streetlights, shadows formed. The gaps between fixtures were dark. No wonder she twisted her ankle.

"Are you all right?"

"Just a bit clumsy. You would never know I walk this street every day in these boots. I feel like an arse." Her cheeks burned from the heat of her blush.

He emerged from the shadows and leaned on the wall of the cinema. This man who kissed her was so cocksure of himself. That man would be removed from her life. She was his and only his, for the taking. The fiery red haired beauty would not be stolen from him. She belonged to him. Of that, she could be assured.

More people appeared on the street and he slinked back into the darkness to remain invisible.

The pub was crowded. People mingled over after work drinks. Music blared from the speakers.

He tapped her shoulder. "You go grab the booth back there in the corner. I'll get them in. What'll you have?"

"Gin and tonic, please."

The floor was sticky in patches under her feet from spilled spirits, mixes and beer. Tonight because the place was full, the smell of ale, faint scent of juniper, combined with assorted body odours, colognes and perfumes was overpowering.

When she got to the seats he pointed out, she chose the far side so she could people watch. But he was the only person with whom she had any interest. His snug fitting, faded jeans accentuated the muscles in his thighs. Man he was fit. Sexy, too, leaning against the bar. He turned, smiled and winked at her and her cheeks got hot. Katherine knew she was blushing but couldn't help herself and she couldn't stop staring at him either.

Melissa's comment about the homeless man scaring her played on her mind. When she encountered him in other parts of Aberdeen, she never paid much attention. Now, he was on her street, hanging out around her store. Business was already down these past six months. That was enough cause for concern.

He sat Katherine's G&T on the cardboard beer mat on the table and eased on the bench across from her. Leaning back, he stretched out his legs, bumping her foot in the process. "Sorry," he responded before taking a slug of his Caledonian 80.

"I-I can't believe I'm sitting here with you. After all these years." Katherine raised her glass but her hand trembled. She had to steady it with both hands.

"I know what you mean." He removed the old-fashioned from her grasp and sat it on the table. He held her hands in his, stroking them with this thumbs. "That day you walked away from me, I didn't think I would ever see you again."

"I didn't go by choice."

"I know. I'll never forget the look on your face when your father yanked you out of my arms at the security checkpoint at the airport."

"Why didn't you stop him?"

"My life was a mess back then. You know that. I wish I had but you would have grown to resent what you gave up or worse, I would have been done for assault."

From the moment her mother and father discovered her relationship with Jared, they were determined he was not good enough for their little girl; her father especially. "I despised them for taking me away from you. I hated Canada. The first chance I got I came back. And then I found you with her. I was back for a while but not seen you. I even went to where you lived when we first met and they told me you moved. What was I to think?"

The wail of a siren pierced the din in the pub. As he turned, the sparkle of a diamond flashed. Katherine brushed his hair away from his left lobe. "You're still wearing that?"

"Been there since the day you deserted me at the airport."

Reaching up, she pulled back her long, copper tresses and revealed the mate to the earring he wore in her upper ear. "Got this piercing after we moved to Canada. First thing I did when I got on my own. One of my many acts of defiance. Believe it or not, I was more of a rebel there than I was before they dragged me off kicking and screaming."

He chuckled at her statement, leaned forward and ran his fingers up and down his glass wiping away the condensation. The action made Katherine wish she were the one he was stroking. She squirmed in her seat. Her parents ruined everything when they took her away.

"As soon as I came back I went to your old place so we could pick up where we left off but the people wouldn't tell me where you were."

"Didn't know that. Guess I started working on the rigs a couple of months after you went. I moved closer to the airport to make a shorter commute." He took hold of her hands and stroked the backs of them with his thumbs. "Truth be told, I didn't expect you to come back. I figured you'd find some guy there about your own age and it would be the end of us."

"Five years isn't a huge difference."

"Your parents sure thought different. Good thing you were sixteen or they would have had my arse thrown in jail."

She smiled. "Don't forget. We got together before that. So yeah, glad they didn't. I would have had to spend those nights at Steph's for real, rather than with you."

"I forgot about that." He hoisted his glass and drained it.

"B-but I thought we were over when I finally saw you after our grad party. You appeared so cozy with that girl."

"Oh her. A mistake. One of the lads on the rig set me up with her. I hoped once I saw you that night, we would have a chance."

"And I thought we didn't because I assumed you were having a good time with her all cuddled together."

"What about you? I could say the same. You looked pretty happy, yourself, with that guy."

"I was. I didn't expect to see you there. You don't know how jealous I was. I guess I got involved with Colin seriously to get my own back at you."

"I never meant to hurt you. Never stopped thinking about you and our time together."

A tear fell from Katherine's eye. Before she could swipe at it, he brushed the droplet away with his thumb. "Tell me, please. I want to know why you're so sad."

She gulped back a sob and answered. "Not long after we got the bookstore, not even married more than a minute – after seeing you and … her, thought we were over. Colin was a nice bloke so when he asked, I said yes. Anyway, we got the chance to buy the place."

"And?"

"He was killed in the London bombings. He went on a book buying trip and didn't come home. He was at King's Cross to catch his train to Aberdeen." She pulled a gold chain out from under her layers of clothing and toyed with the wedding ring dangling from it. "This is all I have left of him." By now, Katherine sobbed uncontrollably.

"I'm so sorry. I had no idea and had no intentions of hurting you." He eased around the end of the booth and gathered her in his arms. "Finish your drink and we'll leave. Take you somewhere and cheer you up."

Outdoors, she began to feel better. The fresh air helped clear her head of the unpleasant memories of her past. "Let's go back to mine," she suggested feeling brazen thanks to being with him again and her passion for him returning. "It's not far. Just over the bookshop." She took his hand and led the way.

Once inside, Katherine shivered with anticipation. The fire in her lower belly intensified. Jared leaned her against the door and fixed his lips on hers as he unbuttoned her mac and nudged the garment down. It landed in a heap on the floor. His tongue found its way into her mouth and she embraced him back. He cupped her breasts and squeezed.

Her heart raced. She tugged at his leather bomber jacket. He released his grip and she yanked the sleeves past his hands. The heavy piece of outerwear fell with a thud. One by one, the buttons of her blouse opened. The combination of his touch and the coolness of the air made her nipples tighten. His fingers found their way inside her lace bra and he flicked his thumbs over the hardened mounds.

Katherine unbuckled his belt and undid the button of his jeans. Rolling the stretchy cotton T-shirt up his firm body aroused her more. He stopped kissing her long enough to haul it off over his head and toss it with their other discarded clothing. While he did that, she removed her top. With the exception of her bra, they were both topless. She snuggled closer and drank in the heat from his naked flesh. "Mmm," she moaned.

His light touch as he grazed her torso brought her out in goose bumps. He clutched the cheeks of her bum and ground her pelvis into his throbbing erection. Kat jumped up and wrapped her legs around him. With their lips locked together, she placed her hands on the sides of his face and explored his mouth with her tongue.

After bumping into furniture and bouncing off walls and door frames, they made their way into the bedroom where he laid her on the king-size bed. He kicked his boots off then put his knee between her thighs, crawled across the mattress, and stretched out beside her. So much time had passed since their last sexual encounter, she sighed in anticipation.

Again, he brushed his fingertips against her flesh, this time starting at the corner of her mouth, over her jaw, down her neck, and body to her skinny jeans. Eyes closed, she waited.

He tried to walk his fingers down her stomach under her denims but they were too tight. Button unfastened, zipper slid down, he struggled again to reach her most intimate place. She raised her hips and tugged at them but he didn't have enough room to work his hand inside. He crawled off the bed, planting kisses on her in the same places.

Her burgundy, knee high suede, stiletto boots zipped at the ankle. She picked up her foot helping him. One boot came off and struck the floor followed by the other. Kat's lips dried and she licked them. Delicious feelings coursed through her body. His hands were on the top of her trousers again. She shifted her bum and the fabric rolled away from her skin.

Hovering over her, he traced his tongue from her matching thong to her breasts. He slipped the sexy undergarment out of the way and took the fleshy mound into his mouth, and flicked her nipple. Fingers entwined in his hair, she held his head entrapping him in her grasp. Her breathing quickened. The fire in her lower belly was now an inferno.

He rolled and pulled her over on her side facing him. His hand worked its way to the waistband of her underwear. She twisted the other way with her back to him and wrapped her leg over his thigh. When his hand grazed her over the lacy surface of her thong, she quivered. Within seconds, his digits were on her naked flesh moving lower. She placed her hand on the back of his and chewed her bottom lip to keep from screaming in ecstasy when the time came.

His middle finger touched her sweet spot and she moaned, "I love you, Colin."

Stunned by the name she called him, he froze. Where did that come from? Scrambling off the bed, he raked his hand through his hair. Unable to look at her, he raced out of the bedroom in search of his white T-shirt and bomber jacket. He found his shirt in a crumpled pile by the end of the black leather sofa. While he turned the piece of discarded clothing right-side out, she entered the room tying her short, plum coloured, satin dressing gown around her. In spite of his anger, he couldn't take his eyes off her. She was so beautiful standing there with her long slim legs exposed.

"What's wrong?"

"You don't know?"

Katherine shook her head and stroked his upper arm.

"I love you, Colin, ring any bells?"

"Oh my God. I apologize." She wrapped her arms around his waist and rested her forehead against his smooth chest.

Reaching behind his back, he took hold of her wrists, extricated himself from her embrace, and pulled his T-shirt over his head. "You really know how to make a guy feel good about what he's doing to you. You were gagging for a shag and I was gonna oblige until you called me by his name." He bent down to pick up his coat. "There were three people in the bedroom – you, me, and your dead husband. As far as I'm concerned one too many. I don't do threesomes."

"Just he's the last man I've been intimate with." She whimpered, stared at the floor, and fiddled with the tie belt.

"The London bombings were over five years ago. Time to move on. That is, unless you don't want to." Fueled by anger, he retrieved his jacket and stormed out the door, slamming it behind him just as something heavy crashed against the other side.

Still raging, he punched the cement wall of the casino building across the street from her home. Afterwards he turned around hoping no one saw. Katherine stood in the first floor window. The room where she called him by another man's name. She puffed on the glass and wrote *I'm sorry* in the mist.

The first drops of rain, splatted on the pavements. He jammed his hands into his pockets and jogged towards the railway station before the skies opened up.

When he arrived, an Inverness-bound train waited. He boarded and sank into one of the seats near the doors since his destination was the first stop.

His hand throbbed. His knuckles were bloodied and bleeding. Extending his arm, he flexed his fingers. In the light streaming in the window, he noticed the bruising had started.

She rejected him. Her body remained chaste. His to own, command, devour. His lips curled into a smile. Mr. Cocksure was not so much now after being knocked back. He knew the sting of rejection. This woman was different. She would worship him and the ground he walked on. She would do anything and everything to please him. Still, the time had to be right to make his move. She must not know his intentions until he was ready to reveal them to her.

Katherine fumbled through her large handbag for her phone. When she finally found it, she tapped out a text message to Stephanie.

Can u come? Important.

While waiting for a reply, she walked to the bedroom and put on her jeans.

Her friend's response awaited.

Sounds like wine needed. B there soon.

Dropping on the sofa, Katherine held her BlackBerry Z10 between her knees hoping he would call her. Impossible because he didn't know her number. She fell over sideways, still gripping the device in the same position.

Of all the times to think of her late husband – when she was about to make love to the man who showed her sex could be a beautiful thing. She was not a virgin when she connected with the man who stole her heart. She had lost her virginity at fourteen with her then boyfriend. The experience was awkward, painful, and completely unpleasant.

Then Jared came into her life. They were in HMV looking at CDs and she backed into him, bringing a stiletto heel down on his instep. He laughed at the time, which mortified her even more and she dashed out of the store, her face crimson with embarrassment. Just the memory of their first meeting made her blush now. Periodically, he mentioned the subject as if the event occurred only a few hours ago.

He was older and had his own place ... well, a room on the upper floor of a house on Castlehill. Sex with him was so different from her first encounter. Her grades slipped because she did not study. She even lied to her parents saying she was sleeping over at Steph's when she was, in fact, spending the night with him.

By the time he arrived at Dyce, Jared calmed down. Knowing he overreacted to her calling him Colin, didn't make him feel any better. The pain had grown steadily worse; his hand more swollen and his knuckles throbbed in time with his pulse.

He struggled to remove the fob from his right front, jeans pocket. When he succeeded, he pressed the button and released the locks. The lights on his black BMW 330 coupe blinked. He didn't remember parking that far from the shelter. The car park at the station was nearly empty now. He turned the key in the ignition and the powerful engine roared to life.

Easing out on the road, he started for Newburgh. If only Kat's parents could see him now ... good job, fancy motor, homeowner. Not anything like the lad they ripped their daughter away from. He needed to apologize to her and hoped she would accept. Those harsh words spilled out before he got his temper under control.

After a stop at the convenience store and off-licence for supplies in Newburgh, he pulled up on School Road outside his house. A magazine wrapped in poly film protruded from the mail slot in the front door preventing the flap from closing. He yanked the periodical out and tucked it beneath his arm before entering. Having only one good hand was awkward enough. The debility was compounded by holding a carrier bag containing medication, a small package of frozen peas, and a few tins of lager.

Once inside, he strode to the kitchen and put his packages on the counter. There was a telephone directory somewhere in one of the drawers. He tugged them open one by one until he finally found it. He planned to call Katherine and apologize.

What name did she go by? All he was certain of was she lived over the specialty store on Exchequer Row in Aberdeen. If she didn't have a landline, he was screwed. He didn't have her mobile number. His knowledge went no further.

Flowers. He could order an arrangement and have them delivered to her at the shop. But he was still in the same mess. Couldn't remember the name of the place. He cursed under his breath.

He could deliver the blooms, not just any, but roses and lots of them, the next day and ask her to forgive him for being an ass. That wouldn't work either. The stores would be closed for the New Year Bank Holiday.

The lights in her bedroom stayed on. He willed her to reappear so he could savour her beauty. Instead, the room plunged into darkness. Damn. Disappointment washed over him.

When a woman the approximate size as his red-haired shopkeeper stopped in front of the downstairs door, he stepped out of the murkiness. She held a cloth carrier bag in one hand, her handbag strap crossing her body on the diagonal. A beanie hat with a pompom hid her hair colour. Who was she and why tonight? The timing was wrong – too soon for him to make his move.

If she had a guest, who knew when he would see her again. Her with those long, slender legs that disappeared under the hem of her short, burgundy dressing gown. He yearned to touch them. Caress them. Kiss them. Make love to this gorgeous woman. He would be tender, sweet and loving until the voices told him to destroy her.

His hand fingered the handle of his flick-knife in his topcoat. He grinned and looked forward to mutilating her with its sharpness. So many options to choose from. He could slash her perfect face, slit her throat or stab her. He could be the last man she was intimate with. When he was done, she would be ruined for any who followed. Or she might be dead.

The idea of sex with her made him hard with desire. He disappeared into the shadows again, faced into the corner, pulled down his zipper and seized his erection. He braced himself in position with his left arm. He imagined her lips surrounding it and drawing his organ deep within her. Turned on more by the thought, he wanked harder. When his release came, his legs weakened. He wanted to scream but couldn't be apprehended with his pants down. He chomped on the inside of his mouth until he finished.

Tears pricked her eyes as memories of her past with her former love rushed back. After today's debacle, she was certain there would not be a future with him. Thinking she had ruined any chance of happiness with him, scorching rivulets streamed down her cheeks and she bawled.

The intercom buzzed shocking Katherine back to reality. "Come on up, Steph," she answered not giving the person who rang an opportunity to speak and opened the door before flopping back on the couch.

"What are you doing leaving the door open. I could have been anyone. You know the cops are searching for a rapist." Stephanie held up a carrier bag. "Two red. That should get us through the rest of the evening." The bottles clinked together as she rushed through the flat to the kitchen.

Katherine lingered on the sofa, numb with grief. In a few moments, a glass of Merlot was handed to her and her friend sat down beside her.

"So what has you in such a state?"

"Oh God, how could I have been so stupid."

"Take a sip and tell me what you're on about."

17

Taking a mouthful, Katherine started. "You remember Jared."

"Not the one you were with when you and your family moved away?"

"Yup, him."

"You can't just leave me hanging. Spill girlfriend."

"Well, I sent Melissa to the post office and to pick up the chalkboard sign when we were getting ready to shut for the day. Who does she come back with, lugging it for her? Him." She paused and took another sip.

"He asked me to go for a drink with him and I agreed. We caught up – more or less. I told him I thought he and me were over when I saw him with that girl in the pub – the very first time I laid eyes on him after coming home. He said one of the guys on the rig fixed him up with her and it was a mistake. About marrying Colin and him being killed."

"He works offshore? He'll be well off. Loads of dosh."

"After our drink, we came back here and we were … we were … and I blew it. I called him C-Colin." Katherine blubbered. "He-he stormed out of here and I'll never see him again."

Stephanie set her glass down on the coffee table and took Katherine's away from her. Wrapping her arms around her, she hugged then stroked her friend's back, and soothed her. "You don't know it's the end between you two. Let him cool off and have a think. If I remember, he did have a temper."

Katherine sniffled and wiped her nose on the back of her hand.

"You always were the ultimate in class, m'dear," Stephanie covered her mouth with her hand and giggled.

Jared opened the fridge and pulled out a tin of lager. Holding the can in his good hand, he snatched up the Paracetamol bottle with his other and strolled to the lounge. If Kat forgave him – that was a big if – he would have to control his anger.

He sank into his leather recliner and leaned back. He held the drink between his thighs, pulled the ring tab on the can, and wrestled the pills open. He popped two in his mouth and chased them down with a mouthful of beer. He forgot the peas on the worktop in the other room. He couldn't remember who told him about using them. Someone on the rig? Something his mother used when his father came home drunk, bruised and bloody? That was a memory he could do without.

Struggling back out of his chair, he grimaced then sauntered to the kitchen. Condensation had already formed on the exterior of the package. He snagged the tea towel hanging on the Aga's rail.

Comfortable again, he wrapped the bag in the cloth and laid the compress over his hand. A few seconds later, the cold seeped through and the discomfort eased. He picked up the remote control and turned on his television and satellite receiver. He flipped through the channels, stopping on Sky Sports and a Scottish Premier League game in progress.

His eyes grew heavier the longer he watched. His knuckles stopped throbbing. At first, he fought to prevent dozing off but eventually slumber won out.

~ 2 ~

1st January, 2011

No signs of life showed in the windows above the store. Why was she not out of bed by now? Was she still sleeping? Did the woman with the carrier bag sleep over? Damn, these bloody, interfering people. First, Mr. Cocksure got in his way – now someone else. Those two needed to keep away from her. They would only put bad ideas in her head. Turn her against him. That would never do. If they succeeded, he would deal with them, too.

A curtain twitched. His heart leapt with excitement. Soon, the drapes were open. She stood in the space between them. Most redheads couldn't wear burgundy, but she could. Her fiery coloured hair didn't clash with the shade of her short, shiny dressing gown. The slightest bit of bare leg showed between the hemline and the sill. She raised her arms and stretched. When she did her robe slid tantalizingly higher up her thighs, exposing even more of those long, shapely legs.

He stepped out from the shadows hoping for a better look. When he did, she turned and walked away. At that instant he hated her. Why did she do that? He wanted to look at her. Drink in her beauty. And now she disappeared. Unless she went out later in the day, he wouldn't see her, or would have to content himself with glimpses of her as she went about her daily routine.

Jared woke with a start. His knuckles throbbed and his head pounded in time with the spasms in his hand. Groggy, it took him a few moments to figure out his location. This was his room. He came upstairs at some point. But when? After returning home, he sat in the recliner with a bag of frozen peas on one hand and a tin of lager in the other.

In addition to the aching in his hand, the loud banging roused him even further from his fog. When the haze cleared, he knew someone was at the front door. He pulled on a pair of flannel sleep pants, grimacing when the effort shot burning pains all the way to his fingertips. His white T-shirt lay in a wad on the chair. He scooped up the round-neck.

"Yeah, yeah, keep your hair on," he said as he came down the stairs turning the garment right side out. A searing pain radiated through his head making him regret talking. Hogmanay after he got away from Kat's place must have been decent.

He was pulling his T-shirt over his head as he opened the door. Two uniformed cops stood there. Wracking his brain, he didn't recall doing anything the night before that warranted a visit from the constabulary today.

"Sergeant McIntosh, Grampian Police," the man in uniform said. "This is Constable Pirie." He introduced his female colleague. "Are you Jared Martin?"

"Yeah, who wants to know?"

"May we come in?"

The WPC's face was red and she dropped her gaze.

He ushered them inside then poked his head out through the opening. At least the local gossip-mongers were indoors and not out gawping and pointing. The street was deserted. After closing the door, he guided them to the lounge.

The frozen peas and towel lay in a soggy mess on the carpet next to his black leather, reclining chair. An empty lager tin sat on the side table next to the bottle of Paracetamol. More spent cans littered the floor. He couldn't remember much of the previous night after he stormed way from Kat's apartment in Aberdeen.

"Sit down. I'll be right with you. Need to go to the toilet."

He took advantage of being out of the room away from his visitors and tugged on a pair of jeans and a denim shirt. The expression on her face when he opened the door in a state of undress made him smile.

When he returned to the lounge, his guests had taken seats on the sofa. "Rough night?" Sergeant McIntosh asked, nodding to the debris. "Your hand is bleeding. Been in a fight?"

Unaware his knuckles were split open again until the cop mentioned it, he checked his hand. Blood oozed from the wounds and trickled down his fingers. He grabbed the cloth he swaddled the bag in and wrapped his hand before sitting down in the recliner. "Took on a stone wall and it won." Embarrassed by his actions the night before, he mumbled his explanation.

"Mr. Martin," Constable Pirie began, "Did you live at 48 Wath Road, Wombwell, Barnsley?"

The mere mention of his former home struck fear in his heart. He escaped there for good at the first opportunity. Why were Grampian Police asking about his childhood home? Beads of sweat formed on his forehead. Bile rose in his throat. He swallowed hard before answering. "Yeah, why?"

"The South Yorkshire Constabulary have been looking for you. You're a difficult man to track down. They enlisted our help when they finally discovered you lived in our jurisdiction."

"Not stayed in that dump in twenty years. What do you need me for?"

"There has been a fire at the residence."

"So? The place could burn to the ground for all I care. Hated the place. Still do."

Sergeant McIntosh broke into the conversation. "A body was discovered in the ruins. Registry office records show the last known owner of the property was a Louis Martin. Your father, I believe?"

WPC Pirie scribbled something in her notebook.

He stood and paced around the lounge. "Still don't know what it has to do with me. Not clapped eyes on the bastard since I left home."

"You're the next of kin. We had to notify you as such. Also, South Yorkshire Police need you to come and identify the body."

"They want me to what?" Freezing in his tracks, the outrageousness of their question overwhelmed him. He glared at the cops. "Are you kidding?"

"No, Mr. Martin. We're quite serious."

Shaking his head, he started pacing again. The detachment headquartered in Barnsley must still have records of the all too frequent calls they made to the house. The neighbours to the right and probably even those across the laneway made many complaints about noise and fights.

"If your father is the one lying in the morgue, you're the surviving heir; therefore, your inheritance."

"I bloody well don't want a fucking thing from him or the estate. Think you should leave."

The uniformed pair rose from their seats. "If you change your mind, you can contact us," Constable Pirie said, handing him a business card.

"Cold day in hell before that happens."

"We'll see ourselves out," Sergeant McIntosh stated, nodding to his partner.

Unbeknownst to him, his fists were clenched and his body rigid. He didn't relax until after the front door latched behind them.

"He's not telling us something," the senior officer said as he eased behind the wheel of the patrol car.

"I agree." WPC Pirie removed her hat as she entered the vehicle. "I noticed some nasty scars on his forearm between his wrists and his rolled up sleeves."

"Theory?"

"Well, he's adamant he wants nothing to do with the place. Left at the first chance. I think he grew up in an abusive home," she said, fastening her seatbelt.

"Most astute. You have keen observational skills," he said, firing the engine. "Mother or father or both?"

"In many cases, the father is the abuser and he pounds on the entire family. The mother usually keeps strum, perceiving if she complains things will get much worse and she'll bear the brunt of the violent outbursts."

"You speak like you have personal experience in this area? Were you abused as a child?"

She didn't answer but turned her face to the window.

Her reaction told him everything he needed to know and more. Instead of pursuing things any further, he put the car in gear and pulled away from the kerb.

A call over the radio ended their conversation. Sergeant McIntosh flipped on the lights and siren and drove off at speed. One day he would discover his colleague's secret, but not today.

Alone in the house, Jared fumed. Picked up one of his empty lager tins and flung the can at the fireplace. In less than twenty-four hours, he morphed into his father. When Kat called him Colin and now thanks to the visit from the cops. Over the years, he spent too much time trying to forget Barnsley and now it had been chucked back in his face. His father's anger. Life after the pit shut down in 1984 became a living hell, as if it weren't bad enough before.

Since the day she stomped on his instep in an HMV store, he loved her. Would never hurt her for the world but did by storming out. But, her calling him by her deceased husband's name? At least he punched a cement wall and not her. How long before he caused her bodily harm? He couldn't bear that.

Remnants of his night in the lounge gathered, he took them to the kitchen, tossed the six empties into the recycling, the bag of thawed peas in the bin, and the bloody tea towel in the wash machine.

After the way he acted, he needed to make amends. He would call her later. How could he do that? He didn't have her telephone number. What was the name of her business? No matter, the place wouldn't be open and likely not until the following Wednesday with the way the Bank Holiday fell. He could drive to her place. An apology would be better done in person, face to face, instead of over the phone.

He shook out two pills from the plastic container and swallowed them dry before returning the jar to the worktop so he wouldn't forget the medication when he left for Aberdeen.

Thirty minutes later, his morning ablutions completed, he was ready to face the day. The back of his hand, save for the wounded knuckles had bruised to a dark blue-purple. The white of the cartilage in his middle knuckle visible through the tears in his skin. He clenched and unclenched his hand but the pain too much to make a complete fist.

He plucked his worn, brown leather bomber jacket off the hook by the back door and shrugged into it, and slipped the bottle of Paracetamol into the inside breast compartment. Jared scooped his keys from the island as he went, and headed out the door.

While he prepared for the trip, the haar had moved in. This didn't occur until later in the year but the North Sea had stayed warmer than normal. Now, it was so foggy he could barely see his car parked on the street outside his house, let alone the shrubs and stone wall on the other side. His usual thirty minute drive into the city, barring accidents and roadworks, would stretch to almost an hour if the rest of the area was as socked in as this.

A black BMW pulled up in front of the business. Mr. Cocksure exited. The security of the cinema entryway provided him with the perfect hiding place. No. No. This is not how it was supposed to play out. She knocked him back last night. He paced in the alcove keeping tight to the building to prevent the red-haired woman's visitor seeing him and begged the voices for advice. How could he deal with his adversary, but they didn't answer.

The man was agitated. Would that work to his advantage? Possibly, if not for the CCTV camera mounted nearby, and the time of day. He fingered the flick-knife in his pocket.

After parking outside Kat's premises, he strode to the door they used the previous night and rapped. No response so he knocked harder. "Kat," he called as he pounded with his fist. Pressed the intercom and still nothing.

When no footfalls sounded on the stairs, he walked to the other end of the structure and tried that door with the same result. Looking up, the telephone number on the shop's signage stood out like a neon sign. He pulled out his HTC android phone and punched in the numerical sequence, unsure if she would hear the ringing upstairs.

After ten rings, he was about to disconnect when Kat's voice came on the line. "Hi. You've reached *As the Pages Turn*. I'm sorry but we're busy and can't take your call, but please leave your name, number and a brief message and we'll ring you back as soon as possible."

"Jared here. I need to speak to you … about … about last night," he said to the answerphone and stuffed his mobile back into his jacket. He returned to his car and as he was about to pull on the latch, the outer door creaked.

Not wanting to appear desperate or needy, he lingered beside the vehicle his fingers grazing the handle. Something wet and sticky oozed down his extremities. Blimey, his knuckles split open again. The idea of a trip to A&E on a bank holiday didn't appeal to him. Wait times were long enough on a regular day.

"I didn't expect to see you today. Truth is, I didn't think I would ever see you again," she said, folding her arms across her chest and leaning against the doorframe.

"Couldn't leave things the way they ended."

"Well, then you better come up." She pushed the door open.

Striding to the entrance, he motioned for her to go in first. It was cold and she was not dressed for outdoors. Trying to figure out if she had anything on underneath, his imagination ran riot.

When he turned to lock his car and set the alarm, he noticed the homeless man on the street by the cinema. Shaking his head, he followed her up the stairs, struggling to keep his hands off her body.

She was so sexy and sure of herself the way she stood in the doorway, her leg exposed by the opening of her long white, dressing gown. Her hair appeared wet like she just stepped out of the shower. Although he preferred seeing her in the skimpy, burgundy one, this one was more practical. She looked pure in this colour. Virginal. She must remain chaste. Mustn't give herself to anyone but him. But, how could he prevent it from happening short of kidnapping her? That would arouse suspicion and create too many unwanted questions.

Watching Mr. Cocksure enter her residence yet again made him bitter. No, furious. He should be the one going in. Not that man. How could he stop them from spending time with each other? She cheated on him by seeing this other man. Just because she knocked him back the previous night didn't mean she would again today.

He toyed with the handle of his flick-knife. Knowing he had a weapon soothed him. Which one would he use the blade on first? Her because of her cheating? Him because he ruined her? Sullied her. Made her dirty. He gripped the piece of bone and cursed.

When the door locked, Jared clasped Kat's hands. "Will you forgive me? I behaved like an ass. I'd never do anything to hurt you."

"You did." She paused then continued, "but you're forgiven."

He gave her hand a gentle squeeze then grimaced.

"Results of your temper tantrum? What a mess. You better let me look after it. Come on. Those knuckles need a good cleaning before they become any more infected than they already are."

She indicated the way to the bathroom. Since he walked through her front door, a nervous but excited sensation washed over her. Regardless of having a previous life with the man now in her home, one she so wanted, she remained unable to bring herself out of the past she had with Colin.

Pulling items out of the medicine chest and the vanity drawers, Katherine took stock of what she had on hand and assembled the supplies on the counter. "Sit down." She nodded to the toilet. "Now let's take a good look at this mess."

When she took his hand he flinched. "Well, you really did a number on yourself when you punched the casino façade," she mused as she inspected his knuckles.

"You saw?"

"I stood in the bedroom window and watched you."

"Feel even more like a daft prick now, knowing you saw me do it. I knew you were there, but after not before."

"Better it than me. I wouldn't have been so quick to forgive if that were the case."

She removed one of the cotton wool pads she used for removing her eye makeup from the package, and poured on some antiseptic. Kat pulled his hand over the sink then dabbed the wet fabric on his wounds.

"Ouch." He yanked his hand out of her grip. "What the fuck is that stuff? Feels like you're pouring acid in there. It fucking hurts."

"Oh don't be such a big baby. You didn't make this much of a fuss when you punched the wall in the first place."

"Yeah, I know."

He held his hand out again and she resumed cleaning the cuts. "You really should have gone to A&E. I think there's at least one broken bone in your hand."

"On a bank holiday? I would still be sat there this time next year."

When the injuries were cleaned to her satisfaction, she applied some antibiotic ointment and covered each knuckle with an adhesive wound dressing. Task finished, she gathered up the bloody bits of cotton she had dropped in the basin and tossed them in the small waste basket next to the vanity. "Want a coffee?"

"Sure, why not."

While Katherine searched for mugs in the upper cabinet beside the sink, he leaned against the worktop. "You want the eejit or numpty one?"

After his temper fit last night, either one suited him – even better than the daft prick he referred to himself earlier. He flexed the fingers on his injured hand. He needed to tell her about his early morning visit from Grampian's finest, despite being certain she wouldn't be interested.

"Still take yours black?"

"Yes," he answered, surprised yet pleased she remembered something so minor all these years.

"Go sit down and I'll bring it over." She pointed to the small bistro sized table.

When he sat, he took the chair next to the wall so he could watch her. "Got something to tell you."

"I think this is more you." She placed the numpty emblazoned mug in front of him. "What you did was stupid but not quite on the eejit scale. That would be me calling you by my hus ...." She stopped in mid-word.

With his good hand, he reached over the table and took hers. "You're not an idiot. I am."

She blushed and bowed her head. For a few minutes they sat not saying a word. Katherine fidgeted with her mug, running her fingers up and down the handle.

"So what did you want to tell me?" she asked bringing the awkward silence to an end.

"I had a visit from the coppers earlier this morning."

"Because of last night?" Her eyes opened wide as she spoke.

"I wish." Looking down at his bandaged hand, he walked across the room.

"What is it?" Within seconds, she stood at his side rubbing her hand up and down his arm.

"A fire in Barnsley at the house I grew up in," he said, his voice devoid of emotion.

"More to it, though, isn't there." She grasped him with her free hand while continuing to stroke with the other.

"If you count finding a body in the house and they think it could be my old man, then yeah, more to it." His temper rose but not to the surface. It simmered, ready to explode at any moment. He raked his injured fingers through his hair.

"So you're going home to Barnsley?" She rested her head on his upper arm.

He shook her off and stomped across the room. "Fuck, that's the last place I want to be."

"Look, I don't know what happened there. You never told me. Maybe I don't want to know," she shot back.

"I lived it and I don't want to know. Had pretty much forgotten about it all until the fucking law landed in at mine."

"Are you sure?" She stood in front of him hands on her hips.

Her dressing gown loosened from her movements exposing enough of the milky white flesh of her breasts to make him want to take her right there. He had to quit thinking of her body and the times they had in their previous life together. Those days were gone. Long gone.

"Did you ever stop and think if you went back there and confronted your past, you could move on?" Katherine challenged.

"Sage advice coming from you. You, who is stuck in 2005 before your husband died." His words spilled out in anger.

"And what would you have me do?" Standing on tiptoes she stared him in the eye. "I loved him."

"You felt that way about me at one time, too. Tell me there's nothing left between us and I'll bugger off. You'll never see me again." He stepped back and put his hands in his pockets.

"I don't want you to leave me." Tears ran down her face.

He pulled her to him and mashed his mouth on hers. He didn't want to lose her either. Back in the day, some of their best lovemaking was after a row. Make up sex the girls called it and they did things they wouldn't normally engage in. Whatever they labeled it these days, he could use some now. He slipped his hand inside her dressing gown and squeezed her breast. Her nipple tightened in response to his touch.

Remembering their time together when they were younger, thanks to the smell of his Hugo cologne, she melted into his firm body. But as things heated up even more between them, she forced herself back. It was wrong. "I c-can't. I don't expect you to comprehend my reasons. I'm not sure I understand them."

Housecoat wrapped around her, she cinched the belt tight.

Did not want to fall out again, no matter how much she wanted him. She walked to the table, gathered their mugs, and took them through to the kitchen. Concentrate on something other than him.

When thoughts of Jared entered her brain, all logic and reason disappeared. Bracing herself against the worktop, she sucked in a deep breath and tried to banish him from her mind. So engrossed, she didn't hear his footsteps. As he put his hands on her upper arms and leaned over to kiss her neck, she jumped in fright.

"I know you don't want to go back to Barnsley, but you must. You have to help with their investigation. Admit it or not, you want to know if it is your father they found in the ruins. If nothing else, you'll have closure," she spewed without turning around.

"Make you a deal. I'll go back on one condition. You come with me," he said spinning her around to face him. "And you need to tell me, make me understand why you keep playing hot and cold."

His steely blue eyes still had the same effect on her after all these years. Katherine nodded. She could tell him right there why, but getting it to sink in was a different story.

"Even when we were together before, you never spoke about your home life, other than where you came from. No mention of parents, siblings, nothing. You kept a lot of things inside for too long. Yes, I'll go with you. Stick by you no matter what the outcome. And I promise I'll do my best to make you understand what I'm going through." She wrapped her arms around his waist and embraced him. This she could do and not feel guilty or like she was being unfaithful.

He hugged her and brushed his lips against her forehead. "I have to go before I do something or I won't be held accountable for my actions." Chuckling, he walked to the door. "Pick you up on Monday morning – say half nine for ten."

She nodded.

As he trotted down the stairs, the door clicked shut behind him. When he pulled the heavy door at street level open, the hinges, in bad need of oiling, creaked. He could do that for her.

Jared fumbled in his jacket for his car key. Once found, he pressed the button on the fob, and unlocked the BMW.

The same homeless person who lurked near Kat's since Hogmanay sat in the sun against the nightclub wall. His presence spooked Melissa to the point he escorted her to Union Street to make her feel protected. Seeing the panhandlers and other displaced people was far from unusual. Having one hanging around practically on his former lover's doorstep irritated him, but the guy appeared benign enough, albeit strange.

Grampian Police patrolled the area, on foot or in their marked patrol cars on a regular basis thanks to the casino across from Kat's and the pub next door. A team of uniformed constables rounded the corner from the pedestrianized section of Shiprow, as if his thoughts conjured up their appearance.

He didn't have to worry about the vagrant any longer. The pair in their hi-vis yellow jackets helped him to his feet and frogmarched him away.

~ 3 ~

3rd January, 2011

Jared threw some changes of clothing in the duffel bag he used when going to the rig. Some things never came out except when the time came to replace them. The trip back to his hometown was something he did not look forward to, and he tried to prolong the agony for as long as possible.

The lone good thing to come out of the journey was a few days with just him and Kat – the two of them alone away from Aberdeen. Maybe it would help her move on with her life and put her past in perspective. But, he needed to do that with his life, too. Was she on to something when she suggested he do this?

About ten o'clock, he pulled his BMW up at *As the Pages Turn*. She waited at the door for him, cabin suitcase beside her. As he walked around the front of the car, she stepped out from the shelter of the doorway to meet him. "Hope you've not been out here in the cold for too long." He planted a kiss on her cheek.

"No. When you texted me and said up to an hour, I waited indoors. Only came out a couple of minutes ago."

He opened the door and helped her in. The coupe was an amazing motor but being low to the ground, made it a bugger to enter and exit. Once Jared had her settled in the passenger seat, he popped the boot and stowed her bag.

He cursed Mr. Cocksure for kissing her. And cursed her for letting him. Cursed the police, too, for taking him away. Kept in custody the last twenty-four hours but not charged with any offences. Time wasted he could have spent here watching her. They stole that from him. Their behaviour was criminal. Not his. Out of habit, he reached into his pocket for the flick-knife. Gone. The bastards seized it. At least they didn't charge him for possessing the thing. Still, he would have to source another one.

No. No. No. She could not go away with him. That was not part of the scheme. The time still was not right. The voices, they hadn't told him what to do. He couldn't make his move without their input. Not until the time was right. And now, the opportunity was gone. She climbed into Mr. Cocksure's car. They were going away together. All his plans destroyed.

Placing his leather gloved hands on his head he paced back and forth in the cinema entryway. He needed to calm down. Revise his plan. Think of an alternative one that would still yield the same results. The beautiful red-haired woman would be his. End of. Even if it required a diversion from his original idea. He would not share her with anyone. She would be his and his alone. And if he couldn't have her then no one would.

When Jared slid in behind the wheel, he twisted in the seat. "Hope this works out. Going back to my past scares the fuck out of me and I'm not ashamed to admit it." Putting his injured right hand on her cheek, he turned her face to him. "It isn't too late. We can both back out now."

"No. We have to do this. You have to do this." Her golden-brown eyes were moist.

He leaned over and lipped her forehead before fastening his seatbelt and starting the car.

Before pulling away from the kerb, he programmed his sat nav with their destination's address. Barring complications like roadworks, accidents, or other traffic delays, they would arrive in Barnsley between half four and five o'clock.

"Turn left on Castle Street then turn right," the voice said.

The warren of one-way thoroughfares around the Castlegate, including the one Kat's business was on, made navigating through this section of town difficult. Not that he minded driving; he enjoyed it, but always hated this part of

Aberdeen. With no traffic lights at the intersection of Union and Castle Streets, turning right was impossible, which was the way the satellite navigation system wanted him to go. Ignoring the directions, he made a left onto the main artery, followed by another one when he reached Bridge Street, and continued along this route to, and through the roundabout before the River Dee.

Misty rain fell, requiring him to turn on the wipers, but even when he set them on intermittent, the glass never got adequately wet to prevent them making noise. As he turned on to the slip road leading to the A90, the precipitation changed to snow. Huge flakes splatted against the window, loud enough to hear them over the BMW's radio.

The further he drove, the worse the weather became. Maybe confronting his demons was not such a good idea after all. It certainly wouldn't do any good if he got them both killed in a motor vehicle accident.

South of Dundee, he pulled into a roadside service, purchased diesel and topped up the wiper fluid. While he did that, Katherine disappeared into the convenience shop. When he went in to pay, he met her coming out. She had a plastic carrier bag in one hand and a paper coffee cup in the other. "Got you one," she said holding up the beverage container.

"Not get anything for yourself?"

"A bottle of water – put it in here."

He smiled and continued inside.

Back on the road, Kat searched for some music on the car's stereo. She settled on BBC Radio 1.

"There are some CDs in the console. Take a look and see if there's anything you like in there."

She pulled them out. *AC/DC, Guns 'n Roses, Van Halen,* heavy metal music which didn't appeal to her.

As they drove across the firth via the dual carriageway on their southbound journey, a northbound ScotRail crossed the Forth Bridge. Rail travel was her favourite mode of transport and she vowed to take the train from Aberdeen to Edinburgh so she could say she travelled over the iconic structure.

Memories of Colin filled her mind. He died the day he was due to return from London King's Cross that awful day in July 2005. Who could say an attack would not happen north of the border in Scotland's capital, or Glasgow, or in her city?

After a stop in Jedburgh for a meal at a cozy restaurant with a view of the ruined abbey, bathroom break and fuel, they got back out on the single carriageway. The tarmac wore a layer of snow, except for the tyre tracks from the vehicles ahead of them. The gritters were not out yet. Still, she was safe with him behind the wheel, realizing he would not do anything to endanger their lives.

By four o'clock, night fell. Out of the city, away from street lights – black as a raven. The snow pelting into the windscreen hypnotized her and she hoped it didn't affect him the same way. It took another three hours to reach their destination.

"Can we go by the house tonight?"

"Not much to see. Just a terraced house."

"I'd really like to see where you grew up."

He glanced in her direction. "Would be better to wait until tomorrow during the daylight."

"I know." She reached over and put her hand on his upper left arm. "Please? We can come back again then."

Jared navigated his BMW through the streets of Barnsley from the motorway exit to his former home on Wath Road. He pulled to a stop in front of the house but even though a streetlight was above them, the visibility was terrible. He put the car back in gear and drove to Badworth Close where he made a U-turn.

"We're not leaving, are we?"

"No, but you can't see fuck all from here." Driving past the first narrow street on the right, he turned down the next one. When he reached the other end of the crescent, he stopped so they faced the house. The headlights shone across the road and on the ruined brick structure.

Plywood covered the windows and front door. A metal construction fence donned in official blue and white tape cordoned off the garden.

He sighed and raked his injured hand through his hair. He hated the house and the memories of living there. Seeing the house he grew up in in that state bothered him more than he expected. He took a long breath and turned to Kat, "Seen enough?"

"Yes." She rubbed his upper arm and shoulder.

Turning back onto Wath Road he drove back in the direction they came from. "A new hotel has gone up near the cop shop so I thought we'd stay there."

When they arrived, he helped her out of the car and removed their two bags from the boot before locking the vehicle.

"We need a room for a couple of nights. Are we too late?" he asked the front desk receptionist.

The tapping of her fingernails on the computer keyboard and clicking of the mouse became audible.

"Can we get a room with two beds?" Katherine asked.

~ 4 ~

4th January, 2011

Being a gentleman, he held the door at the Churchfield headquarters of the South Yorkshire constabulary open for her. The lobby was crowded, dull and dingy. Perfume combined with pungent body odour permeated the air. The carpet and sparse furnishings bore stains and burns. She squeezed his left hand and sidled over to him. The place and the people creeped him out so he could imagine the thoughts racing through her mind. He took her hand off his and wrapped his arm around her pulling her closer.

When they approached the reception desk, safety glass separated them from the office area on the other side. A uniformed constable motioned to a location next to the window.

Pressing the intercom button, he told the reason for his visit. "Jared Martin. You guys are looking for me. Something about a fire on Wath Road."

The policeman typed something into his computer and said, "Take a seat. I'll have someone come for you soon."

Scanning the room, he spotted an unoccupied corner and escorted Kat to the spot. He positioned himself so he stood between her and the others.

A door slammed shut behind them. "Jared Martin," a booming voice called out.

"That's me." He strode across the foyer to the tall, overweight mustached man, clinging to her like their lives depended on it.

"Detective Inspector Wells," the man announced, hauling

up his trousers and tucking in his shirt. "Can I see some ID?"

No uniform? What did CID have to do with this? Not that he cared – just wanted it finished. He complied with the request, removed his driving licence from his wallet, and handed his identification to the detective who looked at it, at him, and back at the document before returning the credentials.

"The morgue is over at the hospital, so we'll have to go there for you to identify the remains, Mr. Martin."

This entire situation had become a gigantic pain in the ass.

DI Wells signed out an unmarked car and escorted them to its location in the car park. "Sorry it's a mess. Only one available."

After he helped Kat in, Jared eased in behind her. Empty crisp packets crunched underfoot and paper coffee cups full of napkins and who knew what else bulged out of the cup holders.

The drive from the station took no more than ten minutes, but the state of the Ford Mondeo made it seem far longer. It was a relief to breathe fresh air.

After a walk down a long, well-lit corridor, they boarded a lift to the basement. "Why are these places always down in the bloody cellar?"

She squeezed his hand.

When the door opened, a wave of chilling cold rushed into the relative warmth of the large car. The plainclothes officer stepped out first and held his hand against the doors to prevent them closing.

A sign indicating the morgue's location was next to an insulated steel door across from the elevator. Was he ready for this? Seeing his father's dead body? No time to dwell on it. DI Wells started down the corridor. Confused, he took Kat's hand again and tagged after the man. The morgue would be the logical place where he would have to make the identification.

The detective inspector pushed the intercom button and announced their presence.

"I'll wait out here." Kat stopped and backed to the wall.

"You're sure?"

She nodded.

"Even staying out here, it means a lot you coming this far

with me. Won't be long."

When he followed the police officer through the door, he shivered. Not because of a temperature change but because he was in a cramped room that resembled a lounge in someone's house. A sofa, a couple of chairs and a table furnished the small space. Boxes of tissues were plentiful.

Installed in the back wall was a window to nowhere. Except it was to the room the bodies were shown. The powerful scent of formaldehyde clung in the air even though air fresheners were plugged into the mains. Choking on the odour, Jared plugged his nose and sucked in a deep breath through his mouth.

A shade on the far side of the glass rose. At the same time, the lights in this room dimmed, those in the other room brightened. An attendant wearing scrubs wheeled a metal gurney covered with blue cloth into position, perpendicular to the viewing pane. The cadaver beneath wore a matching coloured blanket over the torso and upper legs. The arms and lower extremities exposed.

In spite of the macabre circumstances, he moved closer. The man's ring finger on his left hand was missing, as was his father's. The face appeared drawn. This was not his first dead body. The cancer emaciated his mother to the point when she died, she was nothing but skin over bone. And then there was Sharon.

DI Wells motioned and the mortuary worker turned the remains so its left side lie parallel to the window. "Is this your father, Mr. Martin?"

The position of the hand emphasized the short stump from the loss of the digit. When the body was turned one hundred and eighty degrees so the right side was closest to the portal, he spotted the crippled right foot. His father limped. When he was a child, polio had been mentioned as the cause.

An ugly tattoo bearing a bony skull wearing a miner's hat with a broken headlight, complete with a pick-axe sticking out of a gaping hole in the top, adorned the corpse's upper right arm. A shaft opening and round-pointed shovel formed the background of the ink. Again, it matched the family patriarch.

The design frightened him during his childhood. Now, just unease. "Yeah, it's my old man."

"You're sure."

"I said he's my old man. What more do you want?" Leaning forward into DI Wells' face, he motioned to his left eye. "The old fucker gave me this. Think I wouldn't remember what he looked like? Then what about this"? He rolled up his sleeve revealing a number of burn marks. "He did that, too. Sorry if you don't like my reaction. I hated the bastard for what he did to us. I'm glad he's dead." He stormed to the door.

"We're not done yet, Mr. Martin. We have some paperwork to attend to back at my office.

Even though a CCTV camera was mounted atop the pole on the pavement at the corner of Shiprow and Exchequer Row, he took a chance. He skirted around behind and stayed next to the building. The establishment remained unopen. How could she leave her business unattended and unopened?

The sign in the window in the door displayed the usual hours. According to it, the store should be open for trade. Beside that placard, another listed the holiday schedule. Damn. Angry she had gone away with Mr. Cocksure, leaving the shop shut up added to his rage.

When she was surrounded by those granite walls, he was calm. Well, calmer than he was, knowing she was elsewhere and with whose company she was in. Her perfect figure, gorgeous face, and the aura she had about her made life worthwhile for him.

Shielding his eyes to eliminate the glare, he peered in the windows. Blocking his line of sight was a huge red sign with white lettering which read 'Sorry, we're CLOSED'. He shuffled to the next window. Everything inside reflected her style. Sleek and graceful with clean lines, displays tastefully arranged. Bead curtains hung in a doorway. He half expected to see her walk through them but then, she was away somewhere getting up to all sorts with the man with the fancy motor.

Rage bubbled up inside him. He could enter and ransack the premises. Vandalize it, too. Rip books apart with his bare hands. Slash others with his flick-knife. Couldn't do that, the police took it from him. Wank on some. Doing that would destroy her maybe even more than if he used the seized weapon on her. But he couldn't go in the retail space's door. The place was locked tighter than a chastity belt. Not to mention he didn't know the code for the alarm box affixed to the wall inside.

She had done everything to keep him out of her home and business. Damn her.

Katherine knew from the thunderous expression on Jared's face things did not go well. She rushed across the corridor and hugged him. "I'm sorry." She whispered an apology.

He pulled her to him and pressed his lips to her forehead. Neither one moved.

Much as she wanted, she could not take his hurt away. With this experience behind him, he might open up to her about his childhood, whether it was good, bad or indifferent.

"Let's get the rest of this done," Detective Inspector Wells said. "I've got work to do."

"No tea and sympathy from him. He's downright rude."

He snickered.

The drive to the morgue was bad enough but the return trip was worse. By then, the vehicle had a chance to warm up and some of the fetor undetectable before became stronger. An accident meant taking a diversion clogged due to roadworks. Katherine put her gloved hand over her nose and mouth to filter the stench of ammonia, mouldy food, and something putrid that did not bear thinking about.

She reached for the control to wind down the window but no such thing existed. Relief washed over her when they pulled into a bay in the car park. Once stopped, Katherine scrambled out into the fresh air.

When everyone exited the saloon, DI Wells guided them to the lobby. Holding the door open for them, he said, "You need to sign in." The plainclothes officer pointed to the place where Jared had announced his arrival and stepped aside so he could complete the necessary formalities.

After signing the book and getting a badge, he handed the pen to Kat.

"Only family," the cop said, taking an antacid tablet from the package and popping the chewable in his mouth.

"She's my wife."

"We could be in a heap of bother lying," she whispered.

"It's only a fucking visitors' log. If anything comes of it, I'd just as soon that, than leaving you behind with them lot out here." He nodded to the swarm of people in the reception area.

The DI's office appeared more like an over-sized closet. His desk, piled with stacks of file folders – their contents spilled out.

Two plastic chairs faced it and he motioned for Jared and Kat to use them.

After adjusting his trousers as he went, Detective Inspector Wells rounded the piece of furniture and sat. He ran his hand over his thinning hair then rifled through the paperwork that littered the surface. "We'd like you to consent to providing a DNA sample, Mr. Martin. That would prove without a doubt the man in the morgue is, indeed, your father."

"Fuck off. I'm headed back to Aberdeen when we're done here and I have no intention of ever coming back."

"No need to be nasty." He pulled out his tube of Rolaids and removed two, which he shoved in his mouth and chewed noisily.

Jared stretched his legs out in front of him but didn't have enough room to get comfortable.

"I fetched you back here to give you this," he said, passing a soot-covered biscuit tin to him. "Fire department found it in the attic."

His bedroom. Well, after he and his sister were too old to share. Jared wracked his brain trying to remember seeing the object before but nothing, and struggled to remove the lid. The filth and heat from the blaze welded the two pieces together. When he finally succeeded, he discovered a stash of money and a letter in his mother's handwriting. He drew in a ragged breath, unfolded the brittle paper, and began to read.

Dear children,

I'm sorry you had to endure the years of abuse at the hands of your father. When I first met him, he was the kindest, most loving man. Then things changed. I've been tucking this away, a smidgen at a time from the meagre housekeeping allowance he gave me from his paycheck each week.

I planned on saving up enough money to get us away from him where we would be safe but I got sick before I had the opportunity. Had I removed you from the family home and died, you would have only been returned to him. Your lives would have been much worse, had that happened. He would have taken his anger out on you both. In the end, I deemed staying the best thing for us, but I never imagined the sick things he became capable of.

Mum

Tears formed in Jared's eyes, blurring his vision. He folded the letter, put the fragile sheet of paper back in the tin and replaced the lid. Why did his mother have to die? She tried to protect them from his father's drunken rages. Life would have been better had he been the one who perished.

He leapt and walked to the door. "You coming?" He didn't dare look at her. Not now. She couldn't see him like this. Like the scared little boy from his past. He stormed out of the office, through the lobby and into the street.

"Jared, wait." Katherine yelled and ran to get closer to him but he was too far ahead. When she got dressed, chasing after someone was not part of the plan. With no trainers or flats of any kind, she was stuck wearing her stilettos. She stopped once to catch her breath then sprinted after him again.

When she reached the approach to the underground car park, he stood with his back against the wall.

Without speaking, he turned and headed to his car. His behaviour scared her. She never saw him like this. Before her forced move to Canada, he had been quiet at times, but always fun to be around. Her stiletto heels clacking on the cement floor as she raced after him echoed in the dark, cavernous area.

She didn't have her seatbelt fastened when he reversed out of the bay and took off squealing the tyres. On the street, he continued at speed, accelerating at intersections. A couple of times, they came close to running through red lights. "Will you slow down? You're scaring me. I've never seen you like this. Please."

Jared stopped his BMW across from the burnt out house on Wath Road. Nothing changed since the previous night. In the daylight, the caved-in roof and charred trusses bore witness to the extent of the blaze.

He exited the car and walked down the snicket between the two terraced houses to the back of the property. Graffiti adorned the plywood covering the windows. The rear garden the same as always, except for the cordon of construction fence and blue and white tape. No grass, just gravel and a stone walk from the waist-high, wooden gate at the laneway to the back door. Even the recent rains did nothing to dissipate the acrid odours. They lingered in the air, making him cough.

Ready to toss the biscuit tin at the house, he drew back.

"Stop. Have you gone mad?"

When he heard her voice and listened to her words, he dropped his arm to his side. Throwing the can at the house might make him feel better for a short time but not forever. He turned his back to her for a moment and sighed.

With his left hand in both of hers, she stood beside him. The warmth from her warm ones, made him realize how cold he was.

"Take me to the cemetery. I want to see where your mother is buried."

Could he do that? Did he want to go there? "Probably should stop there seeing how I came all this way."

"I think we should buy some flowers to take to the

graveside."

"There are a couple of convenience places – at least there used to be – between here and there."

The first corner shop they drove past did not have wrapped bouquets on the pavement outside the door so he continued until he came to one that did. She scrambled out of the car and across the street, reappearing a few moments later with a bouquet of *fresh* pink carnations.

Jared pulled his BMW through the arched, stone gate at the cemetery. He had not been here since the funeral, but the location of her grave never left his mind. He stopped near what might have once been a cathedral – now in ruins – and shut off the engine.

Taking Kat's hand, he guided her past elaborate tombstones and finally to a simple black, granite one with gold lettering. By comparison, the small monument was out of place.

She crouched and placed the flowers on the ground at the base. "I never knew you had a sister."

"Let's go. Want to get out of here and as far away from Barnsley as I can." He turned and walked back to his vehicle.

When he reached it, he leaned on the bonnet. She joined him and held his injured right hand in hers, put her other hand on his upper arm, and rested her head on his shoulder. "Please tell me."

"My mum had breast cancer. Pretty fucking ironic, don't you think? The old man works in the pit, gets miner's lung and lives to tell the tale. She never smoked or drank but she died of cancer."

"Was just me and Sharon what came to her graveside funeral service. Father couldn't be bothered. Stayed home and got trollied instead. That's when I found out the old man was shagging her and had been since me mum got sick enough she had to go to hospital. Perverted bastard." The nightmare of his childhood rushed back to the present.

Jared shook Kat off and paced in front of the car. "I told her, not to worry. He wouldn't do it anymore. When we gets back home, I go after him. Figured I'd stand half a chance since he'd be rat-arsed by then. Unfortunately, things didn't work out quite the way I planned and I got the worst of it – broken arm, cracked my head on the mantle when he pushed me backwards into the fireplace."

Turning his back to Kat, he rubbed his eyes with his thumb and forefinger. "While this went on, Sharon stood in the doorway screaming at our father to stop beating on me. I was laid out on the floor in a daze but saw my father grab her and drag her upstairs. Tried to stand but couldn't. Sharon's bedroom was above the lounge and when I heard the bed springs squeaking, I knew what was happening, but I couldn't do a bloody thing to prevent it."

Reaching out to him, her heart broke at the sad life he lived as a child. She pulled him back beside her, stroked his face, and pressed her lips on his cheek. "I had no idea things were so bad for you."

Before she could speak, he went on. "The old man worked at Cortonwood Colliery until the miners' strike. He was a fuckin' drunk before but at least when he was off working, it gave the three of us a break from his beatings."

"I'm sorry."

"Easy for you to say. Growing up in a normal family."

"Go on."

"Was the year after the pit shut down, my mum died. I hated her for leaving me and Sharon behind with him."

"How old were you?"

"Just turned eleven."

"You were just a little boy. How did you expect to take on a grown man to protect your sister?"

"When you're a kid you don't think about that. You do what you think is right."

She rested her head on his shoulder again. "You've said enough. You don't have to tell me anymore. I think I can fill in the blanks."

"You wanted to hear it. You needed to know everything so shut the fuck up and listen. The next few years were the same. Didn't matter what I did, it wasn't right or not good enough. If he didn't use his belt, he used his fists. The summer after I turned fifteen. Couldn't tell you what started it. In his eyes, I likely fucked up again. Just know he was fuckin' pissed about something. I remember watching him break the whisky bottle and take a swing at me. Didn't duck fast enough. Got this out of the deal." He pointed to the scar at the outer corner of his left eye and followed the line of the orb's socket towards his nose. Once he passed out, I packed my few bits and kissed the dump goodbye. Never darkened his door again. Been on my own ever since."

"Wh-where did you go?"

"Whitby first. Thought the coast would be far enough away. Convinced a guy there to give me a job on his trawler. Things went okay for about three months until the old man found me. Beat me so bad, it stuck me in hospital. Thanks to him who owned the boat, he went down for assault. When I got well, I headed south. Worked odd jobs, finished my schooling and put myself through University. After, I landed work on the rigs."

"And your sister? What happened to her?"

"Daddy dearest deciding she could be his surrogate wife. Shagged her silly until she couldn't take anymore. I know she got into drugs – hard ones, too, but not them what caused her death. Slashed her wrists. I found her in the bathtub. Had to break the door down to get in there. She died in June – topped herself on Father's Day. Poetic justice, don't you think? Have no idea if the old man felt any guilt or not. My guess is no. Never give a monkey's about us as long as he had a roof over his head and lager in the fridge. Oh yeah, and someone to shag. Sharon's death was harder to take than my mum's. I left home in July."

Jared found himself wrapped in Kat's arms. He could tell she was crying, too. His T-shirt where her face rested against his chest was wet.

Kat lifted her head. His eyes were moist. Sooner or later, the brutality of the situation would hit him. Chinks in his armour already showed. During their relationship before her move to

Canada, he was the strong one. When times were bad he held her together. Now, she would do the same and look after him.

Shifting out from between the BMW and her, Jared exhaled. He walked back to the modest grave stone. His normal, upright posture now hunched over. She wanted to rush to his side, but stayed where she was to give him some time with his mother and sister. From the car's bonnet, the larger monuments no longer obstructed the small family marker. But she monitored his movements, prepared to be next to him when he needed her.

Squatted in front of the stone, he reached out and grazed the cold granite with his right hand. Traced his fingers in the grooves of the engraved print. His shoulders shuddered. Kat moved forward but stopped. He touched his lips with the index and middle finger and pressed them on the grave marker.

Jared stood and schlepped to the car, his thumb hooked through one of the belt loops on his jeans. He hugged her with one arm and settled his mouth on her forehead. "Let's get out of here. I'm ready to head back to Aberdeen."

"Are you …," she stopped. "We're booked in at the hotel again tonight. Makes more sense to stay over and start fresh tomorrow. We'll be making the trip in the dark if we leave now and won't be home until the wee hours. As it is, the sun is setting. Let's go out for a meal. Have an early night. Head out first thing in the morning."

Almost the entire day wasted because of his father. How much longer would that man ruin his life? Things were bad enough before he left home, but now, again? Louis Martin died in the house fire.

After eating out, over drinks and even some laughs, they strolled to their accommodations. Kat checked in with her staff ensuring they would be available to work the next day, even though she made up the rota before Hogmanay.

When she removed her high-heeled boots, she massaged her sore feet and wiggled her toes. Yup, they were still there and functional. At the bookshop, she could toil eight to ten hours in heels and they never bothered her, but on those days, she had the chance to sit and wasn't chasing after someone. Laminate flooring as opposed to concrete and tarmac helped, too.

She had promised Jared she would put the ghost of her past behind her, but not tonight. This didn't seem to be the right time or place. Too much emotional upheaval had occurred. When she gave herself to him for the first time – again – it had to be perfect. Today was far from it.

Stretched out on the bed, TV remote in his hand, Jared flipped through the channels. He found a distraction. Something to take his mind off today's events – a good thing.

Toiletry bag and long, white flannel nightgown collected, she padded into the bathroom.

When she came back, ready for bed, he was asleep and snoring. She extricated the remote from his hand, pulled the portion of the duvet not covered by his body over him, and turned out the bedside light.

Button pressed to turn off the telly, Kat pushed the switch on the lamp to extinguish it, then climbed into the other bed.

His tossing and turning kept her awake. She crawled out of bed, and went to him, planning to climb in and comfort him. Wrapped up in the blankets the way he was, it would have been impossible, not to mention uncomfortable.

She disentangled him from the covers and discovered he was still fully dressed but at least had taken off his work boots. When she undid his belt buckle, he grinned. With some effort, she got him stripped down to his T-shirt, boxer briefs and socks. "Come over into my bed." She whispered so not to startle him.

After a struggle, she helped him from his and settled him in hers, before climbing in and snuggling. She put her arm over him and he took her hand in his, raised it to his mouth and kissed it.

~ 5 ~

5th January, 2011

When Katherine woke in the morning, Jared was spooning her. His chin rested in the hollow between her shoulder and neck. Memories of the nights spent in his bedsit rushed back. The only difference, back then they made love many times over before falling asleep in each other's arms.

She wiggled out of his grasp and walked to the window where she pulled the curtain aside. The sunrise, beautiful in its shades of red, orange, and yellow contrasted with the dark clouds.

While waiting for Jared to wake up, she turned on her laptop and downloaded her email. Most were business related but one from Stephanie with the subject a series of question marks, begged to be opened.

> *Hey Kat,*
>
> *Well, did you two do it? Hope so. After all, you spent two nights together. Details, woman, I need details.*
>
> *Steph*

Leave it to her friend to be so blunt. While she pondered a response, Jared stirred. After what he went through since New Year's Day, he needed the extra sleep but she wished he woke to remove her from this awkward situation.

Hiya,

Only you. We're coming home today. Will text you when I'm home. Not sure what time it will be.

K

He shifted in the bed again. "What time is it?" he groaned.

"Just past six," she said, shutting down her programs and turning the computer off.

"How did I end up in this bed?"

"I put you there. I came back from washing my face and getting into my nightgown and you were having a terrible nightmare," Katherine stood and returned her laptop to its case. "You were tangled in the blankets. Your arms were flailing and you were talking. Nothing coherent enough I could make out anything you said, though. Once I climbed into bed with you, you settled down and slept."

"Come back to bed then," he beckoned, patting the mattress beside him.

"No, I want to get back to Aberdeen before dark."

When she walked by to retrieve her holdall, he reached out and grabbed her. "Just five minutes. I promise I won't try anything. It felt good to hold you like that again. Wake up with you in my arms … although it didn't quite work out that way."

She gave in and slipped under the covers. "All right, but no longer."

He covered her with the duvet and put his arm over her. She hugged him around his waist and snuggled closer.

The promised time stretched to half an hour.

"Mmm, this is nice," she murmured. "Brings back memories doesn't it?"

"For sure. Only one thing would make this better." He stroked her back with his fingertips. "Make love with me, baby. You swore you would let go of your ghosts, if I banished mine."

"I-I can't." She leapt out of the bed, snatched her bag,

dashed to the bathroom, and locked the door. Unable to catch her breath, she gasped. What was wrong with her? She was in a room, miles from Aberdeen and the apartment she once shared with Colin. Why couldn't she give in to her feelings? Deep down, she never stopped loving Jared. Even when she married, he held a huge part of her heart. Now, she had him back and was doing everything in her power to drive him away, which added to her guilt.

"Unlock it," he demanded as he knocked.

Forty-eight hours. His red-haired beauty had been away with Mr. Cocksure for too long. He had spent the last two nights in the multiplex access keeping watch on her business and home. No cars came or went. No lights turned on or back off. Why did she leave with that man? Did she not know she had someone here in Aberdeen waiting for her? Someone who would look after her? Love her?

He needed a new knife but he could not walk into a retail outlet and ask for one. Flick-knives were illegal. Hunting goods outlets carried folding, fillet and fixed blade ones but the one the officers confiscated talked to him. The feel of the handle contours aroused him. Nothing else would do. He wanted – no – needed another switchblade. The harbour. That would be a good place to start. Foreign sailors might carry them. He hauled himself to his feet and hobbled down Shiprow.

The streets were busy but not a lot of people were out walking which worked to his advantage. He could get in and out and back to his position with relative ease.

Wandering down a narrow street between rows of stacked shipping wagons, he heard men's raised voices. Foreign sounding. He approached the fence. Beyond the containers on the dock two men with non-Aberdonian accents argued. One was taller, heavier-set and bald. The shorter one had shaggy, brown hair that covered his collar.

"Hey mate," he called out and motioned for them to come.

"I ain't your mate, laddie," the bigger man said.

He waited until the two shipmen reached the barrier. "The

coppers seized my flick-knife. Do you know where I could score another one?"

They eyed him up and down. "Might. What's in it fer us?"

Bloody hell. How would he pay? "You get me a ripper with a six to eight inch blade and I'll give you a hundred quid."

"Fuckin' thing will cost that much. We need to get something out of this deal," the long-haired man said.

"I keep my gob shut about who I got it from."

"Not good enough." He motioned to the other man and they walked away.

"All right five!"

The men stopped and turned around.

The taller, bald man spoke first. "Money up front. Then we'll score you a shiv. Not before."

"But I don't carry that kind of dosh on me."

"No notes. No knife."

"Okay, I'll get the fucking cash."

"Now you're talkin' our language. We're here in port for a week. Longer if they don't come up with our wages."

"How long after I pay you will I have my switchblade?"

"Depends. Might not be able to."

These men were leading him on. They didn't have nor could they obtain what he was looking for. He started pacing and clamped his leather-clad hands on his head.

"Think we've got a crack pot there. Let's have some fun. Come here, laddie."

He approached the fence.

The tall, bald man leaned forward invading his space. "See, matie. It's a matter of supply and demand. You want the supply. We make the demands."

His eyes darted from one man to the other. They didn't have what he craved. They were toying with him. He was about to step back from the barrier when the hairless man put his hand in his jacket pocket. Shit. Was he reaching for a weapon and going to murder him? That outcome never occurred to him. All he wanted was to find someone who could procure a new flick-knife.

Tall man's hand flew back into sight. The glint of sun on

steel followed the click and swish of the blade deploying. This one was more beautiful than the one he had. The bone handle was lined with grooves unlike his, which was smooth. He longed to caress the object, feel its power in his hands but the man kept far enough away even if he reached through the bars, he couldn't touch it. The man waggled the thing between his thumb and index finger.

"Five hundred quid – pound notes. Take it or leave it."

"I'll take it. I'll take it," he gabbled. "I'll pay ya. I need the bloody weapon."

"Twenty-four hours then the price goes up." The two men walked away laughing.

How could he raise it? He didn't have the resources. No credit cards. No ID. Replacing his knife was going to be a difficult thing to do. Even if he sold his sperm, it would require an awful lot of wanking and even thinking about the beautiful red-head, he didn't have that kind of stamina – not to mention his willie would be rubbed raw. But, oh, that gorgeous woman would be worth every painful stroke.

When he came back from the harbour, an evil idea came to him. What if he got the dosh from the red-haired woman? She must have cash in her place or the shop. If not money, something of value he could sell at one of the pawnbrokers. Wouldn't that be ironic? Her pay for the knife he would use on her later – once the voices told him the time had arrived. His mouth curled into a smile and he chuckled.

Mr. Cocksure's black BMW was not parked near her premises. The placard in the window still read closed. He would wait. Was she upstairs? If so, when it got darker there would be lights on inside.

The bolt scraped as the door unlocked. Jared flung the door open. Kat sat on the toilet seat, her elbows on her thighs and her face buried. Her gorgeous, long, red hair cascaded over her shoulders. Her body convulsed with her sobs.

"Hey, what's wrong?" he asked, kneeling in front of her.

"I-I'm sorry. I'm not being fair to you. You're better off without me," she managed.

"I'm not leaving you." Tears streamed down her cheeks staining them. Even without makeup, she was beautiful. Jared took her hands and removed them from her face, then wrapped his arms around her and assisted her from her resting place.

Once she stood, he held her to him. Wanted to take her right there on the bathroom floor but she'd not thank him for taking advantage. If he hurt her, he would never forgive himself. "I never mentioned a time limit for you laying your ghosts to rest. I'll wait as long as it takes. I need to understand what you're going through."

He dawdled outside the cinema, grateful dusk fell early. The woman's apartment stayed dark. He walked further up Shiprow into the pedestrianized section. A wooden gate at the back of her building was all that separated him from her home.

While he waited for the time to make his move, he positioned himself on the cobbled path. The streetlight on the end of the edifice switched on bathing the street in light. It would be harder to act on his plan. At least no CCTV camera pointed down here.

Now was the moment. He stood and sidled over so he was positioned with his back to the gate. With his right hand, he reached behind and took hold of the ring, gave the latch a sharp turn and the portal opened. Ensuring the street was empty he stepped back through the passage into a courtyard. Wheelie bins and cardboard stood against the back of the building. So close.

A combination lock box hung like a padlock from the stem of the doorknob – loose enough to lift but not so much it could be removed. In the dim light from the office area and the shop on Union Street, he noticed some of the numerals showed wear yet others remained pristine.

Now to determine the order they went in. Did any repeat? Nothing happened when he pushed the buttons in series. Tried various sequences with no luck. If he didn't come up with the right grouping soon, someone would spot him and contact the constabulary. That couldn't happen. Was it a date? If so, what format? Day, month, year? Month, day, year? Was the year two digits or four? He took another stab at it but still no good fortune. He had to calm down – had to think.

In desperation, he made one final attempt. After gulping in a breath, he punched in the numbers. One, nine, eight, two, zero, five, one, seven. The box opened and he exhaled, snatched the key and unlocked the door's deadbolt then secured it back in the case.

So far so good. No one had seen him. His fingers grazed the knob before he grasped it and turned. The door gave way and he pushed it open further with his shoulder. No alarm sounded. He stepped over the threshold and into the corridor. His heart pounded with excitement.

The business office was to his right. A nine-paned window in the door provided an excellent view of the room. He could break the glass in the edge closest to the lock, put his hand through and unlock it but didn't. What appeared to be a CCTV camera in the upper corner of the room pointing to where he stood saw to that.

Damn. If that was video surveillance, it spotted him already. When he tiptoed into the passage, he should have dropped to his knees. He had to believe his imagination was getting the better of him. Regardless of what was in the office, the place would have an alarm system. No. Going in there was not an option.

He crept to the base of the stairs. Motion sensor nightlights illuminated the dark hallway as he walked by. Stepping on the bottom tread, he gripped the banister and ascended. The treads creaked under his weight. The relative quiet made the noise sound even louder.

Standing in front of the upstairs door, he wondered if he had been premature in returning the key to its secure box. Did both locks use the same one? He touched the knob with his gloved fingertips before gripping the brushed nickel ball and turning it.

The door opened. No resistance from the chain proving the residence was empty. She went away with Mr. Cocksure and left her place unlocked. Silly girl knew better. Anyone could wander in, like he did now.

Light from the street filtered through the double French doors making the apartment bright enough, he didn't need to turn on a lamp. He wandered through the lounge taking in the ambience of the room and her taste in décor. It mirrored the furnishings and fixtures in the retail space below.

Floor to ceiling bookcases lined the wall adjacent to the doors. Not much chance of finding something there. At least not an object that wouldn't be recognized missing straight away. He had to be smarter, although a number of the classics on display here would fetch a high price in the right market. At the far end of the room, shelving units displaying pictures, ornaments and other baubles stood sentry against the walls. These had drawers in them and doors below.

One by one, he pulled them open, shuffled through the contents and closed them again. He couldn't make it too obvious someone had been in, going through her things in her absence. But then, she's the one who went away and didn't lock up. She deserved everything she got.

He crouched down and opened the bottom sections of the units revealing expensive China, crystal, and table linens. Things that would sell, but be easily traced, not to mention impossible to remove with nothing other than his coat pockets and hands.

The kitchen, located opposite the French doors yielded nothing either. Wine and spirits in one upper cabinet, beer in the fridge, which was likely bought for Mr. Cocksure's benefit as he didn't seem the type to drink anything so refined.

He went back to the liquor stash and perused the selection. In the back, he found a bottle of 18-year old Glenlivet, and snatched down the single malt. The seal had been broken but no more than the Angel's share missing, and shoved the booze in the left pouch of his overcoat, glad it was deep enough to accommodate the whisky. Afterwards, he put the others back in their original, or as close to, positions.

Next, he searched the bedroom. A birch veneer dresser with large mirror stood along the end wall, a matching chest of drawers bounded by two windows, and a leather club chair next to the partition between here and the lounge. A low-slung king-size bed with lots of pillows where she spent time with Mr. Cocksure, no doubt, nestled between two nightstands.

Anger consumed him again. She would learn her lesson. She would belong to no one else. An overwhelming desire to destroy the love nest took over him. Possible means included shredding the pristine white duvet and leaving a calling card of wanking residue under it or on the surface. At least the former wouldn't be discovered until she climbed under the covers and maybe not before she laundered the bedding. That idea pleased him.

He stomped over to the dresser. Perfume in an atomizer sat between the original bottle on one side and an open jewel chest on the other. Nothing expensive inside. Could he, better yet, should he take a piece? Were any presents from the man with the fancy motor? It would be just like him. Ply her with gifts so she would let him have his way with her.

It would be so easy to sweep his arm over the expanse and send everything crashing to the laminate flooring. For now, he didn't want her to know someone had been there. He had to be more subtle – this time. He went through the drawers.

When he reached the one she kept her underpants in, they popped up when he pulled the receptacle open. The silky, satiny garments were stuffed in and wadded up, not folded neatly as he expected. He took out a handful of her intimates, raised them to his face, and inhaled the fresh scent of the laundry soap she used and the perfume she wore.

Unbeknownst to him, black pants fell when he clutched the fistful. He returned the others to the drawer but as he pushed it shut, he snatched a pair of white, satin, high-cuts and shoved them in with the whisky.

When he walked away, he brushed the ones on the floor with his foot and sent them sliding under the dresser.

His search continued. Nothing of interest was found in the airing cupboard not that he figured there would be. The next room down the hall was furnished like an office. A small desk, chair and filing cabinet lined up against the wall adjacent to the head of the king-size bed.

A wardrobe stood along the opposite end. He checked

there first. An assortment of men's clothes – suits, dress pants and shirts – hung from the rail. A tie rack with an impressive collection fastened to the inside of the door. The drawers held pairs of socks and boxers. Nothing here either. The clothing might fit him, not the new man in her life. She didn't move Mr. Cocksure in. A sigh of relief escaped from his lips and he imagined seeing her lying wounded and her blood staining the white duvet.

He sat down and opened the upper drawer. Pens, pencils, ruler were scattered haphazardly like someone threw them in. A photo of her in a brass frame smiled at him from the desktop. Picking it up, he ran his hand over her face. The voices were noisy. Their speech incoherent, but at least they were no longer silent. The time was coming. He grinned and put the picture down.

The adjacent narrow bin held writing pads, post-it notes and other stationery. When he reached the tall lower box, something didn't seem quite right. A measurement confirmed his suspicions. Six inches from the top to the base and from the underside – one inch. The thing had a false bottom. What was she trying to hide? Or what was he, the owner of the clothes, attempting to conceal?

With a metal letter opener, he worked away prying the foundation up to a height he could squeeze his fingers through and lift. Beneath it – the motherlode. There had to be thousands of pounds in various denominations. His money worries were over. He snatched handfuls of banknotes and shoved them into his other pocket, taking extra precautions not to drop any on the floor.

When he deposited the dagger-shaped utensil back in its proper place, a car stopped out front. Careful to remain in the shadows to avoid detection, he moved to the window. The same black car she left in pulled up and she climbed out. He sneered and rubbed his black leather gloved hands together.

All was not lost. He could still get her. Still have her as long as he didn't panic. That would give him away. The authorities would send him away to some prison or mental health ward – again. He couldn't have that. He had to be patient and methodical. That was the way to go. His one major obstacle was Mr. Cocksure, but a problem easily dealt with.

The voices would tell him what to do. The element of surprise would be his comrade in battle. But, if he didn't leg it out of there – and fast – he would be captured. At the last moment, he noticed the drawer open. A dead giveaway someone had been in the room, he pushed it in.

The drive to Aberdeen, took longer than the trip south. A lorry had jackknifed on the M1 trapping them in the tailback for hours.

Kat climbed out of the BMW as soon as Jared turned the engine off. "Want to come up? Can't promise much, but I can at least make you a coffee and let you rest a bit."

"Sure. Why not?" He retrieved her bag and latched the boot, then put his arm around her waist and walked her to the door.

Her large handbag made it difficult to find anything and she fumbled for her keys. She wished she took them out sooner. It was cold and damp standing out here in the night air and she needed the loo. The temperature change made the urge come on like a thundering herd of elephants.

Racing through the lounge to the door, he knocked one of the small, framed photos to the hardwood. He paused long enough to scoop the piece up and shove it in his pocket. With all the other stuff on the shelves, a small photo wouldn't be missed.

He stormed down the steps and turned to the back door. A sheet of paper floated to the floor, swept off the table in his wake.

When the key slid into the lock, the scraping sound of metal echoed in the silent corridor. The latch clicked when the knob turned. As the door moved, he pulled open the back one and escaped. His heart pounded even harder and faster than when he entered the building. He needed to rest but not here. Someone would find him.

Panicked, he couldn't release the bolt on the gate. He pressed himself against it to catch his breath and calm down.

Once he did, he broke out of the courtyard, closing the access behind him.

While Kat unlocked the door, Jared pointed the fob at the car, locked it, and pushed the button a second time setting the alarm. When she shoved the heavy entryway open, a piece of paper lay on the floor in the hallway. "Funny," she said. "That shouldn't be there."

"Probably blew down when you opened the door."

His explanation was plausible but the table was behind the staircase. It should have been protected from the breeze created by the simple act of opening a door.

Once inside, she put the kettle on to boil and rummaged through the refrigerator. "Nothing to eat, I'm afraid. Want to order a takeaway?"

"Sounds good."

His voice was louder than if he were in the other room. When Katherine turned, she discovered him leaning against the doorframe and jumped. "You startled me. I thought you were still in the other room."

As Jared pulled her to him he mashed his lips down on hers. Before things heated further, Kat pushed him back. "I-I can't." Placing her hand over her mouth, she dashed to the far corner of the lounge.

In seconds, he had his strong hands on her upper arms. "Tell me, please."

"I d-don't know how."

He took her by the hand and helped her to the sofa. When he sat, he eased her down beside him and wrapped his arm around her, holding her close. "Take your time. Talk to me."

"I want you, Jared. I really do. I want what we had before … before … Colin."

"I do, too." He shifted and kissed her soft skin.

"How would you feel if you came home and found your wife in bed with another man?"

"But you said he was dead? London bombings in 2005. King's Cross catching the train back here."

Kat stood and walked to the double French doors leading

to the bedroom. She toyed with the chain she wore Colin's wedding band on. Tears burned her eyes and spilled down her cheeks. "They claim the blast blew him to smithereens. I never got to say goodbye. Never got to tell him I loved him. How do I know they identified the right person? How do I know he won't come through that door?" she pointed as she spoke.

That was too close. He sat down on the cobbles, rested, and pulled out the bottle of whisky. The white satin pants came out at the same time. Despite being under a streetlight, he yanked the stopper from the vessel and took a swig. The smoky, peaty liquid burned all the way down but left a warmth in his stomach and an aftertaste of fruit and oak.

He clutched her underwear in his other hand and lifted them to his face. Being in his overcoat had not affected the scent on them. Before shoving them back in with the wad of pound notes, he inhaled their aroma again.

Because of the huge amount of cash he had, he needed to find a safe place to spend the night. He couldn't afford to be robbed. The money secured in his coat was already spent. First thing in the morning, he would go back to the harbour, find the sailor and buy the flick-knife.

But where to go in the meantime? The enclosure behind the book boutique was sheltered from the wind. Broken down packing material was stacked against the wall for recycling. He could hide behind it and be protected.

What would his red-haired beauty think if she knew he hunkered down on the patio area next to her home? Once again, he crept through the gate and arranged some of the cardboard on the ground. Insulation provided from the cold stone, he lay on the corrugated paper and tugged over another piece fashioning a lean-to under which he would sleep.

Jared leapt from the sofa, wrapped his arms around her, and held her. Now that Kat had spilled her guts out to him, he hoped she could move on.

When her mobile rang, she broke free from his grasp and pulled the phone from her handbag. "It's Steph. I was supposed to text her when I got home. She wondered if we got back safely."

Any chance of a quiet night on their own evaporated. "Think we better give that takeaway a miss for tonight." Disgruntled, he grabbed his leather jacket and shrugged into it. Before leaving, he walked to where she stood, put his right hand on the back of her head. His lips lingered on her soft skin.

After he climbed into his BMW and fastened his seatbelt, he didn't start the vehicle right away. Instead, he leaned back and scrubbed his hands down his face. How could he convince Kat Colin wouldn't return? If he was blown to bits like she said, his DNA would have been used to identify the man. Had he been severely injured but survived with the loss of his hand? Did he suffer amnesia from the shock of the entire incident?

Now he was starting to think like her. No, the man was dead. End of. He fired the engine and drove away from the kerb, determined to find evidence to prove once and for all Colin died in London on July 7, 2005.

About ten thirty, Jared pulled into the driveway at his home in Newburgh. Since Hogmanay, the week had been brutal beginning with the New Year's Day visit from the cops, followed by the trip to Barnsley that revived so many unpleasant memories. The only good thing to come out of it was reconnecting with Kat.

He latched the gate, ambled to his vehicle and unlocked the boot. The soot covered form given to him by the detective sat next to his luggage. After swinging his duffel bag over his shoulder, he salvaged the dirty object, locked the car and entered the house through the door into the back hall.

Once inside, Jared dropped the holdall, walked into the kitchen and set the metal cookie can on the counter. Its shape reminded him of something from his childhood. He pulled a length of paper towel off the roll, wet it, then scoured the lid in a circular motion until the beginnings of a picture appeared. With a fresh napkin, he continued. When he finished, a portrait of the Queen emerged.

This canister belonged to his grandmother. Yarn, darning

needles and a spent lightbulb she stuffed inside socks when she mended them. A tiny woman, she wore her white-hair held back with combs. When the children were too rambunctious, she peered over her glasses perched on her slender nose. She died when he was small. This was one of the few meagre things his mother inherited when his gran passed away.

Jared took a lager from the fridge and took it and the dilapidated biscuit tin to the lounge, and dropped into his leather recliner. He popped the ring-top on the beverage and took a long drink then opened the container. In addition to the letter written by his mother, which he removed and sat on the side table, there were a few pound notes and coins, some of which didn't look familiar.

He picked one of them up for a closer look – a shilling. Had she been planning on leaving for that long? He took out another he didn't recognize. This one a halfpenny. Checking the date on this odd loose change, he discovered they were minted in 1952 – the year his mother was born. So much for his first theory.

Before he placed his mother's letter in the tin, he ran his fingers over the paper, unfolded the sheet and read the woman's words again, hoping to find something he missed before.

His past, prior to meeting Kat, needed to remain where it belonged, but since his trip to Barnsley, his previous life became his present. Everywhere he turned reminders of his painful childhood cropped up in front of him. The closet skeletons had been released and there was no confining them to their quarters. He hoped when he went back to work on the rig, the job would keep his mind off his personal life … at least that part.

What about Kat? How could he prove to her Colin died? Better yet, without coming across as cold and uncaring. From the time they first met in HMV and she stamped on his foot with a stiletto heel he fell for her. Even wearing steel-toed work boots, she managed to tromp where there was no added protection.

It hurt like hell at the time, but looking back on the

incident, she was the only one for him. He would never do anything to upset her, but competing with the ghost of her dead husband was something for which he was not prepared. Still, he couldn't expect to pick up where they left off when so much had happened in those missing years.

After a long day on the road, Jared dragged his feet up the stairs to his bedroom. He had to put his head down. Get some rest. With any luck, the memories of the last five days would evaporate into the mist. All except for waking up in her bed, in spite of the lack of sex.

That night, he didn't sleep well. Visions of a grieving Kat haunted his dreams. He tossed and turned and tangled himself in the sheets. When he couldn't discover the reason for her despair, he got up and went downstairs.

Should he have brought her to his place? The only time they spent together in one of the places he lived was in his bedsit on Castlehill. Her staying in a place overflowing with remembrances of Colin didn't do her any good. Everywhere he turned in the apartment, the man was there – pictures, business awards, University degree. She erected a shrine to the man. No wonder she couldn't accept him as her lover there.

~ 6 ~

6th January, 2011

A door opened. Feet shuffled towards him. He froze, not daring to breathe. His racing heart thumped so hard in his chest he was certain she would hear the rhythmic pounding. Its beat pulsed in his ear that rested on his shoulder closest to the ground. How stupid he was to think he could spend the night here and not be caught. The wheelie bin cover opened followed by a thud and the closing of the lid.

The bare leg of his red haired beauty protruded from her long, white dressing gown. Arousal stirred in his groin. He longed to caress that shapely flesh beginning near her ankle and continuing upwards. Make love with her then destroy her. Cast her aside like the rubbish she disposed. The footsteps grew faint and the lock latched shut. He drew a ragged breath. That was far too close. He must escape from here before someone else came outdoors and found him.

When he calmed down, he shuffled out of the courtyard and down Shiprow to the docks. The twenty-four hour timeframe would soon end. He had to meet the sailor who named the price and would sell him the flick-knife.

Last night's dampness got into his joints making it difficult to move. Sleeping on the cobbles would have been worse. At least the cardboard provided a bit of insulation. He hobbled to Trinity Quay. Once he crossed over the road, he stopped to rest. With nowhere to sit, he had to content himself by leaning against the barrier separating the public roadway from the harbour property. He massaged his hips hoping to work out the stiffness from the cold. The action hurt but he continued.

He took advantage of places to obtain free meals, but had not succeeded in finding a place to spend the nights since he arrived in the Granite City. Next to his red-headed beauty, that was the most important thing. If he hoped to accomplish his mission, he needed his strength. Sleeping rough in doorways, courtyards, and parks didn't do him any good at all.

Rested, he carried on to the location where he would purchase his weapon. Spotting the two men from the previous day, he approached the fence. "Oi." He waved his arm beckoning the sailors to come closer. "I have your money – all five hundred quid."

"The price has gone up. No longer enough." The larger man nudged his companion and they laughed.

"But you said I had twenty-four hours." He threw his hands in the air. "It's not been, yet. I still have time."

"We want to know what you're going to use it for. We wouldn't want to be party to anything illegal." They snickered.

The bigger man's hand shot through the bars and grabbed the front of his outerwear. The Fedora toppled from his head and he was powerless to pick it up. His head rammed into the barrier separating him from his adversaries.

"I think we've got a real nutter here. What's under the balaclava sport?" With his free hand, he grasped the beige fabric.

"Let go." His protest was unsuccessful. "Look here's the money." He reached into his topcoat and yanked out a wad of banknotes. The movement pulled the pair of women's white satin pants out and they fell to the ground.

"We've got ourselves a perv."

"Aye. So there fella, what ya use them fer? Wearin' or wankin'?"

He shuffled to the spot where the garment lay on the tarmac and stepped on them. The sailors could not have them. They belonged to him. And soon, his red-headed beauty, the owner of the clothing would, too. "Here's your bloody money. Now give me the flick-knife." He shoved the handful of cash at them.

A marked squad car drove past the end of the road backed

up and parked blocking the exit before turning and pulling down the street. The three men froze. The last thing any of them wanted was to get nicked. The blue roof lights came on and the siren blipped. Fear filled him as the vehicle approached but instead of continuing towards them, the driver pulled a U-turn and sped off in the opposite direction.

"Ah, give the perv his knife. You sure don't need the bloody thing. We'll keep the cash and the women's underwear."

"No. You can't have them." He put more weight on the delicate, white satin object beneath.

When one man snatched the money out of his hand, the other shoved him back. He lost his footing and staggered. With lightning speed, the piece of intimate apparel he stole from his red-headed beauty's home was scooped off the ground and into the harbour property behind the fence.

Much as he wanted, he couldn't take the two of them on at the same time. His hunger to procure the weapon took over. "Knife. Now." He thrust his chin forward and growled.

The metal and bone object clattered on the street behind him. Before moving to retrieve it, he yanked the balaclava off his head. "You wanted to know what was under it? Now you do."

"Fuck me. Put it back on. Don't need to see that."

A voice from the deck of the ship called out. "Ahoy, lads. They's give us our wages. Prepare to sail out in one hour."

The men turned and ran to their vessel. This was the first time he ever revealed himself to anyone. The scars were as disgusting now as they were back then. Nothing improved over the years. Would his red-haired beauty want him looking the way he did? No matter, he would have her whether she liked it or not. He pulled the hood back over his head, collected his Fedora and strode with his awkward gait to the spot the cutter came to rest.

After he snatched up the switchblade, he admired the workmanship and acquainted himself with his new best friend. A push of the button and the blade shot out. This feature worked far better than the one taken from him. He rammed it into his pocket.

As he left the harbour area, the spring long since missing from his step, returned. He revelled in the horror on those burly, strong men's faces at the sight of him. Two men who had sailed the seas, brawled in bars around the world. He envied that aspect of their lives. The places they saw. The women they shagged.

At the same time, revulsion at his appearance consumed him. Would have served the pair of them right had they got themselves a dose. He snickered. No, he would remain faithful to the red-headed vision of beauty who operated *As the Pages Turn* on Exchequer Row. The sailors could go to hell for all he cared. He got what he wanted from them – the flick-knife. Reaching into his coat, his fingers touched the bone handle and excited him.

He envisioned himself masked, making love with the gorgeous redhead, biting, groping and violating her with his gloved hands, her screaming in agony and ecstasy simultaneously, blindfolded so she couldn't see his disfigurement. That would be even better. He could remain anonymous. She need never know who ravaged her.

Then, he would begin at her neck below the ear and trace the tip of the blade down her body. Not enough pressure to slaughter her straight off, but enough to draw blood. Death would come later ... or not. Start by scarring her so that no other man would want her. His idea of shoving his knife blade-first inside her and tearing her apart so she would never enjoy sex again stayed uppermost on his list.

Now he knew the combination to the lock box on the back door to her premises, he could come and go as he pleased. These evil plans and picturing her naked body under his made him mad with desire. He needed to find a secluded place.

A narrow opening between rows of shipping containers was ahead. From his vantage point, no fence separated him from it. He loped in its direction and collapsed on the ground. Curled up on his side to shield his activities from potential passersby, he unzipped his trousers and gripped his erect member, wishing he still had her satin pants. Now, all he could do was close his eyes and imagine their soft fabric and seductive scent.

~ 7 ~

9th January, 2011

His red-haired beauty never emerged from inside. She maintained regular hours but never stepped beyond the door. Much as he wanted to return to her home with her never leaving – not even to the post office or bank – he couldn't take the chance of entering. Mr. Cocksure didn't come back since he left after dropping her at home after their few days away. Did she knock him back for good this time? He could hope.

Overwhelmed by desire to see the beautiful shopkeeper, the temptation to visit her place dumbfounded him. Could he succeed? Go in and pretend to be a patron? Didn't have to purchase anything – just browse. Worth a try. She would be safe. The voices had not spoken to him and until they did, she would come to no harm. Not only could he see her but be sheltered from the weather. Sleet, lashed down, blown about by the wind. When struck by the pellets, his skin stung like thousands of needles jabbing him.

He took a deep breath and walked from the front of the film theatre around the pole with the CCTV camera mounted on top. When he reached the door, he gripped the handle and rested his thumb on the latch. What was more natural than going into a bookstore? Would she kick him out because of his appearance? Was it worth the risk to spend time with her? Hell yes. He pressed down and pushed the door open. A bell tinkled announcing his presence. Damn. Adjusting his Fedora to keep his face covered, he stepped over the threshold.

There she was behind the counter checking out a customer, but stopped and made eye contact with him. Bowing his head he shuffled to the shelves. An area was dedicated to local authors, others to thrillers and mysteries, romance, cookbooks, children's, literary fiction, and a small section for gently used books.

He slipped down the aisle housing the crime novels. From this vantage point, he could watch her movements yet leave her unaware he was doing so.

When the customer left the store, the red-headed beauty, approached the space he had ensconced himself in. "Can I help you find something?"

No malice. No judgement. A simple, polite question. He didn't dare speak. Instead, he shook his head and turned to walk further away. The scent of her Poison by Christian Dior perfume intoxicated him. The bottle was on her dressing table the night he stole the money.

The clicking of her heels on the laminate flooring grew softer as she left him to carry on. He could steal one of the more graphic police procedurals, but saw his reflection in the convex mirror mounted below the ceiling in the corner near the entryway. A short distance from it was a video surveillance camera. He'd be banged up for sure for shoplifting a lousy paperback that only cost a tenner. If he was going down for a crime, it would be one well worth doing time for.

Her long, red hair fell forward as she bent to tidy a display. He longed to run his fingers through those tresses. Make her relax and once she had, grab her by those locks and yank her head back, exposing her throat. In one swift motion, he could slice her from ear to ear. She wouldn't know what hit her. That would be worth being seen on the camera system.

He wished the voices would talk to him. Their silence deafened him. They had spoken to him up until just before Hogmanay. Not telling him much of anything, but more background noise. Now, he missed their companionship.

Rather than do something impulsive, something the choristers wouldn't approve of, he left the shop and nodded on his way out.

Jared eased his car into an empty bay in the Nexus carpark.

Spending the next fortnight with Kat was preferable to heading off to work.

Inside the terminal building, he had to go through security and have his bag inspected. On occasion, he set off the metal detector because he did something stupid like forgotten to take out his keys or loose change.

Once through this stage, he moved on to a small space with fourteen chairs arranged in front of a screen. Each seat held a life jacket wrapped in plastic. After everyone arrived and settled in, the safety video started.

The film had become so routine, some slept through the viewing. The short movie ended with a still shot of the clothing allowed under the survival gear. He had a T-shirt and shirt on but carried a jumper. It was too hot indoors for so many layers.

Good-natured bantering took place in the room where they dressed into their dry suits. From this point, Jared couldn't wait to exit the building. All this extra clothing was too much. People had fainted from time to time especially during the summer months.

He slung his bag over his shoulder and headed to the waiting helicopter. The door to the cargo hatch was open so he stowed his holdall then took a seat on the chopper. Being one of the first to board, he had a choice of seats.

His preference was the rear-facing one by the door – the easiest to exit from in an emergency. He had no desire to sit in the back row. The guys who flew in these birds referred to it as 'death row'. They claimed if you're going to die in a ditching, that was where you'd be seated.

The first day back on the rig was the worst. Things not completed by the men on the opposite rotation. Prior to beginning work, Jared set his mobile to vibrate. Didn't want all and sundry hearing when he received an incoming call or text message seeing how the devices were to be left in their sleeping quarters during working hours. But if Kat needed him, he didn't want her to have to wait until after his shift ended to ring her back.

Before he could do his own job, he had to clean up their

mess. Why couldn't they do theirs? Because they knew he would be there to do it for them. It pissed him off. At least the other crew didn't leave before his arrived. The same aircraft that transported him and his workmates took those men back to the airport.

At the end of the brutal shift, he didn't join the others for supper but went to bed and collapsed. For a long time, Jared laid on his back, hands behind his head staring at the ceiling in the small cubicle that was his bed, wishing he was with her. Regardless of his exhaustion, sleep evaded him.

Not long after he drifted off, the nightmares began. Finding his sister dead in the bath. The water in the tub stained red with her blood. The knife she used on the floor – its handle and blade caked with the dried evidence of her suicide. He thrashed in his bunk. "Sharon, no," he cried. In his delusion, he dropped to his knees beside his sister's lifeless body, held her hand and wept.

"Jared, wake up." Tristan McKnight shook the dreaming man to rouse him from his sleep. "What the ...?" The space was splattered with blood. He disentangled his roommate from the bedding.

A fist punched out at him and he swerved to avoid being clobbered. The knuckles were swollen, bruised and bloodied. Tristan grasped Jared's wrist and forced his arm down against the mattress. "Snap out of it, for fuck sake." He slapped his cheek with the back of his hand. Before he had a chance to react, Jared clutched him around the neck.

To extricate himself from the chokehold, he let go of the limb he held down and reached for his throat. A pair of terror-filled, blue eyes stared at him and the grasp loosened. "Shite, mate. You bloody near strangled me."

"Th-thought you was someone else." Waking from his nightmare, he mumbled.

"Get your arse out of bed. I'm taking you to the infirmary. What the fuck did you do to your hand? Jesus H. Christ did someone die in here? There's enough blood to be a crime scene."

Tristan helped him out of the upper bunk and into his jeans and work boots. They walked from their sleeping quarters to the medical room in silence.

When they entered, he turned and said, "Punched a wall on Hogmanay. Pretty daft, don't you think?"

The bright lighting in the room blinded Jared. He blinked while his eyes became accustomed to the brilliance. The rig's medic, David Asher, was nowhere in sight. The white cabinets and stainless steel work surfaces reflected the harsh glare.

His hand throbbed as he flexed his fingers sending a searing ache through his injured extremity. Blimey, he should have gone to A&E that night or at least the next day like Kat said. He had done serious damage.

Tristan leaned back against the counter. Jared's finger marks on his neck had bruised. Why had he attacked his roommate? He never turned on any of the guys on the rig before. But then he never dreamt about finding his sister dead in the bath when he was at work. In his altered state, he mistook the man for his father – the man behind his sibling's suicide, and his own years of physical abuse. The trip to Barnsley didn't lay his ghosts to rest. It resurrected them.

"I'm going to find the medic. You stay put."

Jared sat on a stool and rested his arm on a small metal table mounted on wheels. Three gurneys were positioned along the opposite wall separated by curtains. A fourth stood off to one side of the room, its back elevated, with a large overhead light above. No doubt, he would end up on that before the night was over.

"What have we here," David said when he entered the room. "Nasty looking hand you got. Let's get you cleaned up and go from there."

The practitioner was no more than five feet three inches tall. What hair he had left, was thin on top but grey and curly on the sides. He filled a basin with warm water from the sink and squirted something in. "Over there." he nodded to the narrow bed.

While he made himself comfortable, David wheeled the

small table with the stainless steel bowl on it over to the right of the gurney. "Put your hand in this," he instructed.

Submerging his hand in the warm, soapy water stung. He was a complete arse punching the wall. But it was better than hitting Kat. He needed to control his anger. When they were together before, he never once blew up at, or because of her.

After about five minutes of soaking, David came over to inspect his damaged knuckles. Ragged skin surrounded the rupture in the flesh. "I can see even without an x-ray there's a compound fracture there." He pointed to the middle finger joint on the back of Jared's hand. "When did you do it?"

"Hogmanay."

"Just over a week ago. It needs to be set. Once that's done, I'll suture the wound, and start you on a course of antibiotics. But first, I need a picture or two so I can see what I'm dealing with." He escorted Jared to another room and x-rayed his right hand. "You go back out there while I develop these."

He knew Tristan would be waiting, wanting an explanation and an apology. He slunk back out into the infirmary. He owed the man both but he didn't know how to put what he had to tell him into words.

"What the name of Jesus H. Christ were you thinking?"

"I wasn't. Look Tris, I'm sorry. I thought you were someone else."

"More than that, isn't there." He pulled the stool over to the side of the gurney.

"Yeah. A fuck of a lot more."

"You never had nightmares before. Something happen on your last two weeks off?"

Jared rose and raked his hand through his hair. "Went home for a few days. Not been there in years." He kneaded the back of his head as he spoke. "Not thought of the hell hole in years either."

"So what made you decide to go back?"

"The cops turned up at mine on New Year's Day. There'd been a fire at the place and they found someone inside."

"Oh, jeez, man. I'm sorry."

"No need. Anyway, they wanted me to go to Barnsley to

identify the body."

"And?"

"It was my old man. Likely started it himself when he was on one of his drinking binges. He was a drunk. Nasty fucker, too."

Tristan stared at him. He opened his mouth to speak but nothing came out.

Jared pointed to the scar under his eye. "Gave me this. A parting gift, if you will."

David Asher entered putting a stop to the conversation. He put the developed x-ray up on the board and turned on the light. "See," he indicated the broken bone. Already started to heal. To do the job properly, I'm going to have to break it and start from scratch. I can freeze your hand so you won't be too uncomfortable."

"Do what you got to do." When Jared climbed onto the gurney, he sighed.

When the medic injected the needle into the wounded area to numb the pain, he grimaced. The bloody thing was sore enough but the anesthetic burned. At least the freezing took hold quickly. Even with that, the pushing and pulling on the finger and hand hurt. The bone snapped and once that happened, David manipulated it back into alignment. After, his discomfort disappeared.

Sewed up, bandaged, a syringe of antibiotics administered, the ordeal was over.

"I want you to spend the night in here."

Jared stood and started to the door. "No. Prefer my own space. I'll be fine."

Soon after exiting the infirmary, Tristan caught up with him. "You sure about going back to the room? You don't look too good."

"You wouldn't either if you just had someone break a fucking bone in your hand." As white as the gauze was now on his bandaged fist, it wouldn't stay that way for long. He extended his arm. Rig work was dirty, no matter what your job was.

"Don't tell me. You thought I was your father? That's why

you grabbed me by the neck."

"Yeah." He hated to admit the ugly truth of his past and continued down the corridor.

"Who's Sharon?"

Jared skidded to a stop and turned. "Why?"

"You were calling her name out in your dream." The man put his hand on Jared's shoulder. "You can tell me. It won't go any further."

They shared the small accommodation for almost as long as he worked on the rig. Tristan had been employed there even longer. The man was trustworthy. "Sharon was me sister."

"You never mentioned her before."

"She died."

"Sorry to hear that."

Did he go into more detail? Did the man really need to know his sibling committed suicide because of the abuse meted out by their father? He would rather keep those disgusting particulars out of the public eye. Kat knew because she went to Barnsley with him. Insisted they go to the cemetery. He had to tell her about Sharon because her identity was carved on the headstone with his mother's. He massaged the back of his head with his bandaged hand. "Fuck, I miss her. She topped herself on Father's Day. I found her body."

"Jeez man."

With that out in the open, Jared didn't tell anymore about his home life. He told Tristan about his sister and how he received the scar on his face. He twisted out from under his companion's hand and strode back to their shared accommodations.

Albeit awkward, he removed his boots and jeans and climbed up into the bunk. Lying on his back with his uninjured hand behind his head, he let his mind wander. At this moment, being alone was the right thing. He knew his workmate meant well and would keep their conversation in confidence, but this was the easiest way to not have to talk to the man. Someday, he might reveal the sordid details of his childhood, but not now.

At that moment, Jared wished he were back in Aberdeen with Kat. In spite of the rocky start to their reunion, being with her felt good. He hoped this time they would make a go of it. No one to interfere and split them up. But would the ghost of her dead husband be the one who would do just that?

Something she said about the location of Colin's death niggled at Jared. It required some research to confirm it, but the King's Cross railway station was not attacked in the bombings. The underground was. Maybe she was wrong? Confused? Until he knew the answer, it was speculation.

A brilliant idea came to him. What if? What if, he took her to London? Took her to the place where Colin died? Would that work? Would she hate him for dredging up those painful memories? Dredge up? Really? The poor girl lived in the past – lived in the months after the terrorist attacks. He would have to ease his way up to taking her there. If he told her in advance, she would refuse. Jared knew Kat well enough to know that.

It was too late to start looking into the events of July 7, 2005. He would have to wait until after his shift tomorrow. Now he had something else to focus on, his nightmares would disappear.

In a much better frame of mind, he drifted off to sleep.

~ 8 ~

10th January, 2011

The second day offshore went better than the first. The twelve hours flew by. Afterwards, he stopped at the infirmary to have his hand checked over and pick up the antibiotic pills David Asher prescribed. The pristine bandage applied last night was filthy. No doubt, the medic would change the dressing. He had mentioned daily inspections to follow the healing progress and with his fist wrapped, he couldn't do that.

When he reached the dining hall, the smell of curry lingered in the room. Garlic Naan bread and pappadums were on hand to have with his Butter Chicken and Basmati rice. Even though he was in a better mood after a good night's sleep and his idea to help Kat move on, being sociable wasn't at the top of his priorities. Spotting a vacant table in the corner, he walked over and started his meal.

"How's the hand?" Tristan asked as he eased his tall frame into a chair across from him.

"Medic is pleased with the progress. Gave me a bottle of pills to take to keep the infection away." After ripping a chunk off the slice of bread, Jared dipped it in his curry, and stuffed it in his mouth. He hoped his bunk mate would take the hint he wasn't up to talking.

"Good. I'll catch up with you after. Have a game of darts or something."

"Sounds good."

Tristan walked away. Now he had another reason to apologize to the man. Rudeness. He yanked his HTC android out of the back pocket of his jeans and typed.

Will Skype u later.

He popped a couple of Paracetamol to numb the discomfort in his hand and shoved the phone into the left back compartment of his dungarees. A darts match with his roommate was impossible. He couldn't tighten his fist enough to grip anything so small. The cutlery proved difficult.

When he finally finished his meal and took back his tray, Jared headed to the recreation room. One of the computers was vacant. No webcam on this system, but it was connected to the Wi-Fi so he could take advantage of the spare time to research the London bombings.

His mobile vibrated and he pulled it out.

Laptop ready. Talk soon.

Discovering Kat would be available, improved his mood. He went back to looking into the events of July 2005. At first, he didn't quite believe what he had read. Now what? Did he tell her about his discovery? Not yet. He needed to investigate further to ensure the accuracy of the piece. All he knew was it didn't jive with her version of the day. He wished he brought his laptop with him. With the subject matter he was researching, he could be mistaken for plotting another attack, but on a different city and on a work system, no less.

When one of the PCs with a webcam freed up, Jared deleted the history from his session. He cleared the cache, shut the browser down on the computer then powered the machine off. He hoped it would eliminate any trace of his activity. But, did that make him seem guilty? He moved over to the other one. In a few minutes, he sat face to face with Kat.

"What's wrong" she asked when they connected.

Nothing got by her. She could always read him like a book. "Yeah. Hand's sore." He held up his bandaged fist.

"Oh my God," she gasped. "What happened?"

"Long story. Split it open again last night and had to go to the infirmary."

"And?"

Jared raked his injured hand through his hair. "You were right. I did break that knuckle. The medic on board had to re-set the bone. Anyway, don't want to go through that again anytime soon. Even with freezing, still hurt. Infected to boot so he gave me a shot of penicillin or something and I have pills to take. Have to go back so Davey can clean and dress the damn thing every night after my shift."

Kat's eyes moistened knowing she was to blame for Jared hurting himself. Why did she refuse him that night? In all the time they had been together before, she never had. She toyed with the chain around her neck.

She needed to tell him about the street person coming in. Was she making something of nothing? His presence bothered her, but what if he just came in for a short time to get out of the cold?

After clearing her throat, she sighed. "You know the homeless guy that's been hanging around between the cinema and casino? Well, he came into the store yesterday. He didn't do anything untoward or unusual. Perused a few novels, like any browsing customer would do, and left. The weather was cold and foul here so I think he just came in to warm up."

A tall, dark haired man appeared behind Jared. "This your bird? She's quite the looker."

"Kat, this is Tristan."

"Hi," she greeted. His name. Familiar. But from where? Not a common one, at least in this area. She wracked her brain trying to remember. The only other person she knew with that name was one of her regular customer's partners. She swallowed hard and asked, "Your last name wouldn't be McKnight, would it?"

"Yeah. How did you know?"

"You're Cherie Young's partner."

"How do you know her?"

"She comes into my bookstore – *As the Pages Turn* – quite often. She talks about you a lot. Told me you worked offshore but I didn't realize until just now you were on the same rig as

Jared."

The man shook his head.

"If you're talking to her tonight, tell her the crime novel she ordered – *Dead Wood,* by Chris Longmuir came in. I know she's been anxious to read it."

"She spends a bloody fortune in that store of yours." Tristan pulled another chair over and sat.

Perhaps she shouldn't have mentioned the book to him. When she opened for business the next morning, Kat would call Cherie and apologize for dropping her in the deep and murky with her partner. Now, with the man ensconced beside Jared, it was impossible for them to talk.

How did that happen? His conversation hijacked by his roommate. Small world. He smiled when Tristan moved on, leaving the two to finish their visit. The expression on Kat's face said she was also relieved by the man's departure.

"So the homeless bloke was in your place. Don't like the sound of that. The way he's hanging around makes me think he's stalking you." Shifting in his chair, he continued, "I'm with Mel on this one. Not that he creeps me out, but something's not right there."

"I think the two of you have been watching too many crime programs on telly," she answered.

"All the same. Just be careful. I'll sleep easier knowing you're protected. Maybe you should contact the police?"

"And say what? I want the vagrant hanging out on my street removed. They won't do anything with him unless he's done something illegal. Besides, they have more important things to do than worry about a guy who's spending his time between the cinema and casino."

"And coming into your store."

"So he came in. It was cold and sleeting and he needed to warm up."

Jared was not getting anywhere with her on this argument. Still, Kat was naïve and required protecting from herself because of her lack of street smarts. He wanted to say 'the next thing you know, you'll be making him a hot meal' but he changed the subject. "How would you like to do something when I get home?" Might as well float the idea of spending time together out there. See how she would react.

"Just not the twenty-fifth. Steph and I have tickets to a Burns Supper that night."

She didn't shut him down – not yet at least. That was good.

"Did you have something in mind?" Kat scratched the corner of her left eye.

"Not really. Just want to spend time with you. We've got a lot of years to make up for." He didn't mean it that way – implying shagging their brains out twenty-four seven. If he tried to worm his way out of that line, he would only drop himself in deeper. Best to leave it lie and carry on.

"Did you want to go see a film? Vue Cinemas are right by mine. I can see what's playing."

Not what Jared envisioned, but in a darkened movie theatre, maybe he could take a few liberties. Hell, she might even return the favour. He had to stop thinking like that. The rest of the night under a cold shower was not a pleasant prospect. "Go on then."

"Or we could stay in. I'll pick up a DVD."

That appealed to him more than going to the cinema but he would rather be with her at his house in Newburgh. The pictures of her and Colin, among other reminders of her life with him, made Jared uncomfortable.

Kat's mobile rang. The display identified the caller. "It's Steph. I'll talk to you tomorrow? Same time?"

"Sure. Time I got off here and let someone else use the computer. Getting the stink eye from some of the blokes."

"Until then," she said.

He wanted to tell Kat he loved her but it was too soon. Not to know how he felt – he had never stopped loving her – but too early to tell her. He didn't want to frighten her off.

When the screen blanked, he pushed the chair back and sighed. The system he researched the London bombings on earlier was available. Did he look for more evidence? Was there any? Or merely wishful thinking on his part?

"Hi Kat. Want to go for a drink?" Stephanie asked. Not seeing Katherine for some time, it was now time for a proper girlie chat.

"Don't much feel like going out. Why don't you come over here? I've got a couple of bottles of white in the fridge. Besides, I was about to jump in the shower."

Sure, her bestie was busy running her business and needed to catch up with things there after being away for a few days, but only in this last year or so did she start going out other than to work, the post office, and the bank. Now Kat had started being seen out and about, other than work-related trips, she hardly refused an outing to one of the trendy bars in the city.

Well, not before Jared came back into her life. Stephanie was glad her friend had a decent bloke again. She always liked the guy even to the point of being jealous. Kat never went home with any of the blokes who tried to pick her up when the two girls went out, but at least she was no longer stuck in night after night living a nun's life.

"See you in a bit. I need to hear about your trip." Steph pushed the button on her mobile to end the call then shoved the device in her handbag disturbing her sleeping cat, Molly. The foul-tempered, grey striped moggy hissed and swatted at her, claws bared. Unable to pull her hand back in time, Stephanie paid the price. The sharp nails dug in. "Let go." She gave the tabby a swat. The animal relented and scarpered off to another room.

Blood dripped from the cut. The veins in the backs of Steph's hands were prominent and the feline had managed to dig in to one of them. Catching up on the dirt from Kat's trip to . Barnsley with Jared would have to wait. The injury inflicted by Molly needed attention. The beast always was a temperamental sort but now she was a senior, and going blind and deaf, even more so.

Stephanie plucked a tissue from the box on the end table and exercised pressure on the affected area. By the time she reached her bathroom where she kept her plasters and other first-aid accoutrements, the bleeding stopped. Big fuss over nothing? Not when it came to cat scratches. Who knew what nasty germs lurked in their feet and claws. After all, they used litterboxes and peed and pooped in the freakin' things. Yuck.

Steph's stomach lurched. She ran her hand under cold water and poured peroxide over the wound. The foam turned a watery red colour. She rinsed and repeated the process then dried her hand and applied antibiotic ointment. According to the plaster box, small round ones were included. She dug one out and put it over the puncture. Satisfied she would be good for tonight, Stephanie gathered her things and left.

Bottles of wine meant at least one glass, if not more. She had the option of walking or taking the bus to Kat's. The night, for early January, was pleasant so she opted to walk. *As the Pages Turn* was only about ten minutes on foot from her apartment on Crown Terrace.

The Bridge Street Stairs to Guild Street then up Shore Brae past the Maritime Museum, the film theatre to the bookshop. She could go left up Market and cut across the narrow section of Shiprow but at this time of night, best not to take that route. Returning home later, she would call a cab.

Kat picked up the intercom to buzz Stephanie through the security door downstairs. "Thought you would never get here."

"I didn't think I would either. Bloody cat attacked me when I put my mobile in my purse. You should have seen it." She held her hand out. The gauze pad had turned red from the wound bleeding.

"What is it with you two? Both of you with hand injuries."

"What's the scoop with Jared's hand? You told me he punched the casino wall after leaving yours at Hogmanay."

"The daft ape only went and broke his knuckle. The middle one had to be re-set in the infirmary on the rig. And it's infected."

"So tell me about Barnsley. You never did answer my question. Did you two do the horizontal mambo?"

"We slept together but nothing happened."

"But you wanted to, didn't you?" Steph's green eyes glowed with excitement.

"No."

"What? Are you off your nut woman?"

Kat headed to the small kitchen to pour their wine. "Jared was in a bad place. I shared a bed to comfort him. Nothing more." She handed her friend a stemless glass.

"FFS. Tell me," she urged.

"I'm not sure he wants his private life laid bare. Let's just say, he'd rather forget his childhood."

"You can't just stop at that," she said then gulped down her drink. "No holding back. Tell me."

"I don't feel right sharing."

"I swear it will go no further. Pulease ...."

Katherine sipped her Pinot Grigio. "This goes nowhere. I mean it."

"What happens in Kat's flat stays in Kat's flat."

Satisfied Steph would keep their confidence, she began. "There's so much about Jared I didn't know when we were together before. He never talked about his family." She took a drink. "I didn't know he had a sister."

Stephanie spluttered and swallowed the mouthful of wine. "What?"

"Yes, he had an older sibling."

"Had – as in doesn't now?"

"She got mixed up with drugs and committed suicide. Jared found her body." Kat took a sip. She didn't think her friend needed to hear anything else surrounding the circumstances of his sister's death. That part of his home life would remain private. If he wanted any more known, it would be up to him to divulge, not her.

"Wow. Poor guy. That must have been tough."

Katherine walked into the kitchen, and came back with the open bottle of white, and topped up their glasses. "I imagine it was."

"And that's why you two didn't? That would have been the perfect time. Jump his bones and take his mind off his previous life – BK – before Kat."

"If only it were that easy." She knew facing his past and compartmentalizing things again would be next to impossible.

Too much had happened in the years before she met him.

Before they called time on their night, the girls emptied the first bottle and made a good dent in the second.

Stephanie rang a cab. She hugged Kat, promised to call her later and went downstairs to meet the taxi.

Alone, Katherine contemplated her decision to tell her friend about Jared's past. She omitted the sexual abuse his sister endured at the hands of their father. Never mentioned the physical abused meted out by the man.

After she locked the front door, she took the remnants of their girlie chat to the kitchen and walked to the bedroom. Her long, white satin nightgown hung on a hook inside the closet door. She took the soft, silky garment and padded down the narrow corridor to the bathroom.

When she returned, she paused by the window furthest from her bed. No trace of the homeless man who had spent so much time on her street. Kat raised the sash and the floor length curtains billowed from the breeze. She got her laptop and climbed into bed. The clock radio on her bedside table read half eleven. Too late to try to Skype with Jared now. If she emailed him, he would receive it in the morning, or pick up her phone and text him.

Same thing, he likely wouldn't respond until the next day. His twelve-hour shift started and ended at seven, maybe earlier. She didn't want to wake him if he was already asleep. Instead, she checked on the status of a few book orders for the store, shut the computer down and went to sleep.

In the brief moment she stood before the open window, he knew she was naked under the nightgown. The lighting in her bedroom left nothing to the imagination. Her nipples, hard like diamonds poked against the fabric of her clothing. The narrow shoulder straps held the garment in place. How he would love to be with her, but he couldn't get and maintain an erection in the presence of a woman.

Only when he fantasized about them and it enraged him. His switchblade would be his penis. Slipping his hand beneath the band of fabric – first one, then the other – the nightgown would slide down her body leaving her naked in front of him. He would grip those firm, milky white mounds and squeeze them. Not roughly, but hard enough to elicit a response from her. Lift each one to his face, fill his mouth, flick his tongue over her hardened flesh, then nibble.

Start slow and seductive. Trick her into feeling safe, secure and treasured then lay her on her back on the bed and put one knee between hers. Once she responded to his touch, his bites would be harder. Her breasts, her throat would bear witness to his brutality.

He would break the skin with his teeth and taste her blood's copper tang then lick the wounds and suck on them to draw more of her life's fluid from her veins. To keep her from screaming in agony, he would wrap one hand around her neck. Not tight enough to kill, but adequate to prevent her from speaking.

She could thrash under him all she wanted but no one would hear her cries for help. Rape her with his leather gloved fingers followed by the handle of his flick-knife. When he deemed the time was right, remove the weapon, deploy the blade and shove that end into her.

Cut her to bits. As he did, his grip would tighten and he would choke the life out of her. She made him the way he was. She would pay. He would have his revenge. Now, if the voices would talk to him and agree with his plan.

~ 9 ~

22nd January, 2011

The safety meeting took longer than normal. Jared couldn't wait to leave. The fortnight away from Kat was too long. Skype worked but not the same as being together – touching each other, smelling the scent of her shampoo and perfume.

The chopper had encountered rough weather on the trip offshore and diverted, the foreman explained so it would be about sixty minutes late. It could be a lot worse. Could be days instead of hours. This way, he would still see her later that day or the next.

When he landed at the heliport, Jared was anxious remove his survival gear, change into his street clothes, and get to his car. The question was, did he go to Newburgh first or go straight into Aberdeen. He opted to go home. His body odour from sweating in the neoprene suit was pungent and he didn't want to subject her to that. He would make plans to do something with her from there.

Forty minutes after leaving Nexus headquarters, he pulled his BMW into the driveway, happy to be home. Unlocking the side door, Jared pushed it open, and stepped over the threshold. The place had been closed up for two weeks so he left the entryway ajar to air out the house.

Next, he entered the utility room and stuffed the contents of his duffel bag into the wash machine. The notes he made on the few occasions he managed to do some research on the London bombings lay on the bottom of the holdall. They were extracted and sat on the worktop over the front-loader.

Showered and changed into clean clothes, Jared felt more

like a human. He gathered up the papers, stopped in the kitchen for a tin of lager, and climbed the stairs to the spare bedroom where he used his laptop. The broadband signal was stronger in this room than any other place in the house.

But after the shite Wi-Fi offshore, not to mention not enough systems to go around, unless you had your own, anything was better. Now Kat was back in his life, he would take his computer with him. At least then he would be guaranteed of an available unit. One he could use in his room, if he so chose.

Deciphering his notes was something different. Because of his injured hand, gripping the pen was impossible so his usual scrawling script was worse than normal. Instead of wasting precious time doing that, he started over from scratch.

When he typed London bombings 2005 into his search engine, the number of results overwhelmed him. Where to start? The most reliable would be the *BBC News* or those of the reputable newspapers, rather than the tabloids. He began with an article in *The Telegraph* which listed everyone massacred on that day at every location. Colin's name was near the beginning of it along with the others who died on the Tube between King's Cross and Russell Square. On the few occasions he did any investigating using the systems on the derrick, he never got this far. Jared read and re-read the text on the screen. She had it so wrong.

A piece on the BBC's website told of the memorial plaques unveiled the following year at the locations near or where the bombings occurred.

Bring her to his, here in Newburgh, for a few days. During her stay, take her to London where her husband died. Risky? You bet. Worth a try? If it meant helping Kat move on, yes. Worst thing would be, she would hate him and he'd lose her. But, in her mind, with her still being married to Colin, did he even have her to begin with? He opened another tab in his browser and searched the schedules for times and fares.

~ 10 ~

23rd January, 2011

Jared waited until noon before phoning her. Business hours commenced at eleven o'clock so he would catch her there, unless one of her staff worked. Someone answered the telephone on the third ring.

"*As the Pages Turn*, how can I help you?"

The voice on the other end of the line was hers and not the answerphone recording. "Hi, it's me. Put some stuff in a bag and come spend a couple of days at mine."

A long silence greeted his invitation. "I-I can't. I have to run this place."

"I'm sure Mel would love the extra hours. Call her and any other of your part timers and get them to help. Trust me, you need to get out of the flat," he said, leaning against the doorframe to the kitchen. "I know the break to Barnsley was good for you. You can't tell me otherwise."

"But … I don't know. I can't promise you anything but more frustration."

"When we were in Yorkshire, waking up in your bed helped me. Much as I want to make love with you twenty-four seven, if you don't want the same as me, then I won't. All I want is to be with you. Share my house, my bed – with or without sex. No pressure at all. Can you live with that?"

Another long pause. "Well, spending time with you has brought back a lot of good memories. Let me try to arrange things here. I'll call you back."

"I'll be waiting."

Kat hung up the phone. Had she done the right thing? Should she spend time in another man's house? Not just a few hours but overnight? She couldn't deny awakening in his arms felt great and revived wonderful memories of their previous life together.

The rota she had drawn up for the rest of the week had her part-timers in for various shifts. Melissa was on for Thursday afternoon for the late night shopping and on Saturday all day with Josh. He was down for Wednesday and Friday afternoons from three until six plus the day with Mel.

Coverage from nine in the morning until her students arrived after classes was needed. But who? She wanted someone knowledgeable about books and did not already have a job. Cherie. Would she do it? The woman knew the place as well as Katherine, was well-read, well-spoken, and well-dressed.

Melissa and Josh were hard workers and knew her. They would understand if she enlisted her to work during the day while they attended school. She grasped the handset and dialled. The answerphone picked up on the sixth ring.

Cherie's cheery voice came on the line. "Hi, you've reached Cherie and Tristan. We can't come to the phone but if you leave your name and number after the beep, we'll get back to you. Thanks. Bye."

Message left, Kat hoped she would call back soon. Now she knew Jared worked with Cherie's partner, the two might be making up for the two weeks they had been apart. While she waited, she wrote a list of things she would have to teach her – the alarm system, how to disarm it once inside, the till, combination for the safe so she could remove the float money in the mornings.

Was there anything else? Josh and Melissa knew the close routine but she should show Cherie how to do that, too. The chalkboard sign proved to be a problem. Jared helped with it at Hogmanay. Would the personnel at the tourist information keep it at their premises?

As she looked up the number for the visitors' centre, her phone rang startling her.

Four rings before her heartbeat slowed. *"As the Pages Turn,* how can I help you?"

"Hi Katherine. Cherie here. You called and left a message?"

"Yes. I wondered … well …," she faltered, tapping her pencil on the countertop. "If you fancied working a few hours here in the shop."

"I'd love to. When?"

"This Wednesday, Thursday and Friday."

"I'm not sure what Tristan would think. Him being on his two weeks off."

"Sorry, I never thought of that. Jared invited me to spend a couple of days with him. I didn't make him any promises. He knows I have this place to run."

"Let me talk with Tris. I'm sure he won't mind. There are some projects need doing at ours. Never know, with me out during the day, it might be easier for him to finish them. I'll call you back."

"Thanks." Kat hung up, leaned on her elbows, and rubbed her forehead with her fingertips. Finding someone on this short notice was not going to be easy. If Cherie couldn't do it, a temp through an agency would have to be obtained. The idea of a complete stranger running her business didn't sit well but if she was unable to secure someone, she would have to shut. She couldn't, wouldn't expect Josh and Melissa to take time off school to work, not to mention closing took away from the kids' hours. Spending time with Jared might have to wait until another time.

Rather than dwell on what might not happen, Katherine busied herself opening a case of books that arrived the previous Friday. Embargoed until tomorrow when they officially went on sale, she needed to see the cover to determine the most attractive way of displaying the new tome. The publisher included rack cards, bookmarks and a poster in the shipment.

Standing in the entrance of the store, Katherine scanned the room for the place to create the presentation. Nothing could be displayed in front of the till because of the hindrance created for the customers. The far corner would be perfect. Turn the small antique table on an angle at the end of the shelving unit against the wall. Hang the poster above and have the books arranged on its surface. Some of the hardcovers would stand in plastic easels, the others stacked.

The remaining promotional material divided between there and the counter. Satisfied, she had chosen the right location for the display, she slid the carton under the shelf.

When the telephone rang, she hoped the caller was Cherie and she would be able to provide daytime coverage. "*As the Pages Turn.*"

"Tris is fine with me helping you out. Says I spend enough time and money in your store, I might as well start earning my keep." She chuckled.

"Brilliant." Butterflies churned in her stomach – excited but nervous about spending time alone with Jared at his place. "Why don't you come in for nine tomorrow morning and I can show you the ropes."

"See you then." Cherie rang off.

Did Katherine call now to let him know? She couldn't leave before the twenty-sixth because of the commitment she and Stephanie had on Robbie Burns Night. She grabbed her BlackBerry and scrolled through the callers to his number. It went to voice mail. "Hi Jared. Everything is sorted. I'll see you sometime on Wednesday."

Next, she called the tourist information office. To her delight, they would look after the chalkboard sign.

~ 11 ~

24th January, 2011

When Cherie arrived well before opening time, Kat was pleased, confident she had made the right choice. She deactivated the warning device and let her new employee in. "When you enter, you only have a couple of minutes to turn off the alarm or you'll have a visit from the law." The control panel and how to disarm the appliance was demonstrated. "Come in, close the door, key in the code and press the disable button."

Cherie nodded. "Looks easy enough."

"We're small, but I have a CCTV system installed, too. Keeps watch on the customers to make prosecuting shoplifters easier." She drew attention to a camera above the door. "That one captures most of the retail area. The one in this corner gets what the other can't see, and the one behind the counter watches the front door. Can't be too careful these days."

"Y-you're right."

"I haven't put you off, have I?"

"No."

"Just you seem somewhat nervous."

"A lot to take in."

"You'll do just fine." Katherine directed the way to the cash register. "I have a special project today. Sometimes books come in ahead of the official launch date, but they can't be displayed until then. I opened the case yesterday for an idea of what colours will be the best accent."

She slid the box out from under the shelf, and removed a copy of the latest hardcover crime novel and handed it to her newest employee. "I was thinking of setting up the display over in that corner." She pointed as she spoke. "That way, when people come in, it will be the first thing they see."

"What about going with a table covering in the same shades as the book's title?" Cherie suggested. "Have you got something that will make it pop?"

The cover art was in dark colours making the scene look sinister. The banner was in red changing to orange and finally yellow from top to bottom. The author name and tagline were printed in the mid-tone.

Cherie turned the book over in her hand then arranged the novel on the table. She stood back and took in the image. "You've got more experience with this kind of thing than I do, but what if, we move the exhibit to the end of this bookcase? Turn the stand ninety degrees so the narrow side is against the shelving?"

Kat folded her right arm over her waist and tapped her chin with her left index finger. "Go on. I'm liking what I'm hearing so far. The publisher provided a poster. We can put it on the unit above the presentation."

"What about over here?" Cherie walked to the counter and indicated the empty space she had in mind.

"Mmm …, I think it will get lost there. The customers queue up to pay in that area." She applauded the woman's initiative but experience told her, before the workspace where the till was located was a bad choice.

"Got it."

Katherine pushed the bead curtains aside and entered the small office cum storeroom leaving them clacking in her wake. After rummaging in the bins, she came up with a table covering. When she returned, she held up the cloth in front of the table. "A throwback from Halloween but I think the colours will work." The fabric was spread on the surface.

In the meantime, Cherie had fastened the poster to the end of the bookcase. The exhibit started to take shape. Books were stacked in three piles. Rack cards and bookmarks arranged around the display. Those not required there were laid out by the checkout.

Standing back to admire their work, Katherine was pleased. They worked well together. "I think we deserve a break. Want a coffee?"

"Thanks."

A few minutes later, they settled down to mugs of the steaming, hot brew. Now that they finished working, the quiet became awkward. She knew Cherie as a customer but not as a familiar friend. When Kat broke the silence, she asked, "How long have you and Tristan been together?"

"Going on seven years if you count when we first started seeing each other. We moved in to the house on Osborne Place four years ago."

"What about you and Jared? Tris told me you two were a couple."

Complicated. How else to describe it? "We're only just reunited again."

"Again?" Cherie's hazel eyes widened.

"We were together before my family relocated to Canada. My father was high up in the Royal Bank of Scotland and they offered him a transfer. He and my mum didn't approve of Jared's and my relationship." Kat clapped her hand over her mouth. Had she said too much?

"So you two go way back, then."

"Yes. Not long, but it was intense."

"Was he on the rigs then?"

"I can't remember." She wished things could go back to the way they were, but over ten years had elapsed. Too many things happened in their lives. It was doubtful it would ever be the way it used to be. "When Jared walked in on Hogmanay, I was gobsmacked. I thought he was gone forever, yet there he was."

"It's destiny. You two are obviously supposed to be together."

Bringing her mug to her mouth, she tried to hide her smile. Until she exorcised her demons and said her final goodbye to Colin, resuming her life with Jared would never happen. "How do you cope with Tristan being gone for a fortnight at a time?"

"It is hard I grant you. I just become acclimatized to being on my own and then he's home and I have to adjust to having him around again." Cherie sighed.

"I hear you. These past two weeks have been awful. Sure, we talk to each other on Skype but it's not the same. Since he's come home, I've not even seen him yet."

"You will. You're working into a routine. Once you find it, you'll do what feels right for both of you. Give it time."

The two chatted a wee while longer before Katherine called an end to their break. Being a quick learner the rest of Cherie's training went well. Some of the things she showed her were later in the day jobs and by that time of day, Josh or Melissa would be there to help her or do it themselves.

~ 12 ~

25th January, 2011

While the daily, closing routine was completed, Stephanie waited. "Hurry up, will you? All the haggis and good whisky will be gone by the time we arrive."

"A body would swear you've never been to a Burns Supper before." The day's takings were locked in the safe along with the cash register tray containing the float for the next morning. "Let's go. You're not going to give me a minute's peace until we do. Besides, the place I booked us is holding a celebration every night this week. There shouldn't be any danger of them running out. I just thought it would be fun to go on the actual day."

When they arrived at the facility hosting the week-long Burns festivities, the lobby was packed. Coats checked, and complimentary dram in hand, they followed the others to the dining room. Men in kilts, ladies in floor-length, evening dresses with tartan sashes pinned on their shoulders mingled. Seeing the women dressed in this manner made Kat feel under-dressed. She didn't own anything as fancy as the clothes on display here tonight. Her forest green, cashmere jumper, black pencil skirt, and high-heeled, knee high boots were more appropriate on a street corner than at this function.

Stephanie's tartan scarf worn as a sash over her right shoulder and pinned at her left hip over a strapless, black satin dress was classy. Even her shoes – thin-strapped, black, stilettos –amazing.

As a young girl, Katherine attended many of these functions, but always part of the entertainment. Oh, God, she hated those events back when she belonged to a dancing group who entertained the guests. Tonight, although she dressed well for the occasion, there were no expectations to perform a Highland Fling, Sword Dance or any other one for that matter.

Taking her friend by the elbow, Katherine steered her to a quiet corner for a quick girlie chat. Before the opportunity arose, the call came to take their seats.

They paused by the door in front of a large, polished brass easel holding a board displaying the seating arrangements. More than forty tables, in addition to the high one, were set up. Their names showed them at table thirty-nine.

When they entered, matching table sign holders held tartan bordered cards with Burns portraits beside the number. They were next to the back wall about halfway to the head table. She took Stephanie's hand and led the way through the crowded room; their progress impeded many times by people preparing to sit.

Three well-dressed couples already settled were gracious and nodded on the girls' arrival. One of the women looked down her nose at Kat. She smiled and introduced herself and her plus one. "Hi. I'm Katherine Murphy-Whithorn. I own *As the Pages Turn* on Exchequer Row. This is my friend, Stephanie Lindsay. She's a loans officer at the Clydesdale Bank."

Why had she used her married surname when referring to herself? She was not that woman anymore. Why had she done that? A pang of grief stabbed her in the heart and she dashed off to the women's toilets.

Katherine pushed the door open and found herself in a luxurious anteroom. Along the far wall, a granite counter stretched the entire width of the room. Above, hung illuminated mirrors. Leather sofas and armchairs provided places for conversation not to mention, refuge from awkward situations. Her moment at the table suited that. She didn't bother stopping there but dashed to the other side of the room and braced herself against the cool surface.

"Hey, what's up? You okay?" Stephanie asked. She rubbed her friend's back as she spoke.

"Do I look it?" The reflection of her tear and mascara stained face stared back at her. "I'm sorry I snapped."

"What the … happened out there? One minute you were talking and having a good time. Next you're in bits and in here."

"Did you hear how I introduced myself?"

"Yeah, Katherine Murphy-Whithorn. It is your name."

"I haven't been that woman in a very long time. She ceased to exist when Colin died in London."

"Fix your face and we'll go back out there. I explained your situation to the folks at the table. Told them about losing your husband and you never had proper closure. They understand."

Since 7 July, 2005, life had not been kind to Kat. The following twelve months filled with firsts – wedding anniversary, Christmas, their birthdays, property purchase – they had only rented in the beginning – and grand opening. There were more, there had to have been, but those escaped her at the moment.

When she came back, a hand reached over and patted hers. "You're bound to be upset dear. Going through something so tragic at your young age. You're well within your right to grieve. And it will hit you at the most inopportune moments."

A kindness and a hint this woman had gone through something similar – at least lost someone – whether through an act of terror, accident, or disease, reflected in the woman's eyes.

The sound of bagpipes announced the arrival of the special invitees. Everyone stood as they entered. When the last person sat down, a hearty round of applause greeted them.

After the Chairman welcomed the guests and recited the *Selkirk Grace*, the piper preceded the chef and the haggis at which time, the *Chieftain o' the Puddin' Race* was addressed and sliced open. Drams of whisky were poured and consumed.

Waiters and waitresses in crisp white shirts and black waistcoats served the starter course, their kilts accented by matching tartan ties. When her Cock-a-leekie soup didn't contain a big fat prune like some recipes, Katherine sighed with relief. Her father extolled their virtues as he ate a bowl of them every morning. She collapsed in a pile of giggles drawing disdainful looks from the others seated at the table. "Sorry everyone. Seeing the soup made me think of prunes."

Stephanie stared at her.

"You probably think I'm quite the head case. Bawling my eyes out one minute and laughing like a lunatic the next. I assure you, I'm fine and don't suffer extreme mood swings like you witnessed tonight."

Once they finished the first course, the wait staff, with the same efficiency, cleared tables and served plates of haggis, champit tatties and bashit neeps. Someone at their table ordered bottles of red and white wine which they were invited to share in.

During the first entertainment, a small group of girls in Highland Dancing attire, performed. Watching them made Kat feel wistful and wish she was young again so she could dance with them, although when she was about their age, she hated putting herself on display in that manner. At thirteen, being involved in something like this was no longer the 'in' thing. Because her father was a banker and high up in the Royal Bank of Scotland, the members of her clique looked to her for leadership, but some were right cows, too.

Back then, Katherine hated her red hair and received a great deal of torment from schoolmates for being a ginger. Now with the multitude of products available, she embraced the shade and loved how much richer her hair was now compared to back then.

While the Master of Ceremonies recited the *Immortal Memory* speech, Katherine grew disinterested and yawned, not even attempting to stifle it. To her, the evening couldn't end soon enough. In an effort to wake up, she excused herself and went outdoors.

When she was on the front steps, Stephanie joined her. "Everything okay?"

"This time – yes. Hot in there. I'm bored senseless. I hoped some fresh air might revive me."

"Well just don't stay out here too long."

She needed to tell her bestie about Jared's invitation. The girl would be hurt if she heard it elsewhere. Was the idea of spending time at his place the cause of her breakdown earlier at dinner? "Steph, wait."

"What's up?"

"I don't want you hearing this from someone else."

"Quit scaring me. What don't you want me to hear?"

She inhaled and said, "Jared has invited me to his for a few days."

"That's all? Brilliant." She threw her arms around her friend.

"I'm nervous. He says he won't pressurize me but I can't keep putting him off forever."

"Maybe being away from yours?" Steph offered. "So you didn't shag in Barnsley, but you shared a bed. His home could be the one. After all, when you first met him, his bedsit was your passion pit. Conceivable his new digs will be the place?"

"He lives out in Newburgh now. That's all I know. I don't mind saying, I'm scared. Even though he says no pressure, does he mean it?"

"Quit over-analyzing everything."

"Did I ever tell you about the time my parents almost found the two of us in their bed?"

Stephanie stopped in her tracks. "What? No. Never told me squat."

"It was one of my many acts of defiance. Mum and Dad had gone to some cocktail party and would be out until well after midnight. Jared waited down the street in his Land Rover. When their car pulled out of the drive and disappeared, I flicked my bedroom light off and on as our signal. Well, when he came in the door, I blindfolded him and brought him up to the master suite. At first, he hated the location but I soon persuaded him. Anyway, we fell asleep in each other's arms. When the front door opened, we woke up. Talk about scrambling. I sent Jared to my room, fixed the bed and put on my dressing gown. Me wandering about in jimjams wouldn't be suspicious. Lucky for us, they didn't come upstairs right away. When they did and turned out their bedroom lights, I snuck him down the stairs and out the door. His last words to me that night were 'you're dangerous'."

Stephanie shook her head and giggled. "I'm going back in. It's freezing. You coming?"

"In a minute." After Steph went back inside, Katherine rubbed her hands up and down her arms hoping the friction would warm her up.

The sky glowed orange. At this level, the night was clear, but higher the fog thickened and distorted the shape of the light fixtures turning them into deformed, bright fuzzy orbs.

He stood in the shadows over the road from the hotel. Illuminated by the lights, her beauty captivated him. Such a shame she would have to die. Her long red hair shone and her skirt and boots showed off her shapely legs. He had followed her here. She had another woman with her so he couldn't act then. No, she must be alone when he made his move – like she was now.

The time was still wrong. He flexed his leather-clad fingers and fantasized the feeling when he wrapped them around her neck and choked the life from her body. He had something else in mind for her, first. Something that cost him five hundred quid. Pulling his Fedora down over his eyes, he turned and walked away. The time was getting closer. The voices told him so. And they would tell him when it was time to act.

When she entered the dining room, the guests were preparing to sing *Auld Lang Syne*. Katherine took her place at the table, crossed her arms and joined hands with the people on both sides of her.

Overall, the evening had been enjoyable, but she anticipated getting home and into her long, white satin nightgown and going to bed. Maybe once she settled under the duvet with her laptop, she could Skype with Jared but would have to check her email when she got home to see if he tried to contact her.

~ 13 ~

Kat determined she would work until her young tattooed employee, Josh Cameron, arrived. Cherie's training on Monday went well. The woman caught on fast and was a huge help setting up the display for the new book. She might use her more often so she could escape during the school year.

Even though her newest hire was quite capable, she wanted to be there on her first day and introduce her to Josh when he came in for three o'clock. She asked Melissa to come by, also, to meet her before her shift on Thursday.

While Cherie was out posting the cheques to the book distributors, Katherine used the shop's computer to look up ScotRail's schedule. She would go as far as Dyce and Jared could uplift her there and save him driving all the way into the city.

The first service out of Aberdeen after Josh clocked in left just before half-three. The following one departed about twenty minutes later.

Scrolling through the callers' list on her BlackBerry Z10, when she found Jared's number, she pressed the icon to ring him back. "Hi. I'll come by rail to Dyce. I have a few things to do here before I leave. Josh doesn't start until three and I want to be here to introduce him to Cherie. Melissa is coming by, too."

"They don't know her already?"

"As a customer not a co-worker. I think I owe them that much." Kat tidied the card rack. Why don't you plan to pick me up at the railway station in Dyce for three-forty? If I can't make that one, I'll let you know. The next would put me there at four o'clock. Save you driving all the way into the city." She ran her fingers through her long red hair waiting to see if he agreed with her arrangements.

"I don't mind coming for you."

"And I like the train."

"Oh, all right then. Love you. See you soon."

He said those two words. Something she longed to hear for ages. Five years was a long time to go without hearing them. Kat disconnected the call, afraid if she stayed on the line any longer, of breaking down in tears while on the phone.

The anticipation of spending more time alone and away from Aberdeen with him excited her. Would the end result be them making love? She couldn't think that far ahead. Being with him again was the main thing.

Kat needed to pack. In the toiletries and cosmetics department, she kept a duplicate supply in her travel bag. A quick inventory to ensure she had enough of everything would be all she required. Clothing would need to be refreshed, though.

After all, the same things she took on her previous trip away with Jared wouldn't give the right impression. She didn't want him to think her wardrobe extended no further. There was a time when it had no bearing. When all that mattered was spending time with him – most of the time without clothes.

Why did she keep going back to their previous life when all they wanted to do was have sex? Was it because he was sexy and treated her well? Gave her the very first orgasm she ever had? Didn't hurt her the first time they made love unlike her encounter before him. Did things to her she never dreamed of? His hot breath on the insides of her thighs … his tongue in places …

The memories of their lovemaking sessions excited her. Would they get that back if she went to his? Start over like they'd never been apart? She hoped so. At that particular moment, she wanted nothing more.

When Josh entered, the shop bell jingled. "You okay?" he asked. "You look a bit flushed."

Embarrassed, Kat dashed upstairs, exposed in the middle of one of her fantasies. So worked up with her recollections of sexual encounters with Jared, she rushed into her bedroom and threw herself across the mattress. Melissa walking in on her in the midst of a steamy recollection would have been bad enough. But no, it had to be Josh. Young, handsome, jet black hair, piercing green eyes. Could she face him again?

She had no choice because there were things she needed to tell him before she left. Climbing off the bed, she opened her suitcase, packed laundered sweaters, jeans, a couple of scarves, and plenty of panties, and socks. Since the majority of her underwear was matching sets, Kat added the bras to the pile, too. She didn't know what Jared had in mind for meals – eat out or stay home, so tossed dress trousers to the stack of belongings to take with her.

Most of her footwear was not conducive to doing a lot of walking, so she shoved them in her luggage and opted to wear her warm, suede Uggs instead. Wearing stiletto heels when she went to Barnsley at the beginning of the month, proved it. Katherine added a white, cable knit beanie hat and matching scarf and a pair of cozy fur-lined mittens that matched her boots – the latter of which would be useful getting from her street to the railway station.

Plucking her white, down-filled parka off the hook, she checked to ensure she had everything. Satisfied all was in order, she put the garment over her arm, picked up her bag and walked downstairs to the shop.

Cherie came in carrying two bouquets of flowers in bright shades of orange, red and yellow. "Do you have any vases? I think these would look good on the window sills."

Josh's face wore a puzzled expression. His green eyes flashed.

Katherine introduced him to the newest member of the staff. "Cherie will be working the morning shift when you're in school. Her being here won't affect yours or Melissa's times."

"What about my hours?" Mel asked as she entered the store.

Another introduction was made and more reassurances

given. Katherine would never sack either of her students. They worked hard. Melissa found two vases and helped Cherie arrange the flowers. "If any of you need anything, I'm only a phone call away. I'll have my BlackBerry with me."

"We'll be fine. You go off and have a brilliant time."

Kat breathed a sigh of relief when she bolted the door after her. She expected a smart comment about her earlier behaviour. On the street, she extended the handle on her small cabin suitcase and started out, pulling it behind her. The icy east wind buffeted her as she rounded the corner to Shiprow, making her glad she had dressed for outdoor activities. The buildings funnelled the cold off the water up the road rather than protecting her from its frigid clutches. The air was heavy and the fumes from the vessels in the harbour assailed her nostrils.

The concealment of the cinema entrance was the perfect location. He hovered in obscurity. Few people knew he was there. Those who did turned their heads away to avoid eye contact. Were they afraid of him? They shouldn't be. Their existence had nothing to do with the reason he came back to Aberdeen.

When she passed his hiding place, he walked out and fell into step trailing her. Near enough to track her movements but far enough back, she would never realize he followed. Where was she going with that suitcase? Was she going to see Mr. Cocksure? The voices told him to eliminate his opponent. Still, the man was bigger and stronger. How could he do it? They didn't communicate that information. Since the previous night, not a single one spoke to his subconscious.

On her trip to Barnsley with Jared, she only wore her wine coloured mac. Had his car broken down and they had been stranded somewhere, she would have been screwed in such a light piece of outerwear.

The sensation of someone following her overwhelmed Katherine. She stopped. If she was, her pursuer halted at the same time. Her original plan was to take the narrow section of

Shiprow at the Maritime Museum to Market Street. Now, she changed her mind and continued down Shore Brae to Trinity Quay.

At the first opportunity, Kat entered the Union Square Mall to walk to the railway station in the warmth and the odour-free environment it provided, but even that was relative. Some of the shops had their perfumeries near their doors and those scents wafted into the corridors.

As she approached the doorway, second thoughts about this excursion plagued her. After purchasing an open-ended return ticket, she walked through the turnstile to the platform from where she would depart.

He followed her. She went through the barrier. He wandered as close as he dared in an attempt to determine her position. A member of the British Transport Police gave him a look, took two steps in his direction, and he retreated to read the arrivals and departures boards.

As he scanned the screens, he noticed the stairs leading to the far staging areas at the end of the sandstone kiosk closest to the gateway. He climbed them. Checking for more coppers or cop wannabes and finding none, he settled on the bridge over the rails. There she stood on the northbound platform. He begged the voices to tell him what to do but they refused to answer. The train entered blocking his view of her and when it pulled away, she had vanished. Had she boarded?

She wouldn't have gone to meet Mr. Cocksure somewhere, would she? She couldn't. She was his. She would never belong to anyone else. He would see to it. Voices or no voices.

Settling into a window seat, Kat's absence from her business bothered her. Did her staff begrudge her the amount of time she took off since Hogmanay? Sure, some of the days fell on Bank Holidays so she didn't open, but she had only been home from Barnsley a few short weeks and was going away again.

Now Cherie was in the mix. Would they resent working with the woman despite Kat's assurances? Before long, the

ScotRail service approached Dyce. As promised, Jared waited for her. She spotted him leaning against the exterior of the shelter at the unstaffed station, his arms crossed over his chest.

Kat knocked on the carriage window and waved trying to grab his attention but was unsuccessful. When the train came to a full stop, she stood and retrieved her luggage from the overhead rack.

In the midst of the crowd detraining, Jared spotted her long, red hair near the pedestrian bridge. He sprinted in her direction, dodging others coming at him. When he reached her, he put his arm around her and kissed her cheek then took her suitcase.

"I didn't expect it to be this busy, she said, taking his bare hand in her gloved one. "At this time of day, I would have thought everyone would be where they were going."

"You think this is bad, you should see this place around three o'clock after the shift change on the rigs and the guys are getting back to the mainland for their off weeks." Steering her in the direction of Station Road, he said, "Car park was full so I had to leave it up on Merrivale so I hope you don't mind a bit of a walk."

"I'm fine."

A little over half an hour later, he parked the car in front of a white, period cottage in Newburgh. "We're here. Chez Martin," he said, turning to her and winking.

Pleased Jared made something of his life, this came as a total surprise. She expected an apartment similar to hers. "This is all yours?"

"Yup. Every square foot. Well, more than for one person, but … would be great to share with someone special. Maybe even raise a family in. Lots of room and no one shuffled off to the stinking hot attic bedroom."

Did he just imply he wanted her to move in? She hoped not. Just coming to his place for a couple of days was a huge step. Kat didn't know if staying here would even work. Yes, she and Jared had a life together before. One to which she'd like to be able to return. The big thing, was she ready?

She tugged down the zipper on her parka about six inches and toyed with the chain around her neck on which she wore Colin's wedding ring. Why did she have such lousy luck with men? Yanked away from Jared before, then widowed when Colin was killed in the London bombings. Karma? She did nothing to deserve ... or had she?

He climbed out of the vehicle, strode to the front door, and unlocked it. When he came back for Kat, he opened the passenger door and helped her out of the BMW. "You can go in through there while I put the car away. I'll bring your things in from the back."

She nodded and walked to the portico where she stopped and turned to him.

"Go on. You're all right. The place is empty."

The interior of the vestibule was gloomy and she fumbled for a switch. When she couldn't find one, she pulled the door open wider to allow more natural light into the small area. Before going any further, she kicked off her Uggs and sat them in the boot tray under the table on her left. A dark stained, French door took up most of the space in the partition separating the entrance hall from the rest of the house. She turned the knob, pushed it open and discovered a bank of switches on the wall.

One by one, she flipped them on, starting with the one closest to the anteroom which turned on the outdoor light. The one in the middle illuminated the foyer. The walls in there painted a deep shade of blue, explained the darkness in the room. The last one controlled the fixture in the corridor.

When she started into the suite on her right, Jared came through with her bag from the back of the house, startling her.

"Give me your coat and I'll hang it up."

Kat removed her parka and handed the garment to him. "Thanks." He walked out to the back hallway and hung her outerwear on a hook beside his. The simple action made her heart flutter. Why was she so nervous? She didn't react this way as a teen. Being in his bedsit with him when she should have been elsewhere had been exciting – dangerous.

"Go on in. I'll be with you in a minute. Going to take this

upstairs."

The fixture in the hall gave off little usable light in this room. Kat found a switch and when she turned it on, the ceiling lamp illuminated the lounge. A large fireplace stood on the opposite side. Heavy, navy blue, velvet curtains covered the window – the plush carpet the same shade.

A chunky, beige sofa nestled along the wall to her left and a matching armchair to her right next to a wide-screen television and stereo system. Built-in, floor to ceiling bookcases – their shelves stocked with CDs – occupied both sides of the fireplace. Kat walked over and read their artists and titles, having to sidestep a black, leather recliner and side table.

"Well, what do you think?"

"I-I'm not sure. It's not what I expected."

"And what were you expecting? Another grungy bedsit?"

"No. Just not a house. I didn't think you would bother with anything so permanent when you're away so much."

A faded photograph in a pewter frame sat on the mantelpiece. It was of a woman and two children before a house. The little girl in the picture appeared older than the boy. The smaller child was a younger version of the man she was with. No one smiled. Their expressions were serious, as if afraid of something. "This you?"

"Yes." He plucked the object out of her hands and stored the memento back where it belonged.

"Your mum and sister, too?"

"Yes. The only good things to come out of living in that dump. And they're both gone now," he answered, his voice tinged with sadness.

"I didn't mean to upset you."

Jared took her in his arms. "You didn't. Want to see the rest of the place?"

The remainder of the cottage, much like the sitting room, was void of any touches making a house a home. His place was clean and tidy, despite a thin layer of dust, but the house had been sealed up for two weeks.

They stopped at Jared's room last and Kat walked in ahead of him. Her cabin suitcase stood against the wall. Did he expect her to share his bed? A king-size no less. He lived alone, spent at least a fortnight at a time away from home. Why did he need one so large? Her mind wandered and she envisioned the two of them snuggled together under the covers.

As much as her body yearned for his touch, inside and out, her heart told her now was too soon. Reining in her imagination, she continued her perusal of his room. The absence of bedside tables puzzled her. His alarm clock sat on a chest of drawers across the room – far enough away to force him out from under the blankets when it went off.

Jared walked up behind Kat and encircled her waist with his arms. She rested her hands on his. The backs were rough from working. The knuckles on his right hand remained swollen. He moved her hair away from her neck with his chin and nuzzled the now exposed skin. "Hey, I know what you're thinking. I like to spread out when I sleep. Those beds aren't big enough to roll over in, not to mention you got a guy sleeping under you." He held his hands out in front of him to demonstrate the width.

Kat tilted her head giving him more of her to kiss. "How do you know what I was thinking?"

"For the record, you're the first gal I've brought back here ... and a bed this big has more room to shag in."

"This is all I'm here for? A romp in the sheets?" She struggled out of his grip.

"I didn't mean it like that."

"Just how did you intend it to come out, then? And why did you assume I would sleep in here? That's what bringing my suitcase into your room says to me." Grabbing her cabin bag, she stormed out.

"Wait." He rushed after her and caught her as she reached the head of the staircase. "I'm sorry. Don't go. I promised you no pressure." He wrenched the luggage handle from her grip. She lost her balance and teetered backwards. Jared lunged for her and captured her before she tumbled down the stairs. Wrapping his arms around her, he mentally kicked himself in the arse for his actions and gathered her tight to him, loath to let her go. "I am so sorry. I could never forgive myself if I did something to hurt you."

The tension eased from Kat's body but she didn't return his embrace. Certain he ruined any chance of a permanent reunion with her, he pulled back. "You take mine. I'll sleep over here," he said before returning her luggage to his bedroom.

Once he put the bag down, Jared brushed past Kat and down the steps. He needed to get away from her and the accident he almost caused. He spread his hands out on the kitchen island and tried to catch his breath. Anger bubbled over and he swept his arm over the surface sending a pottery bowl crashing to the floor. Blimey, his temper got the best of him again. Kat might be better off without him. She didn't deserve to live with his moods.

Katherine walked into Jared's room and dropped on the bed where she replayed their conversation in her mind. Climbing into bed with him in Barnsley was wonderful – waking up in his arms, amazing. But it was more of a comfort thing for both of them. When he rang her that morning and invited her to spend a few days at his, he said 'no pressure'. Did she overreact? She didn't give him a chance to explain.

With her bag sitting in his room, why wouldn't she assume the worst? Did he plan to take the spare bedroom from the time he phoned her? Oh, God, she was such an ass. Did she stay or did she leave? Was their relationship doomed before it ever restarted? Too many things had happened to them since her move to Canada – one her parents didn't see fit to tell her about until they left for the airport. Up to that point, she thought they were going on a family holiday, not a permanent relocation.

After her arrival in Calgary, she ran away many times. The furthest she got was Toronto. With no means of income and her passport being held somewhere, she had no way of getting back to Scotland. Mobile phone confiscated, snail mail scrutinized or destroyed, it was like being an inmate in a prison, but without bars. Computer access was limited to school or the library – both places with their own set of restrictions. Any chance of communicating with her friends back home evaporated.

Kat resented her father for being the one who took the job in a foreign country just to take her away from her boyfriend. When the man died of a heart attack, she did not cry. In her eyes, it looked good on him after tearing them apart. Before she got her inheritance, she applied to Universities in and around Aberdeen. Anything to come back to the place and man she had fallen for, head over heels.

Things fell to pieces the night he was in the pub with another woman. Devastated, she let Colin into her life while she rebounded. She loved Jared before relocating to Canada and still felt the same way about him. Ached to be held in his arms. Yearned to make love with him.

They bared their souls to each other in the days since Hogmanay. He, to her at the cemetery in Barnsley, and she, to him at her place after they came back. Was it enough for her to move past the guilt of having a sexual relationship with someone other than her deceased husband?

Did Jared's volatility stem from PTSD or even post-concussion syndrome. Living in a violent, abusive home would push anyone to the brink. Finding your sister dead in the bath, right on over the edge. He mentioned the day of his mother's funeral, his father giving him an almighty shove and he bashed his head on the fireplace. Maybe he suffered a concussion in the incident and no one ever knew. Back then, if you cracked your head without drawing blood, and sought medical attention you were considered a wimp. It was just coming into the fore now.

She pulled out her BlackBerry and stared at the blank screen. What should she do? Cut her losses and run away from Jared as fast and as far away as she could? Stick it out and in one of his rages become a punching bag?

The next thing she knew, she had dialled Steph's work number. "Pick up," she urged.

"Hiya. Clydesdale Bank, Stephanie Lindsay speaking."

"I'm in a predicament." Kat kept her voice down, not wanting Jared to overhear.

"Speak up. I can barely hear you."

"I'm at Jared's house in his bedroom."

"You're in there with that hottie and you're ringing me? Give your head a shake."

"You don't understand. I'm in trouble. I'm upstairs. He's down in the kitchen. I don't want him to hear me."

"You're scaring me. What the fuck is going on?"

In all the years Kat had known Steph, the girl had never uttered an expletive stronger than shite or bollocks. She just dropped the F-bomb.

"I'm coming to get you. Where is his place?"

"No. Don't. You'll only make things worse."

"You sound terrified. How could me arriving there to collect you do that?"

Kat sighed. "I almost fell backwards down the stairs. I got mad because Jared put my suitcase in his room. I planned on leaving right then. Snatched my bag and started. When he yanked the thing away from me, I lost my balance. He caught me and kept me from falling."

"You're not staying there another minute. I don't care what excuse you have to give him, just get yourself out of that lunatic's home."

By now, Kat sobbed. "It was my doing. Not his. I jumped to conclusions. He told me no pressure but when I saw my luggage in his bedroom, I didn't once think he would use the spare one across the hall. I wanted out of there." She paused to breathe. "He tried to stop me from leaving to explain. It was an accident. Please, I'll be fine. I just needed to talk to someone. Bye." She ended the call.

Stephanie held the receiver in the air between her ear and the cradle, trying to come to grips with the conversation. Her friend for more years than she could remember sounded petrified which was out of character. Then there was the excuse she made. Not his fault. Hers. Back in the day, Kat swooned over Jared. In those early days did he hold some kind of power over the girl?

Since he came back on the scene at Hogmanay, she

became nervous and jumpy and not her old self at all. Mind you, the poor woman had been different for the past five years after Colin's death. Everyone grieved in their own way. Katherine built a wall around herself, spent ages indoors, never going out, not even to run her business.

Had Jared physically abused her bestie? She lifted the handset and punched in her friend's mobile number. Counting the rings, Stephanie tapped her fingers on the desk, determined not to hang up until Kat acknowledged. With no voicemail, the blasted thing would ring until … someone picked up, or threw the phone against the wall and smashed it, or stomped on the display and broke the screen. She hoped the former would happen and not the latter.

Eighteen rings later, she answered. "H-hello?"

"What's happening? Are you safe? I need to know – now."

"I'm fine. I'm on my way downstairs now to tell Jared I'm sorry for putting two and two together and coming up with six."

"What do you mean, apologize? You don't have a single thing to be regretful for. He should be the one."

She received no response. Bollocks. Kat's behaviour screamed battered woman. If that man did anything to her friend, she would swing for him.

"Please. I'm all right. Don't worry. I have to go."

The next thing she knew, the call had ended and the dial tone buzzed in her ear, increasing Steph's anxiety over her friend's situation. More and more, Kat acted like an abused woman. She hoped her assessment was wrong.

When the awareness of someone watching him became too great, Jared raised his head. The woman he adored and vowed he would never hurt, stood in the archway separating the kitchen from the corridor, holding the handle on her small suitcase. She didn't have anything on her feet other than socks. "Don't come any closer," he warned. "Busted glass on the floor. I don't want you to step on it."

Her eyes moistened with tears. He did it to her. Had he been a split second slower, she could have broken her neck in the fall. Maybe even ended up paralyzed. He thanked his lucky stars he got to her and prevented such a catastrophe.

Moisture ran down her cheek. He brushed the droplet away with his thumb before placing a gentle kiss on the spot. Jared held her. He couldn't lose her. Not now. Not after they only just found each other again after years of separation. Kat was the one good thing in his life since he escaped from Barnsley at the age of fifteen. Her arms reached around his waist and she rested her face against his chest. Placing his right hand on the back of her head, he stroked her long, red hair.

"I-I should leave. This was a mistake. Would you take me back to Dyce so I can go back to Aberdeen?"

Those were the last words Jared wanted to hear. He blew his chances with her – big time. Now he paid the price. "No, you shouldn't." He enveloped her in his arms. "We need to talk first. Then if you still feel the same way, I'll drive you all the way to the city." He relaxed his hold on her, tipped her face upward. Her golden brown eyes were watery. "We'll go into the lounge. Neutral territory, if you will."

Once in the room, he led her to his leather recliner. He paced, raking his hand through his hair. "I didn't do this well. Downright, fucking bad. I assumed when I rang you and told you no pressure, you'd realize I meant separate rooms. I gave you mine because the bed is bigger and more comfortable than the one in the spare. Blimey, had I known things would go this pear-shaped, I would have spelt things out in the first place, but no. I bloody well cocked it up. At one time, we could almost read each other's minds. Guess I thought we still could. Made a right pig's ear of things."

Jared squatted before Kat and took her hands in his. Rubbing the backs of them with his thumbs, he continued, "I'd never hurt you for the world." He sniffed and blinked fighting back his feelings. "Had you fallen down the stairs and been injured, I couldn't live with myself, knowing I was to blame."

She raised her head. "I know."

"I don't want to lose you again. Once was enough. More than enough." He needed to give her some space. Jared rose and walked to the window. Not only that, his emotions had to be reined in. He rubbed his eyes with his thumb and forefinger before scrubbing his hands down his face. If she dumped his sorry arse, who could blame her? He stood in front of the huge paned glass, hands on hips, with his back to the rest of the room.

A pair of slender arms encircled his waist. His heart leapt with joy upon discovering Kat didn't walk out the door and abandon him, even though in his mind, he deserved it. The heat from her breasts warmed his back. His eyes glassy with moisture, Jared stiffened, trying to calm down. He drew in a ragged breath. The two stayed in the same position for some time. About fifteen minutes later, he tipped his head back, inhaled again, and blinked back his tears. He turned around, and wrapped his arms around her.

Kat's beautiful, brown eyes were moist, too. Jared pressed his lips on hers. Not urgent, but gentle and loving. When she opened her mouth and touched his with her tongue, he reciprocated.

Tracing down her neck with his fingertips, goose bumps came out on her skin from his touch. When he reached the open collar of her blouse, he stopped – the caress, the kiss – everything. "I love you," he whispered, his voice husky with desire. "It's not right. You're not ready."

"I am," she protested.

Jared put his hands on her upper arms. "I wish you were, but I can tell you're still not in a position to make such a commitment. And if we cross that line, I don't want you to resent me for taking you over it."

"I would never …."

"It's a chance I don't want to take. I promised you no pressure if you came here. I plan on sticking to my end of the bargain, no matter how much I want you, and have wanted you since …."

Until, Kat laid the ghost of her dead husband to rest once and for all, Jared resigned himself to a life of cold showers and the occasional wank. Now was one of those moments. The woman standing in front of him was gorgeous. It took all his resolve to not take liberties. But he had to. Nothing could happen until she was ready. "Give me fifteen and we'll walk to the pub. Not far. About five minutes. I think we both need a change of scenery."

Jared took the stairs two at a time to the spare room he would call his until such time as either Kat wanted to share his king-size bed or went home. He hoped for the former. He turned on his computer and went back to searching schedules.

Thirty minutes from Newburgh to the railway station at Dyce – forty-five to allow for unforeseen events along the way would be better. Could be cutting things close. Less than fifteen to Aberdeen should there be no delays and plenty of time to arrive at the right floor for the Virgin East Coast to London King's Cross. The earlier they left the more advantageous since the journey took about eight and a half hours.

If they waited almost an hour, a non-stop route was available. The initial leg would still have to be made early to ensure the connections fell into place. Jared pulled his credit card out of his wallet and booked their passage.

Now, he couldn't let the proverbial cat out of the bag too soon. He needed to tell Kat something but it could be worked out over a pint at the Udny Arms or the Ythan Hotel since they were about the same distance from his place, in the opposite directions. He knew she would prefer the atmosphere at the former.

When they reached the tavern, Jared held the door for her. Despite the hour, the area was quiet. He ushered her in that direction and pointed out a booth in a corner. "You want to sit and I'll get the drinks in?"

"I don't think we have to worry about our seats being taken. Besides, I'm just as happy waiting here with you."

"Hi Jared, what can I get you?" the pretty, black-haired barmaid asked.

"Hmm, know you by name, I see. You must come here a lot," Kat teased.

He turned back to the bar. "Well, it is my local. Caledonian 80 for me and a G&T." He nodded to his companion.

"Go take a seat. I'll bring them over."

Because of the lack of custom at the time, they were spoiled for choice for an empty table or booth. Jared put his arm around her and walked her to the location he indicated earlier. Taking Kat to London was heavy-duty stuff. He couldn't just come out and tell her where they were going. She would flat out refuse. This required a wee bit of deception.

She slid into the banquette with her back to the wall. Once settled, he eased in beside her. The girl waited with their drinks while he sat down. She put them on the cardboard beer mats on the table and left them.

Jared took a deep breath, exhaled, then took a slug of his ale. "With the cock up I made of things bringing you to mine …."

"You think I should go back to Aberdeen."

"Fuck, no. Not what I meant at all. What I was going to say was … spending a few days together might be best done away from my place, away from yours. Some place where there are no memories, no distractions. You and me."

"Hmm, sounds nice. What did you have in mind?"

"Already booked the break. And no, I won't tell you because it's a surprise." He leaned back. She believed him – he hoped. Jared hoisted his glass and took a drink and motioned to the bar for another round even though they weren't yet ready.

He waited in the cinema entrance. Once the bookstore ceased operations for the day, he would go back into her home. Snag another trophy. Maybe help himself to more of the cash he found in the desk. The clock in the tower of the Aberdeen Town House chimed six o'clock. Almost time. He strode to the entryway securing the courtyard behind the business, but stopped just beyond the corner of the building. He couldn't enter too soon. He needed to know the place was empty.

When the young girl with the neon streaked hair walked by him, he ducked his head and turned his face to the stone wall not wanting her to know his identity. Whether he succeeded or not, he didn't know but she carried on to Union

Street and disappeared.

Heart pounding in anticipation, he opened the gate and slipped into the inner sanctum. Unlike the first time he went in, tonight was the day she left trundling an overnight bag behind her. He couldn't risk getting captured. He almost did once. He couldn't make the same error again.

A light stayed on in the retail space – one normally extinguished. He pressed himself against the wall and peered in. He didn't see anyone. Did neon hair leave it on by mistake? Or was someone still in there?

After a lengthy wait and not seeing a single sign of life inside, he pushed the combination into the lock box and extracted the key. He let himself in the backdoor. He grinned at her expression knowing he was in her apartment. In her underwear drawer among other places.

In a stealthy fashion, he crept to the base of the stairs. He counted on her leaving the upstairs door unlocked like last time. If not, he'd go back, hope all the locks used that particular one.

He needn't have worried, the stupid girl had left the flat wide open yet again. She should know better. He was not about to tell her. It made life so much easier for him to come and go from her home as and when he pleased and she would be none the wiser.

The first place he went after stepping over the threshold was her bedroom. He gripped the handles and pulled the drawer open. Again, her assorted satin underpants, popped up, released from the constraints of the dresser. He rifled through them having difficulty choosing which to steal. She had so many she wouldn't miss them if he took more than one. He shoved a pair of bright red ones in his deep right pocket and a set of black in his left.

When he moved forward to the room where he found the cash on his first visit, he froze. Someone was downstairs. The electronic beep of the security system echoed through the empty flat. Who was down there? Had she come home? He didn't dare move, let alone breathe lest he be caught.

His heart pounded and the beat pulsed in his ears. If it

were his red-haired beauty, he'd be trapped here once she came up. There was no escape. The only way out was the door that opened into the lounge from the corridor and down the steps. He stood at the far end of the place. No way, he could pass by her.

If that happened, his plan would be pressed into action, whether the voices agreed with his methods or not. She couldn't live to tell who did this to her. He would ensure she was silenced. Wouldn't it be a shock for Mr. Cocksure? Come to visit his fancy woman and find her dead. The idea entertained him. Still, most important, don't get caught.

The bead curtains clacked against each other. His weight shifted and the floorboards creaked. He took a deep breath and held it, expecting to hear footsteps on the stairs. Instead, the sound of the alarm being armed wafted through the space.

He crept to the double hung. The girl with the fluorescent streaks walked down Shiprow towards the Maritime Museum. She either forgot something or came back to turn off the light. Why go that direction? When she left for the day, she went in the opposite.

Enough time wasted, he needed to finish what he came to do. He pried up the false bottom in the drawer and scooped handfuls of notes into his trench coat on top of her intimate apparel he shoved in earlier.

The photo of her on the desktop mocked him. He picked it up, prepared to slam the picture down on the floor and smash the thing to bits. No, that would tell her someone had been inside her home. He took a chance when he pilfered the one from her lounge. Before placing it back in its place, he licked the glass. Until he was ready to reveal himself to her, things had to remain as they were.

He left her residence, crept down the stairs and out the back door. When he reached the window to the office, the lights were now off. Neon hair must have come back to correct her mistake.

~ 14 ~

27th January, 2011

Kat stirred. She blinked a couple of times before peering through one eye at the clock radio. Just after six. Jared had been secretive about today. All she knew was they had to make an early start. What did he have in mind? Much as a long, luxurious lie-in would be wonderful, he was right. His bed was comfortable, but too big for just one person.

Could she see herself living here? Maybe. Someday. But not yet. The commute from Aberdeen to Dyce would be doable, but this was another half hour further out of the city. For now, things would remain in their current state. Throwing the duvet aside, she sighed and climbed out of bed, gathered her toiletries and dressing gown, and padded to the bathroom and shower.

The car park at the railway station had a number of empty bays, but being Saturday and early in the morning, most people were still at home in their beds. "So you're not telling me where we're going?" She asked when Jared pulled his BMW into a vacant one near the shelter.

"Nope."

"So all I know is we're going someplace on the train."

"Yup."

"Not even a hint?"

"No." He turned off the ignition and removed his key from the switch. "Come on. We don't want to miss it."

When he pushed the button on the fob, the boot latch clicked and the lid rose. Kat jumped out, not waiting for him to open her door as he did so many times since their reunion.

Blue skies and bright sunshine warmed her face. The temperature hovered around freezing but her down-filled parka, fur-lined mitts, and Uggs kept the cold at bay.

About five minutes behind schedule, the ScotRail service to Aberdeen arrived.

"That's us."

So, they were going by rail this far. But where to afterwards?

When the train slowed approaching the city, he stood and pulled their bags down from the overhead rack. "Coming?" He took Kat's hand to prevent them getting separated.

Once they de-trained, he scanned the huge screens to determine what platform they needed. He could keep their final destination secret for quite some time. The next leg of their journey showed on the subsequent departures screen. At least two others were ahead of them. Did they find a place and sit for a while? Did he take her shopping? If so, where? Yes, there were plenty of shops in the mall but which ones did she frequent, if any? Jared sighed.

He avoided the British Transport Police so far. In his eyes, there was nothing more natural than watching trains come and go. Since he was young, he had a fascination with them and the people who operated them. As a child, his father took him to one of the smaller railway stations near their home and they watched, counted and recorded the comings and goings from the bridge over the rails. They also played a game of guessing the passengers' destinations. Not they would ever know for sure, short of asking. It was all pretend, which he liked. How was he to know, on one of these adventures, his father would throw himself off a catwalk into the path of an oncoming goods run.

At first, he couldn't believe what he saw. His eyes must be playing tricks on him. There she was, sitting with Mr. Cocksure in one of the small lounges off the concourse. What was she doing here with him? He turned his back to them. He mustn't let them know of his presence. This sighting was coincidental, unplanned, but something to take advantage of. How he wished the voices spoke to him now. Seeing the two of them together, laughing and smiling, angered him. He should be the one sat there with her, not that man.

Fingering the handle of the knife, he pondered the best way to extract his red-headed beauty from the clutches of the man with her. Trains came and went. People arrived. People departed. He no longer had a clear view of the waiting area where she and her companion sat.

Whatever course of action he took, it couldn't be here. Too many witnesses. He could walk up behind her and slit her throat. He could come from behind and stab both of them. First her, then her lover. When they dropped to the ground in front of him, he could slip the weapon back into his pocket and disappear into the crowd and away from the crime. That idea appealed to him, but he couldn't act this soon.

He wanted more from her first. Stabbing her in the back, near her kidneys would do the trick but the end result was too immediate. She deserved a long, lingering death. He would have to do that in a private location. Her flat? Should work. Ensure she was alone, creep in the back door and up the stairs. Rape her. Choke her. Cut her inside and out. And as she lay there dying, do it again then stab her in the heart over and over.

Make sure she was dead. And in the moments before death, those precious minutes she remained conscious, reveal his identity to her. By then, she would be too weak to contact the authorities and finger him for the offense. The voices spoke. They agreed with him. Encouraged him. Now, he needed to find the right moment.

He sat in the benches facing the arrivals and departures screen. From here, watched everyone who came and went. The turnstiles were to his left. He scaled the steps by the sandstone kiosk to the bridge for an unobstructed view. Once he determined where they went, he would go back to the primary level and the boards to see what trains departed from where.

Things didn't go according to his plan. Before he had the chance to watch from a higher elevation, they approached and ascended the staircase. That meant they were going to one of the further platforms. Angered by her leaving with Mr. Cocksure, at least now he had a better idea of their destination. If he could afford it, he might purchase a ticket and follow. Wouldn't that be fun if he booked a seat with them?

He climbed the stairs and waited. A high-speed, Virgin East Coast passenger parked at seven south. They descended and approached the waiting convoy of carriages. Billboards and other barriers blocked his view. Damn it to hell. This was bad. Really bad. Oh, to be a sharp shooter and have the proper weapon. Be able to pick them off before they knew what hit them. But all he had was the flick-knife – something that necessitated close range.

Eight hours after boarding in Aberdeen, Kat and Jared arrived in London at the King's Cross station. "What are we doing here? You know this was where Colin died."

"I know. I'm hoping you can lay his ghost to rest and move on with your life."

Tears pricked at the backs of her eyes. Being so close to the place her husband perished overwhelmed her. The need to flee from this location took over and she started to the carriage door.

Jared grabbed her. "Please. Just listen to me."

"Why should I? You bring me to the one place in the world I never want to go near. And then you expect me to take heed? That's rich. Now let go of me." She jerked her arm free.

"Everything all right here?" the conductor asked.

"Yes." At least he hoped so.

"No," Kat said. Scared, angry, betrayed – she was a bundle of emotions. "Everything is not all right."

When the doors opened, she darted off the train. Where to go? How did she escape? Bumped and jostled by the throng of passengers departing, they swept her along their path. Outdoors, Kat pressed herself against a wall. Her tears flowed and she made no effort to stop them. This was why she never came here before. She couldn't handle being in the city where Colin died. How could Jared be so cruel? Why was he putting her through this anguish? It was wrong. It was unfair.

Before she had the chance to analyze the situation any more, he appeared in front of her. "I know you hate me for this. Can't say as I blame you. I'd feel the same way."

"Then why did you? Why?" In all their time together pre-Colin, he never did anything that even came close to being on a scale similar to this.

"You helped me face my demons back in Barnsley. Let me help you face yours here in London."

Brow beaten? Bullied? Kat didn't know what to think at the moment, but she didn't feel loved. Why would someone who professed to adore her be so uncaring? Bring her to the place she most hated in the world?

"Let's go to the room. It's booked. And before you ask, I got one with two beds so you don't have to worry about sleeping with me."

Kat snatched the handle of her cabin suitcase out of Jared's hand and trundled the bag behind her. As they walked, she stole glances at him. She did love him. Despite this, she still loved him. Maybe he was right. Maybe this was the thing to do after all.

Night settled in. He waited in the entryway of the Vue Cinemas. He secured a couple of cardboard boxes which he broke down. Sitting on them provided some insulation from the cold stone. Her place was in darkness. The shop below brightly illuminated. Not quite closing time, yet. Another half hour or more would pass before the last person left for the day and the book emporium plunged into almost complete obscurity. A nightlight stayed on even after neon hair came back the previous evening and turned out the other one.

The lights went out, one row of fixtures at a time. A tall, thin man garbed in goth attire exited. Who was he? In the times he sat here and watched and waited for the right time to attack, he never saw this person. If not for the streetlight mounted on the front of the building, the man would be invisible.

Perhaps he needed to do that. Adopt a change in appearance. At night clothed in all black, no one would see him. His threadbare overcoat used to be camel coloured. It still was, albeit filthy and worn. His trousers, shoes, gloves and Fedora were dark.

Despite having helped himself to more cash from her secret stash, he refused to spend his money on something frivolous like clothing. Maybe he should purchase a handgun. Somewhere in Aberdeen there had to be someone who would sell him one, no questions asked.

Assured the store was empty, and the man in black now beyond Castle Street, he strolled to the gated access. With a cursory glance, he ensured the pedestrianized section of Shiprow was void of people. He turned the ring on the wooden gate and slipped inside.

This time, he would hang on to the latchkey long enough to have a copy made. He punched in the code and took out the piece of brass. Holding the metal in his hand, he pondered the idea. No, best leave things as is. Keep the status quo. No sense making her suspicious and getting the law involved sooner than need be. For now, he unlocked the back door, and put the key back in the lock box.

Inside the lounge, he shifted a picture here, an ornament there. Nothing too much or moved too far. Subtlety. She might notice things not in their usual spaces. Maybe not. And she may well think she was going off her trolley. He liked the idea. Annoy her until she was beside herself.

When she reported the goings on to friends or the local constabulary or whomever, they wouldn't believe her. All her credibility would be gone. In the kitchen, he took an open bottle of Pinot Grigio from the fridge, and a glass from the cupboard. He drained the remaining contents and stored the empties on the counter. She would think she left them out before she went away. At least he hoped she would. Another check in his quest to drive her insane before he savaged her.

The wine made him dizzy. He didn't drink that much, had he? Only about half a bottle. He drank some of the single malt he pilfered the first time he snuck in. It didn't have this effect on him. But then, he consumed the hard liquor outdoors where he sat in the cinema entrance in the cold. The room spun. He groped for anything to steady himself.

The wooden dining chair he reached for toppled with a resounding crash. If anyone were downstairs, they heard the racket. He wanted to lie down. Sofa? No. Her pristine, white duvet covered bed. Staggering to the bedroom, he made more of a hodgepodge than he intended. He'd put these things back in their rightful places, or close to, but first he needed a nap. He teetered and wobbled the distance to her room and dropped on the mattress.

Checked in and upstairs in their room, Kat plunked her suitcase on the bed furthest from the loo then walked to the window. Their room overlooked the railway station. The street below teemed with people. Here in their top floor room, she was safe from the discovery of finality – of closing the door on a chapter in her life.

What terrified her more was the unknown. Would her relationship with Jared be the same as when they first met? Given what happened to both of them since that time, not a chance. They had changed. Matured.

"Clean yourself up. You're a mess. I want to show you something."

His voice jolted her out of her daydream.

Whether intentional or not, his tone frightened her. His words, the way he said them, were cold and controlling – almost vicious. She was tired and didn't want to fight. With resignation, she removed her heavy outerwear, and tossed the parka on the mattress before opening her luggage and retrieving her cosmetics bag.

Sidestepping Jared, she rushed to the bathroom and locked the door behind her. Her reflection in the mirror showed the state of her face. Mascara and eyeliner stains ran down her cheeks. Maybe she would be better off not wearing any makeup during her stay. Kat pushed up her sweater sleeves and washed her face, applied toner and finished with moisturizer. A hint of blush and freshened lippy and she was ready.

"You were in there long enough. Thought I might have to break the door down," he quipped when she emerged.

"Well, I'm here now. So what do you want to show me?" Kat reached for the down-filled garment but he took hold of it first and helped her dress.

"Let's go."

At least now, he didn't come across cruel like before. He was like always.

"Where are you taking me?"

"You'll see soon enough." He closed the door behind him. "We'll go for a meal afterwards."

Outside the hotel, Kat stiffened when he took her hand. Strange thoughts swirled through her mind. At the access to the subway station, she stopped. "What's here?"

She didn't receive a verbal reply. Instead, Jared put his arm around her and eased her to him. Whatever he wanted her to see, his action was soothing and protective. She let herself sink into the comfort of him being there.

He steered her to the location of a plaque mounted on one of the walls. "Look at this. Colin was down here on the underground going away from you not on his way back to Aberdeen." His voice was soft and loving.

With her fingers shaking, she reached out and touched the commemoration on her late husband's name. "How did you know?"

"I didn't. Not at first. Not until you told me he was killed in the London Bombings. I can't believe you didn't."

Kat spun around and faced him. "And just what do you mean?"

"Nothing. Just all this time and you didn't know."

"It didn't matter. He was dead. I didn't want to find out the gory details – didn't want to hear them. I didn't read the newspapers. Didn't watch the telly. Or look it up online. Colin died on July 7, 2005. I didn't need to know anymore." A strangled sob escaped from her lips, sounding like someone else's cry. Jared pulled her into his arms and held her close. Angry as she was with him for bringing her here, Kat was comforted having him with her. "I want to go home."

"We will, but there's one more thing you need to see

before we go," he said. "I saw a pub around the corner from where we're staying. We'll have a drink, something to eat and go back to the room."

"When are we going home?"

"Saturday. We're booked on the ten o'clock train."

Inside, Jared pointed out an empty table near the inglenook and sent Kat there. The place was busy. He didn't mind standing at the bar, beverage in hand, but he didn't think she wanted to – not after today's revelations.

No, the table in what appeared to be a quiet corner was best. He ordered a pint for himself and a gin and tonic for her. While he waited for their libations, he pondered her reaction to seeing the plaque. He couldn't fathom she didn't know the King's Cross railway station and underground were two different places.

Why did she think her husband was on his way back to Aberdeen? Did he ring? Text? Or tell her his return date and time before he left? Being on the tube and going in the opposite direction spelled lies to him. What was – if anything – the man trying to hide?

Her home appeared like she still expected Colin home any time. She said as much when they came back from Barnsley earlier in the month. When the bartender sat the beverages on the mat in front of him, he interrupted his musings.

Carrying their drinks to where Kat waited, Jared worried if he did the right thing. Why didn't she come to London after the attacks? Not even on the anniversaries to join the others affected by the events. He handed her the G&T. She downed her cocktail in one go and held the glass out for another. He raised the empty, catching the barman's eye. A few minutes later, another drink arrived. "Not so fast this time," he said.

"Don't tell me what to do," she seethed.

He really pissed her off by bringing her here and near the location where her husband died. Reaching across the table, he touched her hand. "Don't do it, please. I know this has been hard for you. I felt the same way about Barnsley when you talked me into going back there."

Her eyes shot daggers into his heart. Had he ruined things between them? He hoped not. He clung to the memories of their good times together and had faith she did, too. "One of their specialties here is fish and chips with mushy peas. Want me to order you a small portion?" he asked – anything to break through the barrier his companion threw up.

"No."

"You should …," he started and paused. No sense. She already made it clear she didn't need him telling her what to do. "You might not want to eat, but I do."

"I want to go back to the room." Kat finished her second gin and tonic and stood. "Key please."

"Give me a minute." He went to the bar. "Can I get a fish supper to go?"

Between the time they came in and now, there had been a shift change and a young girl now worked there. She took the details and told him to wait.

Jared walked back to the table. "I'm sorry if today has upset you. I thought you needed to see the plaque. See the area."

Kat slapped him across the face. "Fuck you."

He caught her wrist before she escaped or lambasted him again. "I deserved that, but don't go. Please. I only brought you here so maybe you would quit living in the past. You're beautiful, bright, vibrant – any man would be lucky to have you. I want to be that man. We were good before. We can be again. You just need to move beyond 7th July, 2005."

Kat stormed out of the pub. Now she didn't know which direction to go. Nothing looked familiar. She pulled out her mobile and typed a message to Stephanie.

In London. I found out something about Colin but don't know what to make of it.

Her finger hovered over the send button while she debated pressing it. Right or wrong, she sent the text.

A few seconds later, her phone rang. Not a reply to her

message, but an actual call.

"H-hello?"

"Okay, what's going on? Why are you there?"

Relieved to hear her friend's voice, she broke down in tears. "First off, I'm lost and don't know how to find my way back to the place we're staying at."

"Where are you now?" Steph asked.

"Outside a pub."

"What's the name? The road it's on?"

Kat stepped away from the edifice and turned around. The information was emblazoned on a plaque on the first floor. "Caledonia Street."

Steph's fingers clattered over her keyboard. "Got it up on the screen. Where's your hotel?"

"Our room overlooks the railway station."

"As in yours and someone else's? Who is with you?"

"Jared brought me here. Said it was to face my demons since I made him go to Barnsley." She choked back a sob.

"Where's he?"

"In the pub. I walked out on him."

"Deep breaths. I see one at the other end of the street. Look to your left. Does it look like the building you see from your room?"

"No. If I look that direction, all I see is a busy dual carriageway."

"Right. What about the other way? Look familiar?"

"Y-yes."

"Walk that way then. I'll stay on the line."

Following Stephanie's directions, Kat continued. When had she had turned from being invincible – not quite the right expression – to lost and vulnerable?

"Your text said you found out something about Colin."

"It may be something or nothing. Why was he on the Tube that morning when he was supposed to be on the train to Aberdeen?" Kat looked over her shoulder when the sensation of someone behind her strengthened.

"Coming to the station?" Steph offered.

"Wrong direction – leaving the King's Cross underground,

not approaching."

"Colin loved you to bits. He'd never have done anything to hurt you."

By now, she reached the intersection. The hotel stood on the other side of Caledonia Street and the railway station facing her. "I hope you're right," Kat said as she slumped into a chair in front of Costa Coffee.

"Fuck. You scared me to death. I came out of the pub and you were gone. I hoped you'd come back to the room but I didn't know what to think."

"You found me. I told you I wanted to come back here," she answered, and stood as if to challenge him, but her voice showed no emotion.

"I'm glad you're all right." He tried putting his arm around her but she spun out of his grasp and bolted for the entrance.

With her current frame of mind, Jared knew to back off and give her some space. He saw her through some rough patches before her parents dragged her off to Canada, but they were mild by comparison. Her lack of feeling scared him. She never shut down like this. Anything would do. Yell at him, slap him, scream, cry.

Later that night, Jared got his wish. Muffled crying roused him. He crawled out of bed and sat on the edge of the one Kat occupied. She had her back to him. Her shoulders shook as she sobbed. He reached out and touched her. She recoiled at first but then rolled over and hugged him with a strength he didn't know she possessed. After extricating himself from her grip, he slipped beneath the covers and held her to him.

~ 15 ~

28th January, 2011

The rumbling and clattering of a bin lorry picking up garbage woke him. What time was it? He sat up. The red numerals on her digital clock read half-six. Early dawn. He must have passed out and slept all night.

He needed to pull himself together and skedaddle. His sojourns into her home had all been done under the cover of darkness. He leapt off the bed. The sudden movement made him light headed. A wave of nausea followed. He lurched to the bathroom making it there in time to throw up into the toilet.

Movements had to be slow and steady since swift ones nauseated him. How much havoc had he wreaked the previous night? There were things he did on purpose, but what about after the wine took hold of him?

He tiptoed to the lounge. A tipped over chair which he righted. Placemats hung off the edge of the table. He moved them back to their places. Now to clear out of here before *As the Pages Turn* opened for trade. He'd come too close to getting nicked. He couldn't be careless again.

Kat woke to the sound of the shower running. The clock radio on the nightstand between the two beds read almost half-seven. She never slept this long even on days she didn't open for business.

When Jared exited the loo, all he wore was the white, bath sheet wrapped around his waist. He dried his hair with the hand towel. "Bathroom is yours. I turned the heated rack on."

Seeing him in that state of undress made her forget about

where they were and why they were there. After yesterday, she deserved to be abandoned in London alone. She threw back the duvet and climbed out from the warmth of her bed.

Once Kat finished in the bathroom, they went downstairs to Costa Coffee for breakfast.

"What is it you want to show me today?" She spread cream cheese on her toasted bagel.

"You'll see when we get there."

"Can you at least tell me where we're going?" She hated Jared being secretive.

He smiled and winked at her. "No. But it does involve taking a ride on the subway."

Terror congested Kat's heart. The Tube. The bombings. What if? What if there was another attack? "I-I can't."

"Yes, you can. I'll be with you. You'll be fine."

She wanted to believe Jared, but now she knew Colin had been on one of the underground trains at the time of his death. She had doubts. Still, she needed to be with him and hoped after the trip things could go back to the way they used to be between them.

The two walked to the station holding hands. Kat tightened her grip as they approached the way in. While Jared bought their tickets, she wandered to the location of the plaque. Staring at it, she toyed with the gold chain around her neck holding Colin's wedding ring.

They began their trek through the tunnels. "Piccadilly Line will take us where we want to be."

Kat nodded.

Once they boarded, he spoke. "This is the one Colin took the day he died."

That same feeling of dread occupied her again and she leaned against him hoping to soak up some of his strength.

Jared scanned the picture of stops over the door. When they moved again after stopping at Green Park Station, he said, "Ours is the next stop."

When they emerged from the subterranean depths, the sun blinded him. Once he got his bearings and using the small map of the corner of Hyde Park he printed at home before they left, he took Kat's hand and they worked their way through the crowded street into the green space.

A skiff of snow covered the ground. The leafy trees which provided shade in the summer stood bare, providing a somber reminder of why he escorted her to London in the first place.

"You okay?"

"I-I think so."

Putting his arm around her, he pulled her closer to him and kissed her beanie hat covered head.

Soon the columns representing the casualties of the attacks came into view. Jared didn't know how she would react to seeing the memorial, but even if Kat didn't agree with him, he knew she had to see it.

When they reached the site, he followed but lagged behind as she walked between the pillars brushing her hand over their cold, metal surfaces. He wanted to give her space to explore the area on her own, but remain nearby so if she needed him he would be there for her.

Kat turned to face him, burning tears streaming down her cheeks. "There aren't any names. Just dates, times and places. Which one is Colin?" She whispered, not feeling right about speaking out loud in the hallowed space.

By now, Jared stood in front of her. He wiped them away with his thumbs. Once he finished, she wrapped her arms around his waist and held him – afraid if she let go, he would disappear from her life, too.

When she raised her head, a figure crouched at the end of the display of pillars flashed in her peripheral vision. Kat released her hold, but latched on to Jared's hand and walked to the location.

She peered over the person's shoulder at the plaque erected on the ground. "In memory of those killed in the London Bombings," she murmured before scanning the names for Colin's. She found what she was looking for. Fingers ran over the raised lettering. What the ...? Why would a complete stranger be interested in her dead spouse? She mustered up some courage and asked, "Excuse me, but why are you caressing my late husband's name?"

The form stood and turned to face her, pushing the hood of her parka down. A pair of oversize sunglasses concealed most of the woman's face. A jagged scar slashed across her cheek from the corner of her mouth and vanished behind the right lens. When she removed the eyewear, a flesh tone patch covered the spot where her eye should be. Her left was green but dull and full of grief.

Kat stared at her. She looked familiar.

"He was my lover."

This lie didn't help her already emotional state during the trip to London. "What do you mean? Colin was never unfaithful to me. Never." Lowering the zipper with one hand, she fished inside the neck of her sweater with the other for the chain she wore. Then Kat recognized the person in front of her. "You're Diana Braithwaite. I remember seeing your face in trade magazines and the book catalogues we either received in the post or Colin dragged home with him after trips here."

"I was. After that awful day, I couldn't bear to go out in public. I sold the business to one of my competitors. Suited me fine. Got a good price and I didn't have to leave my house if I didn't want. Except for my visits to see the doctor and come here after the memorial was built, I holed up inside."

Back in the day, the woman was gorgeous. Confident, too, according to the write-ups in the media. Such a change from the one here today.

When Kat found the piece of jewellery, she pulled the necklace out into the open and dangled the preserved gold band in the other woman's face. "See. My husband. His wedding ring. It's hung here since the authorities returned it to me."

"Ha. That means nothing," Diana retorted. "I always wondered who my competition was. Now I know. You're the red-headed ice queen."

Kat clenched and unclenched her fists before bringing her hand back to slap the disfigured brunette in front of her, but before she followed through, Jared grabbed her wrist. "Let go." She tried to shake free from his grip.

"You don't want to do it," he hissed.

"He's right. I would have you done for assault. An able-bodied person attacking a victim of a heinous crime."

"I don't believe your lies for one minute. If you were having an affair with my Colin, I want details. When did it start? Where? How?"

"Oh honey, you don't want to know that much. I will tell you, it began between the time he bought ..."

"We bought," Kat corrected.

"Yah, yah, whatever. Between then and when you opened for business. We met at the London Book Fair. I used to own a publishing house so attended the event every year. We started out talking books over lunch, then over cocktails. Other than some heavy snogging and groping, nothing happened then. But I gave him my card. We kept in touch. Are you so naïve you think all those trips he made were to buy stock for your store? Oh, no. He came to me. Shared a bed with me. Wanted me. Made passionate love to me. Sometimes at mine, others at the place he stayed in and once in a while, we would drive out to my country house for an intimate weekend. We got away with it for so long because I worked in the industry. I sent him home with catalogues, or books, or both. Said he only married you because he needed the money your inheritance provided. He would have abandoned you in time, but died before he had the opportunity."

Bottom lip quivering, Kat didn't know whether to believe these sentences as the truth or dismiss them as lies.

The woman stepped closer and leaned forward. "He said you never loved him. Said there was always another man in your heart but until he found me, he was willing to go along, if it meant having you, frigid ice woman or otherwise. If he'd not left you before that day, we would still be having our illicit trysts. Your dear Colin booked us a posh room at *The Savoy*, to make up for the accommodations he used near the King's Cross railway station. We were on our way there after checking out of his hotel."

"No. It's all lies." Katherine's stance stiffened and she glared at her adversary.

"'fraid not. We were on the Piccadilly underground line. He had his back to the bomber. We were chatting about how to spend the day – the things we'd do to each other when we got into bed."

Colin had never been adventurous in bed, their bed anyway. Looking back, he was never a great lover. Was that her fault? Did she drive him into another woman's arms? Must have been, otherwise he wouldn't have taken up with someone else.

Diana continued bringing Kat back to the present. "Then there was a bright flash of light. I couldn't see anything. I was covered with blood and bits of bone and brain. A piece of his collarbone pierced my eye and blinded me. The doctors ended up removing it. If not for Colin standing between the terrorist and me, I would be dead now, too. Maybe I should have been the one who died. I'll never see out of that one again. Lost my left arm. By the grace of God they managed to save my legs."

"And my adulterous husband got blown to bits. He got everything he had coming to him." Overcome by nausea, she dropped to her hands and knees. A cold, clammy sensation came over her making her shiver. She tried to gulp in fresh air to quash the feeling, but to no avail. The descriptions were too graphic. Whether real or imagined, she saw the woman take off her artificial arm.

How could she be so stupid? The signs had to be there. Why didn't she see them? Diana Braithwaite was twisted and bitter.

Jared squatted beside Kat and stroked her back. She didn't deserve to find out Colin was a lying, cheating toe rag. Good thing the man was already dead. He would murder him otherwise. "I'm so sorry. My plan was to bring you here for closure, not destroy you."

Diana leaned down to Jared's level, fixing her good eye on him. "She's upset her husband was shagging me. She couldn't satisfy him, but I could and did. What about the two of you? You're quite cozy."

Her gaze bored through him and he squirmed. "I don't

need to justify our actions – emotions to you." He wanted to say more, but showed restraint using all his inner strength to keep quiet. "Come on. Let's go home," he said in a low voice as he helped Kat stand.

Once he had her upright, he encircled her waist with his arm. He pressed his lips to her forehead then turned. "Oh, and not that it's any of your business, but I'm the other man in her heart. We were together years ago before Colin and only recently found each other again."

Guiding Kat away from the memorial, Jared pondered the wisdom of bringing her to London. It had been touch and go – a veritable rollercoaster ride so far with her emotional highs and lows since their arrival in the city. Now, after their encounter with Diana Braithwaite, he had no idea what affect her revelations would have on the woman he loved.

He stopped next to a bench and brushed away the snow before sitting down and easing her down beside him. He wrapped his arms around her and drew her close. Kat's body shook and he knew she was crying. He brought her closer and rubbed her back wishing that simple movement would erase her pain.

A flock of pigeons landed on the path in front of them. One bird perched on the toe of his work boots and pecked at the worn leather. He kicked to dislodge it, but he disturbed Kat instead. Her tear-filled eyes broke his heart and he held her tighter.

Snow started to fall. He leaned back and allowed the flakes to land on his face and melt, all the while keeping her body pressed against his. When he worked on the fishing trawler as a teenager, he learned to read the sky and he knew a blizzard approached. That ability served him well out on the rig, too. If the wind didn't pick up, the weather wouldn't be too bad. "Think we should make tracks, don't you?"

Her head nodded. Jared stood and helped Kat to her feet. Once she was upright, he placed his hands on her cheeks and kissed her full on the lips. She kept her arms limp at her sides. He hoped she would wrap them around his waist. When he teased her mouth open with his tongue, she whimpered. Not the time for a kiss like this – one that in the past preceded their making love. Jared raised his head. "I adore you, Kat Murphy."

Armed now with the knowledge of Colin's double life, he couldn't use the man's name, even though it belonged to the beautiful woman before him. He would do everything in his power to protect her, but failed at his attempt to give her closure.

Huge, white flakes drifted downward. The sky had darkened enough for the street lights to turn on. Holding hands, they walked back to the underground station in silence. The sooner he got her out of Hyde Park, the happier he would be.

When they went back to King's Cross, the Tube was busier. He found an empty seat and settled Kat, then stood in front of her and gripped the high bar. She pulled off her beanie hat and laid the knitted toque on her lap before removing her mitts and putting them inside.

Jared reached out and lifted her chin. Her beautiful, sparkling, brown eyes, moist with tears, were dull and overflowed with pain. He hated seeing her like this. The vision threatened to rip his heart out of his chest.

When the train accelerated, she stood and wrapped her arms around him. He shifted her position allowing someone else to take the vacated seat. He draped his free arm around her shoulders and pulled her tight to him. "I'm sorry. Dragging you here was a bad idea."

"Why? Why did he do this to me? How could he? How could they?"

"I can't answer that." Jared didn't dare mention the C name. He wished he had the answers she deserved and needed. Bringing Kat here to London, to the underground station, and the memorial in Hyde Park would be good for her. He never dreamt everything would kick off the way it did. If she never recovered from the experience, he would shoulder the blame.

~ 16 ~

29th January, 2011

His red-haired beauty walked up Shiprow back to her flat. Mr. Cocksure accompanied her. Damn. Voices or not, with that man around, nothing would happen tonight. Still, she was home.

He stood and leaned against the wall. She smiled at her companion and chuckled as the two strolled by the cinema. If they laughed at him, they would regret their actions. He'd see to it.

Once they ambled past his hiding place, he stepped out of the shadows. His hand reached into his overcoat where he concealed the flick-knife and he fondled the handle. His plans for her put on hold thanks to her fancy man. His brutal act to snuff out her life was one best done in private, when it was just the two of them.

When the door sealed, he advanced from the seclusion afforded by the alcove into the middle of the street. Lights turned on. He needed them to move into a location visible from the road but they didn't oblige.

After the long ride back to Aberdeen, Kat was happy to be home. She unlocked the door and dropped her keys in the wooden bowl on the table to her right – glad to be away from the city of London and the horrible memories of the trip.

Jared sat her suitcase on the floor.

"You gonna be all right? I can stay if you like."

"I think I want to be on my own."

Trailing her fingertips over the furniture, she wandered

around the room. For the first time, she realized how close she came to erecting a shrine to Colin. Traces of the man were everywhere. She picked up a photograph of them in a crystal frame and ran her fingers over their images. Tears blurred her vision. Kat flung the picture at the plaster wall. The impact shattered the glass. "It was all a lie. He never loved me."

Jared dropped his duffel bag, rushed to her side, and wrapped his arms around her. "I think I should stay. Or if you want me to leave, why don't you call Steph? I don't want you here by yourself."

"I'll be fine. I need some boxes from the store. There should be some in the office."

"What about the alarm? I'll set it off if I go down there."

She strode to the door and punched a code into a small control panel on the wall. "There. You won't now."

Against his better judgement, Jared left her alone and went downstairs to retrieve the items she requested. When he entered the darkened office, he fumbled for the switch to turn on the lights. After he illuminated the room, he discovered the boxes but they were already broken down and bound together ready to be put out with the recycling.

Jared searched for a roll of packaging tape and a dispenser. The cartons could be reassembled upstairs. Once he gathered up everything he needed, he started for the door.

After a thunderous crash above his head, he tore to the stairs and up them two at a time. He didn't know what caused the commotion, only the source of the racket came from Kat's.

Jared stopped short in the doorway. One of the bookcases – as in the one that held fragile figurines, other knickknacks and baubles – lay face down. Kat was nowhere in sight. He worried she dropped the cabinet down on herself and she lie injured beneath it. Dropping things as he charged across the room, he breathed a sigh of relief when she wasn't trapped under the object.

A racket from another room sent him in search of the noise. He found Kat in the home office standing in the middle of a pile of men's clothing. "What the fuck are you doing?"

Her expression was filled with rage. She held a garment in one hand and a butcher knife in the other. She slashed the fabric again and again. "Liar. You never loved me. You only loved my money," she screeched.

The shredded rags on the floor were Colin's clothes. "Calm down." He worked his way closer to the distraught woman. "Put that bloody thing down before you do yourself a mischief. I don't want to have to take you to A&E for stitches."

While she was in that state, disarming her was not an option. She would cut him into strips, too. Did he let her carry on? The cheating scumbag deserved everything he got. But, too little too late. The bastard should have been stood there watching her destroy the material things which were more important to him than his own wife.

Jared supposed Colin got his comeuppance the morning of July 7, 2005. Poetic justice in a strange sort of way, but back then, Kat didn't know her husband had a fancy woman. Would it have been easier to deal with had this all come out in the open then?

Separate Ways (Worlds Apart) by Journey played from inside his jacket. He pulled out his mobile. Recognizing the number as being work-related, the temptation to disconnect the call grew. "Yeah," he answered.

"Hey mate. It's Ulrich. I wouldn't ask, but it is important." He didn't wait for Jared's reply. "I need a huge favour. Don't suppose I could ask you to cover for me for a couple of days."

"What's up?" Fuck. Why did he let his colleague drag him into the conversation?

Uli, as they referred to him on the rig, performed the same job as Jared, but on the opposite shift rotation. "My mother is very sick. She needs me home. It would only be until my brother can make arrangements to travel from Poland. We're all she has."

That was all he needed. In the state Kat was in, he didn't dare leave her. But he did ask. Could he get out of it? Should he even try? "I'm in Aberdeen and my car is at the railway station in Dyce."

"Don't worry. If you can do it, Nexus have offered a car

and driver to come and get you."

"I got a couple of loose ends to tie up. Can I ring you back?"

"Yes. Yes, but please do not take too long."

Jared disconnected and shoved his phone back. What to do? He raked his hand through his hair but the action didn't offer up any solution. Could she deal with things easier with him gone. Probably not. During the day, she had her work to keep her occupied, although now, she might not want to have anything to do with the place. Steph. She could come stay with her. He didn't know her number but Kat's BlackBerry lay on the table inside the door where she dropped her keys. She would be in her contacts.

Picking up the phone, he scrolled through her connections until he found Stephanie Lindsay and phoned her.

She answered on the fourth ring. "Hiya, Kat."

"It's Jared."

"What are you doing on her mobile? Where is she? Is she okay?"

"Yes and no." He paced as he talked.

"Why did you do it? Why did you take her to London? You know what happened there."

"When was the last time you spoke to her?" he asked, ignoring her questions.

"Um ... day before yesterday when she walked out of the pub on you. She sent me a text saying she found out something about Colin."

So she hadn't contacted her friend after their visit to the memorial in Hyde Park. "Look, I have to go in to work. I don't want to leave Kat alone. I need you to come stay with her for a few days – maybe longer."

"You're scaring me. What's happened?"

"It's best coming from her."

"I'll throw some stuff in a bag and be there in no time."

"Thanks, Steph. I owe you."

Jared ended the call and pulled out his HTC android. Selecting redial, he rang Uli back. "I can be ready in an hour." He disconnected and sighed, still not convinced it was the right thing.

Kat walked through the lounge into the kitchen carrying the butcher knife. Now would not be the time to mention his returning to his job early. The handle clattered in the stainless steel sink. Seconds later, she traversed the room again – this time with large, green bin liners in her hand.

He stood a better chance with her now she didn't have a weapon, followed and found her picking up the shreds of Colin's clothes and shoving them into the receptacles. "Here, let me help you," he offered.

"No. I can manage."

Walking around the end of the desk, he raked his fingers through his hair. "I don't know how to tell you this."

"Tell me what? You're dumping me? You took me to London and now I'm a complete basket case because of what happened there, you're leaving me?"

"You daft mare. No." He put his hands on Kat's upper arms. "I'm sorry about all that. If I could erase the past and the hurt Colin caused you, I would."

She bowed her head. "I know."

Jared lifted her chin with his thumb and forefinger. Her eyes filled with tears – again. Why did he tell Uli he would cover for him. "I don't want to leave you on your own in this state, but …."

"But what?" she asked. A tear escaped from her left eye.

He wiped her face. "Been called in to work. Should only be a couple of days. I got hold of Steph and she's going to come stay with you. I don't want you to be alone."

Kat put her arms around Jared's neck and drew his mouth to hers. Her tongue found his and flicked over it driving him mad with longing. He gathered her up and carried her into her bedroom where he eased her down on the bed and lie beside her.

His fingertips traced down her cheek to her jaw stopping at the collar of her sweater. Jared gave her breast a gentle squeeze before continuing to her waist and up over her bare flesh under the garment. Her skin came up in goosebumps at his touch. When he slipped his hand inside the lacy fabric of her bra, the unthinkable happened. Kat wriggled out from underneath him.

"It-it's too soon. I can't. Please don't be angry with me."

Sprawled on his back, Jared bristled. She led him on again. It had become a habit with her. While he lay there, he took deep breaths to calm down. He should have known she was far from ready. Her world collapsed in the previous forty-eight hours. The truth was a lie – a big fat one at that. He could have stopped things from going further but didn't. Maybe the time apart would be good for both of them.

He didn't have time to stew any longer. The intercom buzzed. Steph would be there to look after her now. Kat not being by herself made him feel somewhat better.

A car horn honked. Jared climbed off the bed and sauntered to the window. It might be the driver they sent to take him to the Nexus terminal at the Aberdeen Airport.

Mr. Cocksure laid his red-haired beauty on the mattress. Did they? Did she remain chaste? Or had this man ruined her? That was his job to do. Not someone else's. He would be far better at it, too. His hand went to the flick-knife. The thought of her making love with someone else angered him. Sullied or not, he would be the last one she was intimate with.

As he stood in the street, the door opened. He scampered into the cover of the casino. His nemesis exited, but in the meantime the same woman who turned up once before arrived. He could handle two women. She could be his first victim. Slit her throat from ear to ear and as she lie bleeding to death, have his way with the owner of *As the Pages Turn*.

Using a dirty knife on her conjured up more evil thoughts of disease. Hepatitis, HIV, any number of STDs. Make her ill so she would die with something foul. Perhaps force her to perform oral sex on the blade. He'd cut her up there, too. The longer he stayed nearby, the more perverse his fantasies became.

After Jared left, Stephanie surveyed the damage in the sitting room. Overturned bookcase, smashed baubles littering the floor, a shattered picture frame and a torn photograph. The mess would wait. She needed to know what happened. He didn't tell her much other than it would be better coming from Kat. He was with her, so they were still together, or were they? She went to the kitchen, opened one of the bottles of red wine she toted from home, and poured two glasses.

When she entered the lounge, she handed one to her friend. "Okay, spill. What the hell happened in London." Stephanie plopped down on the sofa. "Talk to me."

"It was awful."

"I can imagine. Come sit," she said and patted the cushion beside her.

Kat positioned her wine goblet on the coffee table and sank on the couch. "Every time I think of it I cry. And then I get angry. And I hate him."

"Not Jared I hope. You two are good together."

"But for how long? I can't … can't give myself to him. I feel like I'm cheating."

Stephanie shook her head. "You can't be unfaithful to Colin – he's gone."

"But he can cheat on me," she replied and knocked back the glass of Merlot.

"Rewind. We've not talked since the day you walked out of the pub on Jared. You sent me the text …." Steph rummaged in her purse for her mobile and searched for the texts from her friend. "You said 'I'm in London. I found out something about Colin but don't know what to make of it'."

Kat took a deep breath. "Well, turns out he was on the underground going the other way. That was why he was killed in the bombing. If he was where he was supposed to be, he wouldn't have been."

"Well maybe he planned to buy you something from one of the upmarket stores before coming home." He bought you stuff before on his buying trips.

"No. I was the last person he wanted to be with. Discovered he had a bit on the side."

"What?" Steph leapt to her feet. "You can't mean that. Colin loved the socks off you."

"And every stitch of clothing off this *Diana Braithwaite*," she spat, angry he had cheated on her but more so at herself for not discovering the deception.

"Good thing he's already dead, otherwise I'd kill him. But how did you find out?" Stephanie, gobsmacked by her friend's revelation, walked around the coffee table and sat on Kat's right.

"What if I'm the reason he strayed? When I met his fancy woman, she made sure I knew he never cherished me. Why did I agree to marry him in the first place?" she cried.

"Give your head a shake. None of the bad stuff that happened with Colin was your fault. So when Jared pops the question again, you're saying yes, right?"

"What if he never asks again?"

"Come on. He loves you. Now tell me everything about your trip."

"Y-yesterday, he took me to the 7/7 memorial in Hyde Park. She – that cow – well, what's left of her, was there. She said she and Colin were on their way to *The Savoy*. He booked them a room. They first met at the London Book Fair and things started shortly after that. She told me …."

Stephanie wrapped her arms around Kat and tried to comfort her bestie. "And you believed her?" Blunt as the statement was; it needed to be asked.

"Too many things make sense now. All the extra trips. Him not caring if we made love. Oh, and she said he was only with me for my inheritance from my father." Her tears flowed like the water over Horseshoe Falls in Canada, soaking Steph's sweater.

"Let it out, hun," she said rubbing Kat's back as she spoke.

Her friend was a walking disaster area in the men and relationships department. If what the other woman said was true, then the poor girl had lived a lie since her wedding day – maybe even before. With Colin dead, the proof would never be found.

Back in the day when Kat was with Jared, she covered for her so she was able to spend more time with him. That ended in tears when her parents discovered the lies and dragged her away. They could have eloped when she turned sixteen, but she was fifteen so that option went down the sewer and he was lucky they didn't have him charged.

Stephanie helped her to her feet and ushered her to the bedroom. The unfortunate lass was exhausted. Maybe a good night's sleep would do her the world and she would be ready to cope with the fallout in the morning.

After settling Kat into bed, Steph tidied the mess. When she put items in their proper places on the shelving units, the spot where a photo always sat remained vacant. Had she moved the picture to a different location? Broken the glass and disposed of the snapshot frame and all? With the state she was in, there was no reason to cause any further upset so she didn't say anything.

~ 17 ~

30th January, 2011

Kat woke disoriented. She patted the bed beside her. No one there. Her stomach lurched and she dashed to the bathroom where she threw up. Another wave of nausea came over her accompanied by a cold, clammy sweat. After a long time spent hugging the porcelain, she was able to stand without the room spinning. She seized her toothbrush, squeezed out a generous dollop of toothpaste and brushed. She needed to remove that awful, bitter taste from her mouth.

The bottle of Paracetamol was in the kitchen. When she walked through the room, a blanket covered figure moved on the sofa. Had she and Colin had a row? Had he gone to the lounge to sleep of his own volition or had she sent him there?

"What time is it?" The body under the covers moaned.

It was Steph's voice. The fog in her brain disappeared. Jared had called Stephanie to come and stay because he had to leave. Colin was dead. Killed in the London bombings. He was a cheat. Katherine had met the other woman at the 7/7 Memorial in Hyde Park. She cursed Jared again for taking her there.

She removed the container of painkillers from the cupboard over the sink and retrieved a glass from another unit. How much red wine did they drink last night? There was an empty on the coffee table and two more here on the counter. Not the normal 75 cl bottles but full litre ones. She opened the fridge and pulled out her BRITA jug.

"Pour me some of that, too, please."

Steph stood in the doorway to the small kitchen clinging to

155

the doorframe. "Stop the room from spinning."

Kat poured and handed the glass to her friend before getting another for herself.

The cold water gave Katherine a headache but she gulped the liquid down anyway. She knew all the wine the previous night dehydrated her. This was the worst hangover she had in years. Not since she drank herself into oblivion when word her husband had been killed came. Why the sudden fascination with him? Was it because she had been to London where he died? Whatever the reason, the sooner she thought of something other than him, the happier she would be.

The mess from last night's destructive spree was gone. Wrecking anything and everything related to Colin was cathartic. Steph must have dealt with the cleanup. Her stomach turned somersaults like a fish splashing in a bucket of water.

Covering her mouth with her hand, she bee-lined to the toilet. Up came the two Paracetamol she took. So much for getting rid of her headache using drugs. Next the dry heaves set in. Kat wanted to crawl into a hole and die. If only Jared were here. He would look after her. But he was hundreds of miles away. He went offshore to fill in for some guy on the opposite shift. Damn him. When she needed him the most, he abandoned her.

"I'm going home," Stephanie croaked when Kat shuffled into the lounge. "I feel like a Scania knocked me down and ran over me. I need my bed."

"I hope you didn't drive here last night. You're apt to get done for drink driving."

"Best not light a match near me for days. Still enough alcohol in my system, I would be a fire breathing dragon."

Kat's friend's attempt at humour didn't go unnoticed. Stephanie could be half-dead and she'd still find a way to crack a joke – not necessarily a funny one but a laugh nonetheless.

"I'll text you later. See if you managed to rejoin the human race." She threw her raincoat over her arm and staggered through the door.

When it shut, the sound of the latch setting sent daggers of torment through Kat's head. Out of character for her, armed with the knowledge her downstairs doors were locked, she ensured this one was secured and put the chain on as well. Ice bag. She had one. Not used the thing in years.

Where would she have stashed the cold pack? She shuffled into the kitchen. Cutlery and other utensils rattled as the drawers opened and closed inflicting still more misery. God, she was such a sadist. If she survived the day without dying of alcohol poisoning, she swore she would never drink again. Yeah, right. Nothing in with the linens in her wall unit in the lounge. Only tablecloths, napkins and napkin rings.

Things on hooks hung on the inside of the airing cupboard door. In there? The quest would be all for naught if she had no ice. Best check that first. Kat stumbled back to the other room and opened her small refrigerator. In the freezer section, a tray of frost encrusted cubes was trapped in the icy grip. She wrestled the container out of the compartment and continued her search for the elusive object.

One of these days, she would have to defrost the cursed thing but not today. If necessary, a decent sized plastic, zip seal one wrapped in a tea towel would work. Still, she preferred the one which was missing.

Her warming closet was in the hallway by the bathroom. Hot water bottle, a hosepipe that attached to the faucet, why she kept the stupid thing she didn't know, swung and slapped the surface when she opened the door. If she couldn't find her ice sack she might be able to make the other work.

That entailed breaking the frozen water into small enough pieces to shove them through the neck and create more misery and suffering. About to give up her hunt, her fingers grazed something on the upper shelf. She stretched and captured the object.

With the bag stuffed, Kat padded back to her bedroom and crawled under the covers. She burrowed down until all she left exposed was the top of her head. The cooling relief the cold pack transferred to her aching head, welcome. She drifted off to sleep and embraced the dark oblivion. Maybe after a few more hours slumber, she would feel less ill.

The woman who arrived last night before Mr. Cocksure made his exit staggered out the front door. Right away, she put her hand up to shield her eyes. The bright sunshine made him happy he had his Fedora. Not only that, but the sun warmed the pavements and the buildings' cladding, making the day more pleasant to spend time outdoors. She carried on past him and disappeared around the corner. He strode down the road. When he reached the Maritime Museum, he spotted her on the narrow section of Shiprow leading to Market Street.

With it being Sunday, the store wouldn't be open for business – at least not until later in the day. It gave him plenty of time to enter the apartment, give her a scare and leave. The Fedora and balaclava covered his head and face. His overcoat shielded his body and his leather gloves concealed his hands leaving no fingerprints behind.

She wouldn't know who he was. But he couldn't speak to her. That would run the risk of her recognizing his voice. Silence. That would be more threatening than if he spoke. He jammed his fists in his topcoat and loped back up the hill.

Aberdeen came to life. Church bells pealed. People ventured out into the streets – many dressed in their Sunday finery. His clothes were the same no matter which day of the week. These were all he had – all he carried with him when he returned to the Granite City.

He hovered by a bollard on the road's sweeping curve, careful to stay out of the range of the CCTV camera. To the right, Exchequer Row and the front façade of her business. Ahead, the pedestrianized section of Shiprow led the way to Union Street and the vacant building the housed the former Esslemont & Macintosh department store on the far side. He started in that direction.

The gate to the courtyard behind her shop was ajar. Was someone back there? He poked his head inside around the door, but the area was devoid of people – just recycling and wheelie bins occupied the space. Whoever left via this exit hadn't locked up properly after themselves.

Once he slipped through the opening, he secured the door and listened for the clunk of the hasp falling into position before creeping to the lock box and punching in the combination. He held his breath as he opened the small safe – afraid the key might not be there as on previous occasions. Seeing his means of entry inside, he exhaled with relief.

Going in whilst his red-haired beauty was within those four walls was the most daring thing he'd done. On his other trips into her home, the place had been empty. Would this backfire on him? When he tried to insert the piece of brass, his hand shook. He missed and dropped it. He retrieved the item and this time, slid it into the slot. He turned the knob and pushed the door off the latch. Now he had the portal open, he replaced the opener in the safe and clicked the lid into place.

Because the doors were solid, the corridor was blanketed in darkness, even though it was midday. He closed it behind him, careful to make sure he didn't make a lot of noise.

As he crept to the bottom of the steps, the motion sensor nightlights illuminated his path. He ascended one tread at a time, hoping none of them creaked. If she discovered him too soon, his plan would be ruined. It must not happen. When she was away from home, worrying about making noise was a non-starter. It didn't matter. No one would hear him.

Upstairs, he reached for the handle and opened the door. Anticipation coursed through his veins. He nudged it with his shoulder, but the chain prevented the entryway from opening more than about four inches. Damn. Damn it to hell, anyway. How did he sneak inside? Any other time she never locked it. Did she only secure the premises when she was home? He could break the door down but the plan was to creep in quietly. Use the element of surprise to his advantage. She ruined things for him – again. The red-haired woman would pay for this.

Angry as he was, he couldn't kick off indoors. He descended the stairs, but not with the same caution he used when he climbed them. Same with when he left via the back door. He slammed the solid slab shut behind him with no care to the racket he created.

He dashed across the courtyard and out into Shiprow. Leaning against the wall, he gulped in air trying to calm down. The voices grew noisy, displeased with the turn of events. The perfect opportunity to eliminate her was taken away from him all because of a length of chain.

Stephanie stumbled up the stairway to her apartment on Crown Terrace. The sunshine did nothing in aid of her hangover. If anything, the intense brightness lasered its way into her brain and made her feel worse than she did before. Not expecting to be so hungover, and being wintertime, not to mention the call to go stay with Kat came in the evening, she never gave sunglasses a thought. She couldn't remember if she even owned a pair anymore.

Molly rubbed against and between her legs in figure eight formations. The cat's movements impeded her progress despite Steph's feeble attempts to shift the animal out of the way.

Less than five minutes after getting home, the aromas from the Vietnamese restaurant wafted through the air. Stephanie clapped her hand over her mouth and darted to the bathroom. She wretched a few times but nothing came up. Did she dare attempt drinking something? She ran water into the highball she kept on her toothbrush holder and took a sip. After pausing to see if she could keep it down, she tried a bit more. So far so good. She took the tumbler and wobbled off to her room.

Water glass deposited on the nightstand, she crashed crossways on her bed. To her chagrin, Molly jumped up and rubbed around her some more. Steph swatted the cat away, snatched the pillow and buried her head. The two friends had some great girlie nights over the years but never had they consumed so much red wine. The worst for creating a hangover.

Kat opened one eye. The illumination outside her window had changed. How long had she slept? The clock radio said half two in glowing numerals. She sat up. Her stomach didn't lurch from the movement. The ice bag landed on the bed next to her. She moved the waterproof sack to the bedside table beside her face-down BlackBerry Z10.

When she retrieved her mobile, the light was flashing. She touched the screen and swiped upwards. The email symbol showed four new ones and there was one along the message box. Hoping it was from Jared, she tapped on that icon first.

Hope Ur OK. H8ted 2 leave U last night.

His text made her smile. She typed her response and hit send.

Better now than earlier. Hangover from hell.

She laid back in bed not expecting him to respond. He sent it to her about half-six. Now early afternoon, he would be back at work and not able to reply. The worst of her morning after illness gone now, Kat threw back the covers and climbed out of bed. Her head still ached but at least the nausea passed. She staggered to the kitchen and took two more Paracetamol. After having a shower, she would be right as rain.

Undressed, with the water running at the correct temperature, she stepped into the tub. She braced herself against the wall under the spray. The gold chain bearing Colin's wedding band dangled between her breasts. She should have taken the bloody thing off and chucked it in Diana Braithwaite's face in London, but something prevented her from doing so. Did she still have a misguided loyalty to the man who only married her for her money and had a longstanding affair from the early days of her marriage? If she did, she needed her head examined.

Scrubbed, hair washed and conditioned, Kat turned off the faucet and reached for the heated rack for her long, heavy terrycloth dressing gown. Once she donned the garment, she grabbed a towel and wrapped her hair in the fabric. Cinching the tie belt as she went, she padded back to the bedroom.

Standing in front of the dresser, the jewellery sparkled in the mirror's reflection. Taking a deep breath, she reached behind her neck. Her hands shook as she tried to unfasten the clasp. When she succeeded, she laid the chain on the chest of drawers. There would be plenty of time to decide what to do later. For now, she congratulated herself for having the strength to finally remove it.

~ 18 ~

4th February, 2011

Kat left the store under Melissa's charge so she could prepare a special meal for Jared. He departed the next day and a fortnight would pass before she would be with him again. She planned something with wine, starting with an aperitif, although a couple of tins of lager would satisfy him.

Table set, taper candles in holders in the center, created a romantic setting. But tonight would be memorable – in more ways than one.

The sauce simmered on the hob, salad greens washed and prepared in the fridge. All she had left to do was cook the pasta and garlic bread.

With things under control in the kitchen, she walked to her closet to search out something to wear. After a great deal of debate with her conscience, she chose a teal coloured, long-sleeved satin blouse and her skinny jeans.

After their meal, Kat started to clear away the dishes. As she scraped the remnants off their plates and put them in the dishwasher, Jared came up behind her, placed his hands on her hips and drew her backwards into him. He turned her around, removed the cutlery she held in her hand and dropped it in the sink. "Those can wait." His breath was hot and moist in her ear.

She tipped her head back. His steely blue eyes filled with longing bored into her soul. Putting his right arm around her waist, he pulled her tight to him; his body on fire with desire. When his mouth touched hers, their tongues met. His left hand found her breast and he squeezed it before moving to unbutton her shirt.

Katherine's breath quickened when he slipped his hand inside her lacy, black bra and grazed his thumb over her nipple which tightened at his touch. With his lips, he brushed his way across her cheek to her jaw. At the same time, he traced his index finger down her chin, throat and breastbone. Goose bumps formed at his caress. When Jared cupped his hand around the milky white mound, she moaned.

Taking his hand, she guided him to the bedroom. Inside the double French doors, she pushed the ceiling light button then turned the small knob dimming the lights. Next, she removed her blouse and laid the satin shirt over the arm of the chair.

When she unbuttoned her jeans, he stopped her. "Let me," he said, his voice husky. He tugged down the zipper.

As Jared peeled the denim over her hips, he dropped to his knees and nibbled her bare flesh to her black, lace thong. His moist breath puffed on her skin. Soon she stood there in just her undies, her trousers a rumpled pile on the floor. He helped her step out of them and carried her to the bed where he laid her down. While he stripped down to his boxer briefs, she shoved the duvet away from where she lay.

Knee between her calves, he crawled up the mattress, licking and kissing her as he went. She arched her back and undid her bra. Jared guided the straps down her arms and removed the piece of intimate apparel. Kat's nipples tightened from the change in temperature, but his contact made them rock hard.

Too soon, he traced his tongue down the length of her torso. She placed his right hand to her chest to take the place of his lips. His hot, steamy breath rasped against the fabric of her thong. He nibbled the inside of one thigh then the other. Kat squirmed under him. She'd not had sex with any man in over five years and it was way more since she made love with Jared.

Distracted by what he did down there, she didn't notice his hands were no longer on her breasts – until, they reached her underwear. She raised her bottom and he eased them down.

Rising to his knees, he slipped the lacy fabric down her legs. Once they were around her ankles, he held her right calf in his hand and pulled her one leg out. Kat dangled her other foot off the edge of the bed and they fell off.

He leaned over her and mashed his mouth down on hers. She parted her lips in response. His hand traced down her body pausing to squeeze her breast before moving further. When he reached the area now uncovered, he dipped his hand between her thighs and stroked. If he didn't soon make love to her, she was going to explode. He stabbed one finger into her and followed it with a second. As he moved them in and out, alternating between fast and slow movements, his thumb teased her secret spot.

She embraced him and with her feet worked away at the top of his underwear, pushing them down.

He drew back. "You're not ready yet."

"I am." She nodded to reinforce her words.

In the seconds Jared took to undress completely, her desire level heightened. He plunged inside her. Kat dug her fingernails into his shoulder blades. His strokes were rapid, frenzied and she kept pace with him raising her hips to meet each one. It was like they had never been apart. Their bodies still compatible – in sync – after all these years.

When they climaxed, they did so in unison.

Kat wrapped herself in the duvet and walked to the dresser. The fire in her lower belly now diminished from inferno to smouldering. Her fingers brushed the wedding ring she wore on a chain since the authorities gave it back to her after Colin's death. She moved to the window. The city stood quiet below her, the orange glow from the streetlights interrupted by the cool white of the new replacement LED fixtures.

Now she could move on with her life and proved it to herself by making love with the man she fell for all those years ago. She had finally let go of the past.

"Hey, you jumped out of the bed almost when we finished. What's wrong?" He joined her and laid his hands on her upper arms.

"Nothing."

"Are you sure?"

"Positive." Kat leaned back into him.

A figure stepped out of the shadows of the cinema access. The same person who had taken up residence in her neighbourhood, sleeping rough in that location or on the opposite side of the street stared at her and made a slashing motion across his throat.

At the same time, Jared brushed her hair away from her neck and touched his lips on the spot he cleared.

Kat jumped.

"You're shivering. Come back to bed and I'll warm you up."

His kiss was not the reason behind her reaction. The creep's actions caused it but she couldn't tell Jared. He would run off half-cocked and do something stupid. No, she had to keep this to herself, at least for now.

"I didn't hurt you, did I?" He put an arm around her waist.

"No. "I'm fine."

"If I did, I'm sorry, just wanted you so bad since I saw you at Hogmanay."

"I told you. You didn't." A tear slid down her cheek. She couldn't hold back.

"Hey, what's wrong?"

"Oh Jared," she turned and buried her face in his smooth, muscular chest.

"What's the matter?" he gathered her into his arms and held her to him.

"I don't want to lose you," she sighed. "I love you. I never stopped."

"I feel the same way about you. Marry me, Kat."

"Please, hold me."

He moved her hair away from her neck and kissed her pale flesh before pulling her closer to him. "You never have to ask me to do that."

"Don't ever leave me. I don't know what I would do without you."

"No intention of ever leaving you. You can count on it."

He touched his lips to her forehead. "Come back to bed."

~ 19 ~

5th February, 2011

Jared woke early in the morning. At first he didn't know where he was. Kat was in his arms, her nakedness pressed against his body. He was in her bed. Feelings of desire stirred inside him. They had made love the previous night. It was almost like old times. He propped himself up on one elbow. Her long red hair splayed out over her pillow. With a light caress, he trailed his fingertips down the centre of her body, his thumb stroked her right nipple which tightened at his touch.

"Mmm," she sighed and rolled on her back. The duvet slid down, exposing her breasts.

He ran his palm over her flat stomach, his brush light. Her skin came out in goose bumps under his hand. He bent down and flicked his tongue over it. She moaned and parted her legs. Invitation accepted, Jared slipped his hand between them and stroked until she became moist and slippery.

When she was ready, he climbed on her and pushed inside. He laced his fingers through hers and held her hands on the pillows on either side of her head. He pressed his mouth on her lips and she returned his kiss. Unlike the night before when their lovemaking was hard and frenzied, this was slow rhythmic strokes – relaxing by comparison.

Afterwards, they cuddled, her spooning him.

Kat luxuriated under the covers. The warmth of post orgasmic bliss washed over her. Now that she broke past the barrier and accepted him into her yet again, she craved more. Jared did things to her Colin never did, or couldn't. Her husband never fanned the fires of her animal lust the way this man did.

The shower turned on. He had to fly back to the rig today. She didn't want him to go. She wanted him to spend the day with her, making love like they did when she spent time at his bedsit prior to her parents' intervention.

Rather than remain in bed daydreaming of sexual intimacy with Jared, she climbed out from beneath the duvet, and put on her short, plum coloured dressing gown. The least she could do for him with all he did for her since walking back into her life at Hogmanay was cook him breakfast so he didn't go off to work on an empty stomach.

The Super Puma was scheduled to depart from the helipad at half two. If all went to plan, they would reach the Alpha Ecosse between three-fifteen and four o'clock. Before that, Jared, along with the members on his shift, had to sit through the mandatory pre-flight safety meeting and watch the video. He viewed the bloody thing hundreds of times. Nothing changed from one screening to the next. Maybe if something did, he and the rest of the crew wouldn't be quite so bored. A couple of the guys nodded off. The rasps of their snoring soon followed.

His mind wandered to Kat. The previous twenty-four hours with her were like those from before her move to Canada. He wanted to stay with her today and forced himself to leave her bed.

The film ended. Jared and the others breathed a collective sigh of relief. The last stop before boarding was to put on their survival suits. They were big and bulky, hot, and a pain in the ass, but if something happened during the flight, the neoprene garments would keep their body heat in and the water out.

Once he had his suit on, he stepped outside to the tarmac. The temperature inside too warm to stand around in rubber gear. "Okay, George?" he asked when the lone female on their crew exited the building.

"Yeah, just some days I wonder why I thought of getting into this field."

Jared put his arm around her and gave her an affectionate hug. "You and me both." Her head didn't even come up to his shoulder. Until then, he didn't realize how short she was. Other women worked on the Alpha Ecosse besides her, although they functioned in the domestic side of things. Not Georgia. She toiled along with the men in a harsh environment.

If anything were to happen to him en-route to or from the oilrig, after losing her husband in a violent death, Kat would topple over the edge.

"You found someone, haven't you." She looked up at him through her bright blue eyes, veiled with long, black lashes. She smiled, showing her dimples.

"Yes and no." His posture stiffened.

"Someone special?" She turned to face Jared.

He knew she wore contacts. No one had eyes that shade. Not that he didn't like the colour. If he didn't reunite with Kat, and Georgia wasn't involved with Andy, he might have fancied his chances with the girl. She was attractive enough. George reminded him of Kat's employee, Melissa, with the neon colours she dyed her hair. With her dark complexion, courtesy of her mixed race parents – and black hair, the flashes of brilliance suited her. "Everything all right with you two?"

"Yes, other than it's hard to have a relationship on the rig. No privacy."

Jared didn't have a chance to respond. The rest of the crew, including Andy Pascoe, exited the building.

Kat sat at her dining table toying with the basket of fruit. She removed an apple, examined the produce from all sides. Should she have ignored Jared's proposal? Did he ask her only because it was the first time they made love since before her move to Canada? She pondered his question and her reaction.

Before Colin, she would have jumped at the opportunity to marry Jared. But now, she was an adult, and adults didn't leap into things with both feet. They went about life in a logical manner. Still, she loved him, but the idea of commitment scared her to death. Her husband cheated on her. Jared worked in a dangerous field. What if she married him and he died? No, she was happy continuing their relationship the same way.

~ 20 ~

7th February, 2011

Katherine stepped through the door of the coffeehouse on Union Street and scanned the patrons for Stephanie. The eatery was busy at this time of day, which was good to see. Quite often in the weeks after Christmas and Hogmanay, restauranteurs and retailers suffered. No one had any money left for extras. The credit card bills from the holidays had arrived in the post and people were shocked to discover how much they spent.

The aroma of fresh ground coffee beans filled the bistro. The espresso machine hissed and belched out vapour as it brewed another cup. On its own, it was stronger than she preferred, but a cappuccino on a cold winter day wouldn't go amiss.

The modern, exterior façade contrasted with the classic décor within the four walls. Exposed stone and brick along with heavy wooden trim, counters, and tables made the establishment feel homey. Overstuffed sofas and chairs occupied a far corner.

Stephanie waved to her from a table near the fireplace and she navigated her way between the furnishings to the location. A wood fire burned in the grate. They didn't spend a lot of time together since Jared got home from covering for one of the guys on the opposite shift. Not that he controlled her or wouldn't let her see her friends, but when he was home, she liked to spend as much of her free time with him as she could.

They lost too much time when she was in Canada and during her sham of a marriage. Bad enough, he just got back

171

and had to turn around and leave again for his regular offshore rotation. Still, Katherine was thankful for the time she spent with him since they reconnected at Hogmanay.

"So why are you grinning like the cat that got the cream?"

"Let's order first." Kat removed her mac and hung it on the back of her chair then unwrapped her pashmina leaving it over her shoulders but off her chest. Her hair stayed under the knitted scarf. She wanted to tell her good news but before saying a word, did her friend notice anything missing from her usual attire. She chose her ivory wrap jumper with the plunging, but not indecent, V-neck on purpose.

Soups, salads and assorted sandwiches carried by bustling wait staff passed by their table, the flavours lingering in the steam from the hot bowls.

Despite the eatery being busy, the girls didn't have a long delay before their orders were taken. The drinks came first served by a girl with short black, curly hair. She deposited Kat's caramel cappuccino before her and a black tea in front of Stephanie then disappeared into the crowd.

"Okay, you're absolutely glowing. Spill."

Out of habit, Katherine raised her hand to the spot on her chest where Colin's wedding band rested all those years. The chain she wore no longer there. Even though she took them off four days ago now, it had become second nature to her to toy with the gold hoop when apprehensive. "Jared asked me to marry him."

Stephanie grabbed Katherine's left hand. "Where's the ring? He can't propose without it. What did you say? It better have been yes."

"Didn't give me one."

"What? He needs his head examining."

"But he did ask me after we made love."

"You finally? Wow. I'm so happy for you." She jumped up, leaned over the table and hugged her friend. "I need details. Well, not those ... hey, where's your gold chain? Colin's ring?"

"They've not been around my neck since before Jared came back last week." She sighed. The past was back where it belonged.

"You didn't say … what did you tell him when he asked?"

"Nothing. I asked him to hold me."

"You didn't say a word. Not even how's your mum? Kiss my bum?"

Katherine shook her head. "He didn't say anything at the time. I don't know how long or even if he'll ask again."

"If he loves you as much as I think he does, he'll take things slowly. Might have been the post-shagging glow made him ask."

"God, I hope you're right. Taking off that blasted chain and making love with him was a huge step for me," she murmured, lowering her head. Tears burned her eyes. "I'm scared. What if he cheats on me? What if something happens to him? What if I'm the one who ruins things between us?"

"Quit torturing yourself with 'what-ifs'. You do, and you'll never have a relationship with Jared or anyone else."

Committing to another man, after discovering Colin's cheating from pretty much the beginning of their married life, would not be easy. Steph was right. No sense living in doubt, but she needed things to move at her speed, in her comfort zone. Pressure to go at a faster pace only frightened her more.

~ 21 ~

16th February, 2011

With Jared's twelve-hour rotation over, he headed straight to the shower. His job was cleaner than some of the others out here, but far from white collar. He hoped the Internet connection would be better than the last few times he tried to video chat with Kat using Skype. The signal dropped out so often he gave up. Tonight he had an important question to ask her so the Wi-Fi had to work.

Once he cleaned up and had a bite of supper, he strolled into the recreation room. Gym equipment filled one corner, tables, chairs and sofas occupied the floor space in the centre of the spacious area.

A huge flat-screen TV was mounted on the wall near the fitness facilities. A DVD player and discs, and satellite receiver were on a stand beneath it. Six dartboards hung opposite the computers. Not all the systems had webcams and the ones equipped were the most popular. Every one of them was in use.

He eased into a chair beside Brad Gilbertson who chatted with his wife. "Hi Lesley," he said and stuck his head over his workmate's shoulder.

"Hello Jared. Can I finish talking with my husband now?"

He winked and started a game of solitaire to keep him occupied while he waited. The guys spoke to their wives in hushed tones, not that he tried to eavesdrop. The PCs were close together so to have a proper conversation, you needed the room to be quiet, at least on the same level as at home with the telly turned on. He might have a temper, but at some point before her death, his mother drummed manners into him.

A loud whoop from the seat next to him caught his attention. Brad leapt out of the chair sending it toppling backwards. "That's brilliant." He turned around. "Lesley's going to have a baby. I'm going to be a dad," he yelled.

Congratulations, handshakes, and back slaps followed.

While Jared waited for his colleague to finish his conversation with his wife, he sent a text to Kat advising her that he would be online in a few minutes. Many times his first attempts to reach her failed. The advance notice ensured her computer was on and she had the application running.

"Love you, babe. See you soon," he said and logged out. "All yours now, Martin." He stood and whacked Jared's shoulder.

Brad was the only bloke on this shift who called everyone by their surname. All the others used first names. Jared didn't mind. He had grown accustomed to it.

"How are you doin'?" he asked once he and Kat connected via the video chat.

"Not bad … all things considered." She twisted a lock of her hair in her fingers.

"I miss you." He leaned closer to the computer screen.

"About time you got yourself a woman." Steve Norton said, pressing his cheek against Jared's.

He gave him a shove. "Fuck off."

Soon the room was filled with smooching noises.

She lowered her head, embarrassed by the guys' antics.

"See what I have to put up with?"

"How'd you land such a hot bird?" Carter asked.

"I'd tell you, but I'd have to kill you."

The feed froze. Kat's mouth gaped open like she was in the middle of a word.

"Marry me, Kat."

"I-I can't." She rested her chin in her hands.

"I'm not like him. I would never do that to you. Please say you will."

A tear escaped from her eye. Jared wished he were next to her to wipe the moisture away, hold her, and make all the hurt caused by Colin disappear. But, he was stuck out here in the middle of the North Sea.

"I know you're not. You wouldn't. You're getting ahead of yourself. Our weekend in London brought everything back. Our last time together was a huge step forward for me."

"I'm glad you took it."

Kat nodded.

"The trained monkeys are starting to get restless. I best get off here. I'll see you soon. Love you."

"Love you, too." She kissed her fingertips and touched them to her computer screen.

After Jared logged off, that final image of their video chat lingered in his mind. He left the room with a smile on his face and headed to the sleeping quarters where he would have a bit of privacy, since most of the guys who worked in the tin can stayed behind in the recreation area.

Stripped down to his boxer briefs, Jared climbed the ladder to the upper bunk and crawled under the covers. He knew Kat needed time to recover from the pain and her distrust in men. He hoped to be the one to help her move beyond the past.

He asked her to marry him again. Doing it online was impersonal but he asked. She called Stephanie. As soon as her friend answered, she blurted out, "Jared proposed again. This time when we chatted on Skype."

"And you said, no. Quit torturing yourself woman. You know you want to be with him. You've always wanted that. You loved each other then and now. What's so hard about saying yes?"

Katherine dabbed her eyes. "I know. We were good together once upon a time. The sex was amazing but then I was young and impressionable. I was no longer a virgin when we did it the first time but I might as well have been. He was kind and gentle. Took his time with me. When I got dragged off to Canada, he was all I thought about. I never had relations with anyone the whole time I lived there. Blokes called me a tease. Ice princess. How did I know then I'd never find a lover so compatible? A man who did things to me I never dreamed of? Maybe I never gave my body to Colin – at least not completely. I know I never gave him a hundred percent of my heart. Jared still occupied a piece of it. Maybe it's why Colin went looking for sexual satisfaction elsewhere. Even his fancy woman referred to me as the red-headed ice queen."

"I thought you got all this self-doubt, self-hatred out of your system weeks ago."

"I don't know. I'm so confused these days. I'm a mess."

~ 22 ~

19th February, 2011

Katherine decided to surprise Jared by meeting him at the helipad when he arrived from his shift offshore. She double-checked his flight's arrival time against the Inverness-Aberdeen railway timetable. A long wait on a cold but sunny Aberdeen day would not be pleasant so the closer together she could coordinate the two events, the better, but she still needed to leave herself time to walk the distance. Not to mention, she wanted to be waiting for him when he landed.

Since the revelations earlier in the year, Katherine spent as little time in the bookstore as possible. Being there revived too many unpleasant memories. Still, she could not bear to sell the business. Cherie proved a godsend to her during these times, being happy to come and fill in on short notice.

A few people lingered in the open air by the cinema to her right. Pedestrians disappeared around the corner of the granite building housing her premises up the pedestrianized portion of Shiprow, while others appeared having travelled the street in the other direction.

The casino, on the opposite side of Exchequer Row looked empty but inside the outer walls, business boomed. Katherine shoved her hands further into her parka and shivered. Rather than continue on Shore Brae, once she reached the Aberdeen Maritime Museum, she traversed the narrow section of the cobbled roadway leading to Market Street. From there it was a short distance to Union Square and the adjacent transportation hub.

Over two months had elapsed since his return to the Granite City. Frustrated with the uncooperative nature of the voices, he paced at the intersection of Trinity Quay and Guild Street. They should have told him what to do, when to do it, and how to get her at her most vulnerable. Nothing. Sometimes, they had been noisy when he plotted out his plans for her, but they never agreed with him.

A flash of red hair rounded the corner. Certain it was her, he stopped pacing and stared. With her back to him, this woman could have been any other woman with ginger hair. Still, she carried herself the same way as the one on which he wanted to exact his revenge. He couldn't let her out of his sight. Being near the mall, bus terminal and railway station; the streets were crowded.

When she disappeared, he jumped to see over the heads of the people obstructing his view. He spotted her crossing to the shopping complex's narrow, secondary doorway. Horns blared and drivers shook their fists as he sprinted across the road in the middle of the block.

He crossed against the light in front of one of the Stagecoach buses to reach the entrance she approached. When the operator jammed on the brakes, they squealed, but he remained undeterred. The red-head could not vanish.

Union Square wouldn't be a good place. Too many people. Witnesses. No, he required a secluded location to torture and destroy her. Someplace with an easy means of escape. Would he be able to persuade her to climb up to the gantry bridge?

He couldn't do some of the things he wanted with her, but if others thought they were a couple in love, he could stab her, even give the knife a twist before pulling it out and running. Her demise would come quick. She wouldn't have time to scream. Maybe a startled cry, then drop to the ground, dead. No, she deserved to be punished and suffer a long, lingering, painful death.

He trailed her through the mall to the concourse. Was she going to see Mr. Cocksure again? Damn her. She passed through the turnstile. Where was she going? He sprinted up the stairs to see which platform she went to from the overhead bridge. Only certain trains came and went from there. She stood beneath the 6N sign. That was the one to Inverness. Was she going there? He needed to board that passenger service and follow her. When he arrived at the ticket office, he was out of breath. "Inverness." He tried to gulp air into his lungs.

"One way or return."

It didn't really matter. He might only ride as far as she did. De-train and pursue her when she exited. Two people getting off at the same stop was common. He would blend in with the scenery and schlepp along behind her.

"Return." He mumbled and dropped some cash in the tray under the window.

When his tickets finished printing, he snatched them and his change. The digital board indicated the arrival was delayed but expected in the next five minutes.

He walked through the gated access and followed her, staying far enough away she wouldn't spot him yet near enough to watch her movements.

When it finally arrived at the station, she boarded the middle carriage from the rear doors. He climbed aboard the last car from the front. From here, she was visible. He bided his time and waited for her to make her move.

It was a short wait to find out her destination. She rose as the passenger service slowed for Dyce – the Aberdeen Airport stop. A southbound train pulled in on the adjacent track. Distracted by it, she almost got away. She walked by where he stood near the doors and once she passed, he exited.

A number of men carrying duffel bags also got off here. Guys who worked on the rigs, no doubt. Is that what Mr. Cocksure did? Was he flying home and she was meeting him here? Keeping his distance and other pedestrians between himself and her, he fell into step with the group.

Never a plane watcher, he was fascinated by the size of the jets taking off and landing – their bulk defying gravity to climb into the sky, or come back to land without crashing. Helicopters took off and landed, too. Everything perfectly orchestrated. So engrossed in the activity overhead, he almost missed seeing her walk into the car park at the primary terminal.

He had to be careful. He had managed to avoid detection so far; did not want her to spot him and become suspicious now. Not now he was so near to finding out the reason for her coming here.

Despite running about ten minutes late, Katherine still had time to traverse the distance from the railway station to the helicopter company's headquarters. Dyce, located further inland, was still cold but without the dampness from the harbour. Loosening her scarf as she walked, she continued.

The airport was a hub of activity with jets and choppers lifting into the air and others returning to the ground. Some of the fleet sat on the tarmac near the hangar. She checked the time. His flight should land any minute. Kat hoped to get next to the barrier separating the small car park from the helipad. There did not appear to be any security and the gate was for vehicles. She crossed the street, slipped between the barriers to the high, barbed wire-topped, chain link fence.

The distinct sound of the aircraft grew louder. Shielding her eyes from the sun, she raised her face skyward. When the chopper dipped low and made its descent for landing, the Nexus name showed on the fuselage. This should be Jared's flight. Katherine checked her watch again to be certain.

When the passengers disembarked, she clutched the fence. "Jared," she called out not knowing if he could hear her.

One of the men in orange, survival suits broke away from the group. "Kat." He walked to her. "Brilliant to see you. Wait here. I won't be long. Get out of this uncomfortable thing and after a quick debriefing we'll be off." He couldn't kiss her on the lips through the mesh but did plant a tiny one on the part of her fingers on his side.

Damn. She did come to see Mr. Cocksure. He recognized the man's face straight away. Now what did he do? Return to the station with his tail between his legs? Admit defeat? Never. Not in his lifetime. He would have the woman with the red hair if it was the last thing he did.

Bloody voices. Why didn't they speak to him? Before he returned to Aberdeen and began his research and surveillance of her bookshop, they were in constant contact. Now they were silent. Oh, there were some rumblings from time to time, but nothing concrete. Seeing her so infatuated with Mr. Offshore Worker raised the temperature of his blood to the boiling point. He needed to get her away from him – on her own with no one to protect her – but how?

When Jared disembarked on the tarmac, he memorized the call letters on the fuselage – T-BLUE. He would remember that ride forever. Flights to and from the rigs in the North Sea were never smooth but none spooked him like this one did. Maybe it was because Kat was back in his life.

Before they found each other again, no one awaited him – only him which suited him fine. But now, he had a reason to come home even if they didn't live under the same roof all the time. They at least managed a few nights together either at his in Newburgh or hers in Aberdeen.

By the time Jared got out of his neoprene survival suit, and sat through a debriefing meeting, over half an hour had gone by. Thirty minutes Kat spent waiting for him. When he exited the building, he discovered her still standing by the fence. She hadn't moved the entire time.

He strode over to her and pulled her into his arms. In seconds, his lips were on hers and he searched for her tongue. The longer their embrace continued, the more the events of the journey bothered him. Jared began shaking.

"What's wrong?"

"Fuckin' flight from hell. Thought for sure we were going to crash."

Kat pulled back from him and stared into his eyes.

"Come on. The car's in the next carpark up the street. Let's get out of here. Go back to mine. I could use a shower and I'm knackered." He started walking to the place where he left his BMW.

When they arrived at his vehicle, he stowed his duffel bag in the boot and helped Katherine into the passenger seat.

Easing in behind the wheel, he sighed and scrubbed his hands down his face.

"How bad was the flight?" She reached over and put her hand on his.

"The fuckin' thing shook and rattled from the time we took off. There were a couple of almighty, loud bangs and I swear we dropped a thousand feet. I was sure we were going to ditch."

Kat's brown eyes were full of concern. Did he tell her his fear? Afraid he would never see her again? Scared with everything Katherine had been through since the beginning of the year, something happening to him would push her over the edge. It was bad enough she had lost her husband in a violent manner.

He did not want her to go through the same thing if he died en-route to or from the rig. A crash would be one of the worse ways to go. Their air taxis didn't fly as high as passenger jets so when the bird went down, you would be alive the entire time and know everything that was happening. Impacting the water, if you were lucky, would finish you off on the spot. If you survived, he didn't want to know.

Jared leaned over and kissed Katherine's cheek. "You'll think I'm a fucking marshmallow but I can't bear the thought of not being with you. I don't want to die."

"None of us do."

"I don't want to leave you alone. One senseless death is enough for anyone to go through. You don't need me dying in a helicopter crash." He leaned forward and rested his forehead on the steering wheel.

Katherine sat in stunned silence. Jared had always been the strong one in their relationships – this one and their previous one. She had never seen him show the fear that lurked beneath the surface. He would have learned to cover it up as a child growing up in an abusive home. Whatever he required from her, she would see he got it.

"You don't mind if we go back to mine? I'll take you to yours later."

"My place is with you."

Jared raised his head.

They drove to Newburgh in silence. Katherine didn't push him to talk. It made for a long car ride, but he needed to process the terrible flight and move on. She didn't mind flying – reckoned it to being on a train in the sky. This time of year, lounging on a beach somewhere hot and sunny would not go amiss.

If the timing was right, she and Jared could go to the Caribbean or Mediterranean on his off duty time. Maybe she would suggest a trip after they got to his place. But after his flight from hell, this was not the time to broach the subject.

When they arrived at Jared's, Katherine curled up in his recliner, remote in hand ready to watch some telly, but her mind refused to settle. She walked to the window and opened the heavy drapes, letting the afternoon sun into the room. Dust motes glittered in the beam of light. The warmth created from that simple action soon removed the chill from the air.

A few magazines, stacked in military precision, lay on the coffee table. Katherine bent over to inspect them. Among them were a well-thumbed issue of *Performance BMW*, *Land Rover Owner*, *Top Gear Magazine*, and an old, but well-preserved copy of *James Bond Car Collection*. Selecting the one related to the vehicle he owned when they met, she flipped through the pages as she returned to the recliner. The stiff suspension, spare tyre mounted on the bonnet, it provided the most uncomfortable ride ever, although back then, it was what they did once they reached a secluded location that mattered.

The shower running in the downstairs bathroom stopped. He appeared in the doorway, a large towel wrapped around his waist.

"Feel better now?" she asked.

"Much. See you found some reading material. Sorry there isn't more. Not much into it these days. Did enough of it when I went to school. Need to put my head down and grab a couple hours kip then I'll take you back to Aberdeen."

"Do you still have your old 4x4? The one like this?"

Katherine held up the publication and turned the picture around so he could see the image.

"Sure do. Keep it in the garage out back. I'll show you before I take you home, if you want. Think I'll fix the beast up and drive it in the winter. The Beemer is nice but it's fucking shite in the snow." He walked to Katherine's side and kissed her forehead.

"You don't mind being here with me sleeping for a while? I know there isn't much to do. My laptop is in the spare room, and satellite telly although this time of day there might not be a lot on."

"Don't worry about me. I might go for a walk. You get some rest." Kat enfolded him in her arms then pointed him in the direction of the stairs.

She stood at the bottom as he ascended. She could lie down with him, but it would result in sex, not a bad thing, but he needed sleep. Dark circles formed below his steely blue eyes. Time with his head down should eliminate them. When he took her back to the city after his nap, did she invite him to stay overnight?

What to do with herself while he slept? Afraid of waking him if she used the computer or staying in the house for that matter, Kat opted to go out. Closing the back door behind her, she shrugged into her coat as she moved.

Jared's house was handy to the trunk road. Only the church stood between his place and it. She strode off in that direction. There didn't seem to be much to the right other than some houses. Left was the direction they walked to the Udny Arms the previous month. More commercial than residential made it more appealing. At the University of Aberdeen's Oceanlab campuses, the sidewalk ended. From there, Kat followed the cycle/walking path. About twenty minutes later, she found herself standing on the bridge over the River Ythan.

The wind whipped strands of hair in her face. She struggled to keep her tresses under control. The tide was out and the clouds had broken up. The sun peaked out and its rays provided warmth and comfort. The view of the estuary was amazing. The sand stretched for miles. Kat pulled out her mobile and selected the camera function. She photographed the vista including the North Sea then crossed to the other side to take still more pictures. Gulls and ducks floated on the water and walked on the sandy shore.

This scenic place would make the perfect location for a selfie of the two of them. They should walk out here together some time. Much as she wanted to spend more time savouring the surroundings, she had to make a start back. If he woke to an unlocked house and her not there, he would worry. She didn't want to cause him any further stress.

When she checked the time on her phone, she was surprised over an hour had elapsed. Kat shoved the device back, crossed to the path and strolled back to Newburgh and Jared's house.

The return trip to the village was not pleasant. This time, she walked into the stiff breeze. The earrings in her pierced ears magnified the cold and projected its frigidness from the front of her lobe along the posts and against the back. The occasional gust made the headwind harder to cut through. It would be a long trek back to the warm house.

When the latch clicked, Jared walked to the back door. "You look half frozen," he said.

Kat's face was rosy. "It was colder coming back than going out." She rubbed her gloved hands together.

Touching her cheek with the backs of his fingers, he shivered then folded her into his arms and held her. "Where have you been?"

"I walked up to the bridge and back. It's gorgeous up there."

"Can't say I noticed."

Kat pulled back from him. Her golden brown eyes stared in disbelief. "You mean you don't pay attention to the beautiful landscape so near to where you live?"

"The only beauty I'm concerned with is standing in front of me. I was making a coffee when you came in. Want one?"

"Sure." She hung her parka on one of the hooks in the hall while Jared waited for her.

He took her to the kitchen. "Go stand by the Aga. Warmer there than anywhere else in the house." He was being a fusspot but keeping her warm, safe and adored motivated him. If it meant protecting her, he would give his life to save hers. "We'll have this, then I'll show you the Land Rover, and after that take you back to yours."

"Why not throw a few things in a bag and spend the night? You're taking me there anyway. We can pick up some wine on the way and get a takeaway when we're ready to eat." She smiled in her sultry and seductive way.

At this rate, they wouldn't even finish their coffee. He would have her upstairs in his bed shagging her brains out. They might not even get that far. He needed to rein in his hormones. Their first night of unbridled passion happened after the trip to London, one short day before he had to leave. He craved to be with her in that way again.

The sex was even better than when they were together before her parents took her off to Canada. He hoped she wasn't getting her own back on her dead husband and she would always respond to his touch the same way. Spending a night with Kat would prove or disprove his revenge theory. One night. Takeaway? Rather go out for a meal instead. Show off the beautiful woman on his arm. He could do that – might even have something other than jeans and T-shirts in his wardrobe. Come back to his on Sunday. Get some things done at the house. "You stay here near the stove and drink your coffee. I'll go throw some stuff together."

Jared stopped in the utility room and dumped the contents of his duffel bag on the floor. The clothing went into the wash machine, but he left the door of the front loader open, not about to start a load of laundry now.

Holdall over his shoulder, he took the stairs two at a time to his room. He packed jeans, white T-shirt, plaid flannel and long-sleeved cotton dress shirts and chinos, underwear, socks – dark and work – along with a pair of black leather boots.

A bit over the top if they opted to stay home and order in but he still preferred taking her out. His toiletries were in the ground floor bathroom where the shower was located. He would grab them when he went back downstairs.

Kat sat on the counter next to the Aga holding her mug in both hands. "That didn't take long."

"Still have to get the stuff from the loo but otherwise, ready when you are." He walked to her, took the cup from her hands and hugged her. She responded by wrapping her legs around him and pulling him closer. He nuzzled into the hollow between her shoulder and neck. Keeping his head on straight being this familiar with her was hard. The scent of her perfume intoxicated him. Seduced him. "You finish here and I'll go and pack the rest of my shite." He backed away from Kat and rushed out of the room.

Jared braced himself against the sink. A new person formed his reflection in the mirror. No longer the surly one who stared back at him for years when he shaved or brushed his teeth. This one smiled. Happiness glowed in his eyes. The old one was sad, angry, and sullen. He much preferred this guy.

"Whenever you're ready," Kat said.

He jumped. "You startled me. Not expecting you to be stood there." Had he done something to be embarrassed about? Didn't think so. He took his razor, toothbrush, toothpaste, shower gel and deodorant and shoved them into his duffel bag.

After locking the house behind them, Jared stowed his luggage in the boot of the BMW. "Now, ladies and gentlemen, the moment you have all been waiting for. The grand unveiling." He extended his left arm in the direction of the garage, folded his other across his stomach and bowed.

Kat giggled. She slapped his shoulder. "You fool."

He lunged for her but she scampered out of his reach and ran to the stone wall at the back of the garden then turned to face him and taunted. "Think you can catch me?"

Two long strides and he caught her and hugged her. "Not much of a challenge. You didn't put up a fight. I think you wanted me to get you. And now I'm going to tickle you." He captured her and jabbed his fingers into her rib cage.

Kat shrieked with laughter. She bent down and twisted to escape from him but he kept hold of her. The more she squirmed, the more he tormented. "Okay, okay. I give." She crashed on her side to the cold, hard ground.

Jared struggled to keep his balance, but he went down, too. Landed on her. Something cracked beneath him. "Are you hurt? I'm sorry." He scrambled to his feet and helped her up.

"I-I think so." She brushed leaves and other debris from her clothing and grimaced.

"I did, didn't I?" Worried he had caused Kat a serious injury, he raked his fingers through his hair and paced.

"It was horseplay." She rubbed her upper left arm and shoulder and leaned against the garage.

He apologized again, stepped forward, and took her hands in his. "Forgive me. Please. I didn't mean to hurt you. I would never do that."

"Look. It was an accident. Accidents happen. Now show me the Land Rover."

Jared unclipped the carabiner holding his keys from his belt loop. He searched for the one which secured the padlock. Once he had the latch undone, he swung the barn doors open and stepped aside allowing Kat to enter first.

His old 4x4 took up most of the space. A single lightbulb hung from a wire suspended from the rafters. A piece of string with a weight on the end dangled from the flex cable. Jared pulled the cord. The grimy fixture didn't give off a lot more light than the open doors did.

Kat walked to the back of it, brushing her fingertips over the canvas tarp cover as she went. More than once, she gripped her injured arm. It pained him to see her hurt knowing he was the cause. When she returned to Jared's side, he reached up to the roof and yanked the tarpaulin towards them.

A cloud of dust pervaded the room, choking them. He pushed her out of the garage and followed her. Performing such a theatrical unveiling maneuver wasn't one of his better ideas. Coughing and spluttering they stood outside the storage building waiting for the dirt to settle.

Kat rubbed her sore shoulder and arm. She hoped Jared didn't see her action. She knew he would never hurt her on purpose.

She started things by teasing him. If anyone was to blame for the sequence of events, she was.

The longer they waited in the fresh air, the more the old Land Rover materialized from the artificial dust storm. Kat took a few steps forward. The vehicle was forlorn and neglected. The army green paint had faded. Spots of rust, like scabbed-over sores, speckled the surface – the white hardtop yellowed. The poor thing was ready for the scrap heap not the carriageway. "Does it even run?" she asked.

"Sure does. Want to hear it?"

"No, I'll give it a miss. I'm just gobsmacked with the state of the exterior, you're thinking of putting the old thing back on the road. Wouldn't pass its MOT, would it?"

"Not like this, needs some work."

"Some? A miracle more like." Kat walked into the garage. Raising a hand to shield the glare from the ambient outdoor light, she peered inside then reached for the door handle. When she yanked the door open, the hinges creaked in protest. The interior was terrible, far worse than when she rode in it when she should have been at school.

The upholstery had dried and cracked. Kat ran her hand over the once smooth surface, now as rough as coarse grit sandpaper. The gash in the passenger seat cushion that dug into the backs of her thighs when wearing her rolled up uniform kilt, was now joined by more.

She picked at the slash igniting a fire in her lower belly. The things Jared did to her in this vehicle. And in this spot. And sometimes when he was driving. She had sat with her legs parted and he slipped his finger in through the leg of her pants. She almost orgasmed at the thought.

"Climb in."

Jared's words snapped her back to the present. She slammed the door. "No, we probably should get going." Her cheeks hot, she bolted past him and outside.

Confident her shoulder or humerus weren't broken in the fall, Kat massaged her arm again. Regardless, she would have a huge bruise from the impact with the frozen ground. When they arrived at her place, she would take a closer look. Jared brooded in the driver's seat. Despite all her assurances it was an accident, she would need to do a lot more to convince him.

Grazing sheep meandered in the fields beside the road. Early season lambs frolicked on the farmland. Tufts of wool stuck to the inner barbed wire fence surrounding the pasture. One of the areas of roadworks they drove through stopped them next to the field the livestock occupied.

They had barely said two words to each other since leaving Newburgh. The car radio provided background noise. Was this the time to broach the subject of a trip – the same day as Jared's flight from hell as he called it? Would he entertain the idea of flying to a tropical resort? The only way to find out was ask.

She took a deep breath and swallowed. "I know it's too late to book a holiday for these two weeks, but why don't we go to Ibiza or Tenerife, or even the Dominican or Cuba? Spend some time in the sun away from this god-awful cold and damp. What do you think?"

"No." His answer was sharp.

"You didn't have to bite my head off," she spat. "I just thought it would be nice to get away some place hot – just the two of us." Kat folded her arms across her chest. His flat out refusal stung; made worse by the tone of his response."

"I'm sorry. I hate flying. Back and forth to the derrick is all I can handle. Fuck. A flight to the Med is at least seven hours. The Caribbean, double that. I don't fancy being stuck in one of those cigars with wings for that length of time. The ride to the rig is bad enough but I know it's the only way I can commute. The transporter or the Tardis haven't been invented yet."

When they neared the roundabout at Bridge of Don, Katherine instructed him to go left. "I spotted a Tesco through the trees. We can stop and get wine there."

He grunted and entered the correct lane to make the turn.

With his mood, she regretted inviting him to stay with her. She might have been further ahead sticking with the original plan of him taking her home and going back to his. Oh well, too late now.

Inside the Supermarket, Katherine selected two bottles of Jacob's Creek Shiraz. Before they left that section of the store, Jared snagged himself a six-pack of Caledonian 80.

When the black BMW pulled up in front of the bookstore, he stepped back into the shadows of the cinema entrance. Mr. Cocksure exited and opened the boot. He removed a bag. No, that man could not spend the night with the red-headed woman. He sullied her once already. Their relationship must end. He must find a way to prise her away from the man with the fancy car.

She climbed out of the passenger seat and looked around. She appeared nervous. She had no reason to fear him. He wouldn't harm her. Not yet, anyway. The wind whipped strands of her hair and she reached up to tuck an errant shock behind her ear.

Her simple act of securing her ginger locks filled him with longing. It should be him doing that for her. She joined Mr. Offshore Worker at the rear of the car and removed two Tesco carrier bags. He pushed down the lid and set the car's alarm then put his arm around her shoulder. She winced.

The bastard had hurt her. Anger bubbled up inside him filling him with rage. He wanted to tackle the brute and beat him senseless for harming her. She was kind and beautiful and now injured thanks to the lout. That was his job to do. No one could take it away from him. She was his to annihilate. He would mutilate her before killing her. She could be assured of it. She just didn't know what the future held in store for her. He took a step forward but stopped.

They had reached the lower door. If he became careless, they would see him. He retreated into the shadows. Being seen was not in his plans. He couldn't afford that. He made a few errors in judgement since taking up his position on Shiprow. Getting himself carted off by the Grampian Police was one such mistake.

His red-headed beauty and Mr. Cocksure disappeared

behind the door. Infuriated it was Mr. Offshore worker with her, he kicked the wall. When there was no pain, he walloped the bricks again, this time with the other foot.

Inside, Kat took the bags to the kitchen and set them on the worktop. Her shoulder hurt. She needed a minute to herself to get a look at the extent of the wound. She had a hard time removing her outerwear because the joint had stiffened. She slipped into the bathroom, latched the door behind her, and contemplated setting the lock. In the end, she didn't.

Taking advantage of the wide neckline, she eased the jumper away from the affected area and looked at the reflection in the mirror to assess the damage. An enormous, angry, red, blue and purple bruise developed there and extended down her arm.

Jared knocked and stuck his head around the corner. Kat yanked the garment back into place hoping he didn't see.

"You okay?"

"Y-yes." Her cheeks burned from the flush she knew formed from her lie.

When he reached her side, he pulled the large neck of her sweater aside, and planted a soft kiss on her injury. "I'm sorry I hurt you."

~ 23 ~

21st February, 2011

Jared waited until after the normal morning commuter traffic slowed before leaving for Aberdeen. After she rejected his first proposal the night they finally made love, and again when he popped the question from offshore, would she ever say yes? Still, he would wait. Sooner or later she had to. He hoped today would be the day. Maybe not asking with a ring kept her from accepting his proposal.

He knew he wanted to marry her and had for a long time. They should have eloped to Gretna Green or elsewhere in Scotland far from her home before her parents dragged her off to Canada. He regretted his lack of action at the time. Now he was trying to make up for not having the bollocks back then.

When he arrived in the city, Jared parked his BMW in the Harriet Street Car Park. He took a big enough chance shopping for this important purchase so close to where Kat lived. She knew a lot of people and her friend, Steph, worked at the Clydesdale Bank about halfway between the bookstore and the place he intended buying the engagement ring.

After he left the shelter where he secured lodgings for the previous night, he bumped into Mr. Cocksure walking in the opposite direction on Union Street. What was he doing here? He let him get a short distance ahead then turned and followed him. The pavement was crowded and he used it to his advantage to pursue his quarry without detection.

The man walked at a rapid pace and he had a difficult time keeping up with him. He lost him briefly in the throng of people waiting at a bus stop but once he pushed through them, he had no difficulty spotting him. And just in time. He disappeared into a shop near Union Terrace Gardens.

He followed behind. When he reached the location, he paused. Inside, Mr. Offshore Worker stood bent over display cases. He had stopped at a jewellery store. If what was happening, or was going to in the near future, he had to act fast. His red-headed beauty would never marry this man. She would die first.

While Jared perused the cabinets searching for the perfect ring for Kat, the two sales clerks watched his every move. He supposed to them he looked like someone going to rob the place in his worn leather jacket, jeans, shaggy hair and stubble. When he saw the one with six accent diamonds on either side of the one-carat princess-cut center stone, surrounded by smaller ones the same as those on the ring's shank, he made his decision.

"What size do you need?" one of the girls asked.

Taken aback by the question, Jared couldn't answer. He had no idea. "Don't know, but if it comes to here," he said holding out his right pinkie and pointing to a spot about halfway between his first two knuckles, "I think it'll fit."

When the clerk handed the ring to him, he slipped the band on his finger and into the position he hoped was Kat's size. "This is the one."

"Sir, this piece is over thirteen thousand pounds," the girl said.

"I know. I'll take it." He took out his wallet, pulled out a stack of ten, twenty, and fifty pound notes and a credit card.

"W-would you like it gift wrapped?" the other salesperson asked, eyes wide at the nonchalant way he accepted the price.

"Just a box. Nothing else."

When the purchase concluded, Jared tucked the package into the inside breast compartment of his leather jacket. He rehearsed this moment for some time. Before returning to his BMW, he walked to a nearby florists' and bought a dozen long-stemmed, red roses and a single white bloom.

If the traffic light gods looked favourably on him, he would reach *As the Pages Turn* in about ten minutes. Because of the number of one-way streets between the car park and the bookshop, he needed to take a longer roundabout way to get there. And then there was the usual snarl of Aberdeen traffic. Between red lights and jay-walking pedestrians, it was going on half an hour before he arrived at his destination.

Jared sat in his car near the nightclub next to the cinema and waited for someone to go in. He assumed with other people in the room, Kat might be more inclined to say yes.

A customer entered. He started the BMW and eased the vehicle to a stop outside her establishment. Before climbing out, he reached back for the flowers he stowed on the passenger seat.

The Victorian shop bell jingled when he pushed the door open. Katherine was busy with Melissa, one of her part-time employees. She flashed a brilliant smile in his direction.

Jared put the bouquet behind his back as he approached. He hoped she didn't notice the bunch of blooms yet. "Hi beautiful," he said, placing the wrapped bundle on the counter.

Her eyes welled up as she fumbled with the wrapping. Making her cry was not on the agenda. "They're gorgeous," she said when the paper surrounding the roses fluttered to the floor.

"Just like you." He leaned forward and kissed her cheek.

"I'll take them to the back and put them in water for you, Miss K."

"No. You're fine, Melissa. I'll take them upstairs in a few minutes. I've got the perfect vase up there."

The customer who entered before Jared approached the check out. Time for the rest of his surprise. Pulling the velvet box out of his jacket, he knelt on one knee and opened it. "Katherine Murphy, will you make an honest man out of me by becoming my wife? We should have done this years ago before you moved to Canada rather than lose all that time.

"I-I don't know what to say." Kat couldn't take her eyes off the sparkling diamond.

"Say yes."

"Ooh, Miss K," Melissa gushed. "How cool was that? Proposed to in your shop. You just gotta say yes."

"I … it's … I'm …," she babbled.

"I want to go to sleep with you in my arms and wake up with you there every day of my life. I know when I'm offshore it won't be possible, but with you as my partner, I'm willing to give that up and take on something different here in Aberdeen. There are plenty of onshore support jobs."

Tears pricked at the backs of her eyes. How could she refuse? She waited over five years to have a physical relationship with a man after Colin's death. She might still be celibate had her first post-Colin experience not been with Jared. That was where things got complicated.

Before her parents dragged her halfway across the world to take her away from him, she fantasized about being his wife. But she was a teenager back then with no responsibilities. Now she was older – been widowed. Could she go through the ordeal again? Jared worked in a dangerous environment. Things had been learned from the Piper Alpha disaster, but was it enough?

Colin died during the terrorist attacks in London. He was on buying trips to the city before without incident. It was dumb luck he happened to be in that area on the day. She broke out into a cold sweat. The room swam in front of her eyes. A panic attack. She'd not suffered one in a long time and never one this bad.

Making love with him was one thing. Marrying him was different. Marriage meant the final goodbye to her deceased partner. When it was sex, it was like she and Colin had broken up – gone their separate ways – but remained friends.

Jared took her left hand and slipped the diamond on her third finger. When he reached the second joint, he stopped, aghast at the sight. There, in the place he intended to put his token of commitment, was the set from her dead husband. Why didn't she take them off when she removed the chain holding his wedding band from around her neck? After everything she found out about the man, she couldn't still love him, could she?

He had been patient with her since he stumbled back into her life. For how much longer, he didn't know. He knew he loved her. That's what mattered.

Kat gripped the counter. She closed her eyes. Her legs gave out and she collapsed.

He vaulted over the ledge and caught her before she fell. Melissa wheeled the office chair over and Jared sat her on the seat and lodged her head between her knees then squatted in front of her. Never in his wildest dreams did he expect this type of reaction to his proposal.

Kat took a long time to renew their physical relationship. Maybe asking her to marry him was too much too soon. He pushed the ring the rest of the way on her finger, pleased he got the size correct. The ones from Colin dwarfed by the large diamond and its setting. The movement roused her from her faint. "Are you feeling better? Fuck. You scared me."

Still leaning forward, she tipped her head back. Her face was pale; her eyes wet with tears.

"You all right, now?"

She nodded.

"Get her some water, Mel," he ordered.

The young girl dashed into the office, bead curtains clacking against one another in her wake.

He took her hands in his. They were ice cold. Jared lifted them to his face and kissed them then stroked the backs with his thumbs. "Don't scare me like that again. Please."

The strong Katherine he knew from their previous relationship was gone – replaced by a weaker, vulnerable one. He hoped in time the old Kat would return. Some of her reactions resurrected childhood memories. His father abused his mother and him physically, his sister, physically and sexually. Had Colin been that kind of man?

Jared had a temper. He flexed his right hand. The scars on his knuckles from punching the cement wall of the casino were red and angry. He broke at least one of them during that episode and now paid the price. His joints ached in the cold, damp weather, which this time of year occurred daily.

Melissa came back with a bottle of water. Jared dismissed her with a nod as he removed the cap and handed the plastic container to Kat.

Her hands shook as she raised the drink to her mouth. He steadied them with one of his while she drank.

"I can't," she spluttered.

He raked his free fingers through his hair.

"I can't marry you. It's too soon."

"You don't have to decide now. Take your time." Despite the knock back, he still loved her. He hoped one day she would change her mind.

Kat set the water bottle on a shelf under the counter and started to remove the diamond.

Jared laid his hand on hers. "You keep it. I want you to have it."

"But …."

"No buts; it's yours," he said and pressed his lips to her forehead. "You don't have to wear it now. Put it away and when you're ready to say yes, start wearing it and I'll know." He handed her the box. She slipped the ring off her finger and installed the platinum band into the velvet slot. "I'm serious. I'll wait for you." He kissed her again, stood and walked out.

Kat broke down when the door sealed behind him. Why had she told him she couldn't marry him? Colin had been gone for over five years. Why couldn't she move on past that and build a new-old life with Jared?

"Melissa," she called.

"You want me, Miss K?" the teenager appeared from one of the aisle with an armload of paperback novels.

"You can take the rest of the day off. I'll pay you your full wage but because we're slow, I'm going to close up."

"Is there something wrong?"

"I-I'm fine." Kat was anything but. All she wanted to do was crawl into her bed and stay there.

"But the new shipment of books came in. You wanted me to stock the shelves."

"Look, just go home," she snapped.

Melissa's eyes widened.

"I'm sorry. I didn't mean to be so harsh. Please just go. Meet your friends. The racks will keep for another day."

"If you're sure."

"I am."

"Promise me you'll be okay," Melissa said grabbing her jacket off the tree and shoving her arms into the sleeves.

"I will be."

When the door shut behind her, Kat turned the sign around to show closed, and locked the shop. Jared told her to take her time. He would wait for her. What if she never said yes? Would it be fair to him? Should she give back the ring and say goodbye?

Since their reunion, the first time they made love felt like all the time and distance between them vanished. They were back to the way things were when she was a teenager, a bit younger than Melissa, prior to her parents dragging her away. Had they taken her someplace in England, Scotland or Wales, she would have run away from home and back to Aberdeen to be with Jared. But when the move was to Canada, halfway around the world, it became downright impossible.

She texted Stephanie.

Done something stupid again. Can u come? Bring wine.

While she waited for a response, she turned out the lights, clutched the bouquet of roses, and went upstairs to her flat by way of the office doorway. As she shut the door, Kat tossed her handbag on the couch. The velvet chest fell out and landed on the floor under the coffee table. She reached for it, but before her fingers touched the surface, she pulled her hand back.

Can't. Have customer in 5. Will come when done here.

How long before Stephanie could leave the bank? Better yet, could she before closing time? At least being self-employed, Kat had the advantage of coming and going as she pleased. She had Melissa, Cherie and Josh to run her book empire when she couldn't be there. Steph worked in a financial institution and had to maintain their business hours.

She bent down, retrieved the ring box, and opened the lid. The diamond sparkled. Jared spent a small fortune on this. She didn't deserve anything so extravagant. She wasn't worthy of him. It would only be a matter of time and he'd walk out on her for good with the way she kept pushing him away. She shouldn't punish him because of her insecurities. He had been too good to her from the time they met and continued to be.

To take her mind off things, Kat sought out the crystal vase. She took it and the flowers to the kitchen where she prepared and arranged them. When finished, she placed the array on the center of the dining table.

Impatient, Stephanie waited for her client to arrive. She needed to get to Kat's place and find out what this stupid thing was. The analog clock on her wall read three fifteen – well past the appointment time and still no one came. She snapped her pencil in half frustrated by the situation. She was about to leave when her phone rang, announcing the customer.

A handsome man with chiseled features strode into her office. Dressed in a navy blue, three-piece suit, white shirt and striped tie, his appearance was impeccable. He extended his hand to her. "I'm terribly sorry I'm so late. The traffic was horrendous."

She shook his warm hand and showed him to a chair in front of her desk. "So what can I do for you today, Mr. Jones?" The name was too common. If the file started on him was legitimate, then why did he come all the way here to her branch of the Clydesdale? There were plenty of banks in Dundee where he could conduct his transactions.

"Call me Simon. My father is Mr. Jones. I'm looking to expand my business to the Aberdeen area and as such, I'd prefer to have a bank in the city where I'll be operating."

His explanation made sense to her but something about him didn't feel right. But, his sun kissed skin and piercing green eyes made her want to believe every word that came out of his mouth. "And what line of business are you in?"

He flashed a smile. His straight, white teeth sparkled. "Well, since you asked, I'm in the tanning trade."

As in hides? Most of that was done in countries with cheaper labour markets. She folded her hands and leaned forward. "Leather?"

"No, no." He chuckled. "Salons. Beds, spray tans. That sort of thing." He pulled a brochure out of his briefcase and slid the advertisement across the desk to Stephanie.

She leafed through the glossy magazine. If this was his business, and legitimate, he would do a booming trade here in the city. She knew a number of women, some from here at the bank, who did so before going on holiday to hot, sunny locations.

"I'm hoping to be up and running inside of three months. I've put an offer in on a location pending financing. I'll need to borrow enough to cover the mortgage on the property and the equipment, supplies, etcetera."

Stephanie stifled a yawn. Whilst she could look at this good-looking man seated opposite her, she longed to find out what Kat needed. Yes, work came first, but sometimes, friendship trumped it and this was one of those times.

Simon produced another file and put the folder on the desk. "My financials for the last five years. I know you can't make a decision today, but I look forward to doing business with you, Miss Lindsay." He snapped his attaché case shut and stood.

"Thank you for choosing our bank." She rose, shook his hand and escorted him to the door. "I'll be in touch with you soon."

Nodding, he turned and walked away. Even from behind, he was handsome – buff, like he worked out on a regular basis. With his physique, gyms rather than tanning salons were more appropriate. God, the man was fit.

She waited a respectable length of time before picking up her mobile and shooting a quick text to Kat.

Customer gone now. On my way.

Stephanie pulled her bag out of her bottom drawer, stuffed her phone into it, and snatched her wrap off the tree by the door, tugging it on as she strode. Grateful Kat's was only a five-minute walk from her work, she set out. What had started as a sunny, mild day had turned overcast and the temperatures plummeted. The dampness hung in the air.

When she arrived at the shop, it was closed. She walked to the side entrance, through the gate to the courtyard. Steph didn't like coming in this way, but retrieved the key from the lock box and let herself in the back door. "What did you do now?" she asked when she stormed into the flat.

Katherine raised her head; her eyes red and tear-filled.

Not a good sign. Something dreadful had happened or would. "Are you okay here or do you want to go to the pub?"

"Not here. I've already closed up for the day and sent Melissa home."

"You're sure."

"Yes. I need the fresh air."

Stephanie positioned her friend's mac over her shoulders and grabbed her handbag from the sofa. She didn't force her friend to tell her what happened. That would wait until they each had spirits in hand.

Kat stepped over the threshold at the neighbouring pub. Despite the early hour, many people, mostly men from the harbour, propped up the bar. Maybe this was not such a good idea. That coupled with the fact Jared brought her here for a drink at Hogmanay. Tears ran down her cheeks. She knew she looked a mess. Since he left, she did nothing but cry.

G&Ts in hand, they found a table in the quiet, back corner. Why had she said no – again?

Once settled, she pulled the velvet box out of her bag and planted it on the table. "J-Jared g-gave m-me this."

Stephanie reached out and opened the chest. Her eyes widened. "Holy engagement ring." She paused. "You told him *no*, didn't you."

She nodded. "I love him. I really do. I can't take the last

step. I'm so afraid if I do, something bad will happen to him. I mean, look at my track record. Graeme, well that was a total disaster. One I want to forget forever. Pretend like it never happened in the first place. I can't believe I got mixed up with the freak. Then Jared came along and my parents saw fit to end that by shipping us off to Canada. I missed him so much all those years. I came back for Uni and on the night of our graduation, I saw him with someone else, but discovered later it meant nothing. In the meantime, Colin who cheated on me got himself blown up. Who in their right mind would want to get involved with this walking disaster?"

"You're not a washout. You had some bad breaks but Jared loves you. He'd die for you and you well know that."

"He says he'll wait for me and I can keep the ring until I'm ready. Said he'll know when he sees it on my finger."

"See? You two are solid. You were before and you will be again." Steph reached out and patted Kat's hand.

"I hope you're right. I'm afraid I might have said no once too often." She leaned forward and bowed her head.

A patron entering the bar piqued her curiosity and she recognized him. "Psst, don't look, but isn't that the guy who's been hanging out near mine?"

Steph turned her head in that direction. "It's him. Seen him before when I've come to yours. Odd duck isn't he?"

"Fingers crossed it's all he is. Melissa is freaked out by him. He came into the shop one day but I put it down to him being homeless and cold."

"You never mentioned that. Good bloody God. He could be dangerous."

"I talked about the incident with Jared on one of our Skype calls. He said the same thing. Told me I was too naïve for my own good."

"I think he's right. You see this guy hanging about your place again and you call the cops. Do you hear me?"

"I do, but they won't do anything. Don't you watch the news? The police say a stalker has to do something before they can act."

"And by then you might be dead."

"Let's just go back to mine. You're scaring me with this talk."

~ 24 ~

5th March, 2011

The overcast skies matched Katherine's mood. She hated saying goodbye to Jared when he went back to his job offshore. Most of his latest home time was spent together at his house in Newburgh where she incorporated her ideas and made the house more like a home. Nothing overboard or extravagant, but subtle things like throw pillows in bright colours for the sofa in the lounge, pillar candles on the fireplace mantle, and a funky wooden bowl for the coffee table.

Jared's kitchen, on the other hand, was a tug of war. She would rearrange things to make it easier and logical for her and he would put them back in their original places where he liked them. His bedroom continued untouched. She didn't want him to think she was overstepping her bounds so left his domain alone.

Two weeks apart bothered her. She worried every time it would be the last. That feeling of foreboding worsened after his rough flight. What if the bloody thing ditched and killed everyone onboard? She couldn't lose him – not that way.

Leaning over the island with her coffee, Katherine planned the rest of her day. After seeing him off, she would return to the railway station and commute from Dyce to Aberdeen, and revert to her life in the urban setting and the bookstore.

The only thing she had against Jared's house was the location. She grew up in the Granite City, and stayed in a large metropolis when her family moved to Canada. Newburgh was over half an hour away from where she lived on Exchequer Row in Aberdeen. Shopping was limited to a convenience store and off-licence, and a butcher shop. At least there were a couple of pubs where they could enjoy a drink and a meal out, both of which were within ten minutes on foot.

Jared sauntered in to the kitchen and dropped his duffel bag on the floor before folding his arms around Kat and holding her next to him. She leaned her head into the hollow between his chin and collarbone and willed him to stay.

"I wish you didn't have to leave today."

"Me, too. But the time will fly by. And we can Skype each other."

"I know but it's not the same." Her resigned sigh came across as angry which wasn't how she intended.

Jared kissed her before gathering his bag and walking to the back door. Shrugged into his leather bomber jacket. Her eyes were glassy with tears. When she reached him, he pulled her close again. "I don't like this anymore than you. I'd love a trade what didn't take me away from you so often for so long at a time."

Kat nodded and slipped into her down-filled parka.

Her attitude over his leaving spooked Jared. Sure, she always hated the day he had to fly back to the rig and saying goodbye, but today she clung to him. Why was it so different from any other time he left for work? She acted much like after her world fell apart when he took her to London. Frightened, vulnerable.

A storm rolled in off the North Sea. Not ideal weather for flying. Still, he had a job to do, one he enjoyed once he got there. The commute, not so much. Rain, driven by the high wind, lashed against the car windows. Despite having the wipers on full speed, keeping the windscreen clear was impossible. At least it was light out. Making the trip in the dark didn't bear thinking about.

"I'll drop you at the train on the way?"

Kat didn't answer.

Jared took a quick glance to his left. She had her head turned away from him as if she were looking out the passenger window. He reached for her hand but she pulled away. "What's wrong?"

"I don't want you to go. I have an awful feeling something bad is going to happen."

"You never said. Do you want putting down at the railway station?"

Kat shook her head. "I'll come to the airport with you and walk after you're in the air."

"You'll get soaked." Concerned for her well-being, he protested although he knew it was a losing battle.

"I have an umbrella in my handbag. I'll be fine."

Over an hour after leaving Newburgh, Jared pulled his car into a parking bay at terminal one. The drive had taken twice as long because of the bad weather. After he turned the ignition off, he handed the keys to Kat. "Here, you keep them. I'm not going to need them. You can meet me here when I get back." He folded her into his arms as best he could with the console and stick shift between them. "I love you Katherine Murphy."

Her response to him mashing his lips on hers was immediate. No teasing her mouth open with his tongue this time. He wanted to shag her one last time but when he woke, she had already left his bed.

Despite his misgivings, he opened the driver's door.

"Please don't go." Kat clutched his hand.

"I have to." Climbing out, Jared hated leaving her in this state. He sauntered to the boot and retrieved his duffel bag. "Lock up when you go."

The Super Puma taking them to the Alpha Ecosse sat on the tarmac. With the passenger compartment door open, he had difficulty reading the call letters. He walked to a different vantage point and sighed with relief and entered the building. This was not the chopper involved in the flight from hell.

Katherine bowed her head and let her tears flow. She couldn't explain the bad feeling she had about today. She was never so frightened. Things were good between them, not the same as when they first got together back when she was a teenager, but better. She took a long time to get over her parents dragging her off to Canada and away from him. Even longer to recover from Colin's death in the London bombings. Finding out the truth about her husband was like getting kicked in the stomach.

Her track record with men was dismal. She lost every one she had a serious relationship with, and through no part of her own. Well, maybe Jared before her forced move to another country halfway around the world from him. Steph covered for her as much as possible but in the end, the web of deceit disintegrated. She couldn't lose him in a helicopter crash. Not now.

Voices snapped her out of her reverie. A parade of oil workers wearing orange survival suits walked to the aircraft. Katherine unbuckled her seatbelt and scrambled out of the car and over to the fence. She hungered to see him once more before he departed. Wiping the tears away from her eyes, she blinked hard to keep more from forming.

He broke away from the others and came to the barricade. In the short time she stood there, the heavy rain pasted her long, red hair to her head. In her haste to see him again, she had left the umbrella in her handbag.

"You're going to catch your death," he said.

"I needed to see you one last time." A tear escaped and she dashed it away with the back of her hand. "I-I love you."

"I love you, too."

"Come on Jared. You're holding up production." A female's voice yelled from the group queuing up to board.

"Keep your hair on."

It was impossible to tell who had spoken. The survival suit made everyone look more or less identical, but the girl had shoulder length, shiny, jet black hair with electric blue foils at random intervals, and a dark complexion. She was too far away to see her eye colour. Katherine guessed she was of East Indian descent. A woman boarding with a full complement of men added to her apprehension.

"Got to go. Can't hold them up any longer."

"Phone or text me when you arrive. I need to know you got there okay."

Jared walked to the chopper. Before he climbed aboard, he paused and extended his arm in a wave then disappeared inside.

Gripping the chain link fence, her knees weakened. She lingered there until the helicopter lifted into the sky and vanished from sight.

Dejected by Jared's departure, Kat trudged, slumped and head down, back to the car. She retrieved her handbag from the floor behind the passenger seat and took out the umbrella. After she removed her small carry-on suitcase from the boot, she locked the vehicle and began the arduous walk to the railway station. At least she didn't have long to wait in the small, outdoor shelter.

The first thing Katherine did when she boarded was remove her soggy outerwear. Even her white, roll neck jumper was soaked. With the thickness of the sweater and the camisole beneath, she wasn't starring in her own wet T-shirt contest.

Not long after getting into the warmth of the carriage, her teeth began chattering and she shivered. If she didn't catch pneumonia from her drenching, it would be a miracle. A long soak in a hot bath was in her future once she got home.

As the train slowed on its approach to Aberdeen, Katherine gathered her things and, much as she hated to, put her waterlogged coat back on. Once on the concourse, she worked her way through the crush of passengers waiting to board and outdoors. After being in the relative warmth, the cold, damp air chilled her to the core. The rain stopped but the skies remained overcast. She raised the handle on her cabin bag and pulled the suitcase along behind her as she tramped the distance to her residence.

Rather than go into the bookstore, she went to the other end of the granite building, unlocked the door leading to the accommodations above and ascended the stairs. Despite the place being empty, she was glad to be home.

Katherine deposited her keys in the bowl on the table by the door, hung her parka on the rack and carried her bag to her bedroom. Even though her handbag was drenched, her phone had somehow stayed dry. She checked to see if she had any missed calls or text messages then placed her mobile on the dining room table, walked to the bathroom, drew a hot bath, and turned on the heated towel rack.

Squeezing a generous dollop of lavender bubble soap into the cascade of running water, the calming scent infused the room. Foam appeared. She needed something to help her relax and overcome her bad feeling about Jared's flight to the rig. Kat removed her wet clothes and climbed into the large bathtub. She lowered herself into the hot water and inhaled the fragrant steam. Soon she submerged herself to her chin. The heat permeated her cold skin and she started to feel warm.

After taking a deep breath and holding it, she dunked her head under the water. Her already soaked hair wouldn't get any wetter and until then, it was the only body part she hadn't plunged beneath the surface.

Little by little, her anxiety dissipated. She remained there until cooled to the point of being unpleasant. Standing up, Katherine hooked her toe around the chain and pulled the plug. She reached for the bath sheet on the towel bar and wrapped the warmed fabric around her body. Her long heavy dressing gown hung on the back of the door and once she stepped out of the tub, she put it on, then tied her hair in a smaller cloth.

When Katherine padded out to the lounge, the light on her mobile phone was flashing indicating a missed call or message. She swiped the screen to life.

Made it safely. No need 2 worry. Will Skype U 2night abt 8.

Between the lavender bubble bath and Jared's text the stress and feeling of foreboding vanished. She couldn't wait until their video chat later that night. With no plans to go anywhere, Katherine donned a pair of flannel pyjamas and fuzzy slippers.

She gathered up her laptop and its power supply from the bedroom and took them out to the dining room table. Kat would surf the net as a distraction until the appointed time arrived.

Not normally one to drink on her own, she opted to open

the Shiraz she purchased for her and Jared to have. He preferred lager to it. After she opened the bottle, she brought it and a large goblet back to the room.

Most of the news online was too depressing so she went to the jigsaw puzzle site and occupied herself doing puzzles while she waited for him to make contact.

When the Skype call came in, Katherine was ready. His face appeared on her computer screen. The same girl she had seen at the helipad stood behind him leaning over his shoulder. A couple of the guys walked by the webcam and said hello as they passed through its range. But not her. She stayed put.

Not able to show jealousy, at least in front of this person, how did she best handle the situation. Another bloke saved her any further embarrassment when he came on the scene. "Hi Kat," he said then pulled the girl with the jet black hair and dark complexion into his arms.

Katherine gulped down a mouthful of wine. "Who is she?" Her insecurities bubbled to the surface. She tried to keep her emotions under control but after seeing this beautiful girl draped all over Jared, it was difficult.

"Her? Oh, that's just George. Her real name is Georgia."

"She's pretty."

"Not as gorgeous as you are. You're not a bit jealous now, are you?"

Busted. "Sort of."

"Nothing for you to worry about. I told you I would never cheat on you. I keep my word. You should know that by now."

"I know. Just, she's so attractive."

"She and the guy who pulled her off me are together. Likely off to find a quiet place for a shag. Not much chance of that happening out here. No such thing as privacy."

Jared's last comment made her blush and giggle. She had only seen pictures online of the offshore accommodations and the recreation room from her Skype calls with him.

"So are you going to make an honest man out of me and accept my proposal, Katherine Murphy?"

An alarm went off on the rig saving her from answering

him.

"Sorry. Gotta go," he said and signed off the computer leaving her staring at a black screen.

Kat woke in the middle of the night and reached for her phone. She brushed its surface with her fingertips and sent the Z10 crashing to the floor. She didn't bother turning on the lamp. Now she would have to figure out where her mobile landed. Leaning over the edge of the mattress, she fumbled for the errant device to no avail.

She squinted to protect her eyes from the sudden onslaught of brilliance when she touched the metal base of the table light on her nightstand. The phone, face down, lie on the laminate halfway under the bed. When Katherine retrieved her BlackBerry, she checked to ensure there was no damage.

Satisfied with the results of her inspection, she swiped the screen and opened up her text messages. Nothing from Jared. Now she was scared. Had something happened to him? What caused the alarm to go off? Fire? An explosion? Her imagination ran riot as she came up with possible reasons.

Unable to think of any, she returned to the vision of Georgia draped over him. Maybe his casual marriage proposal was a ruse. Maybe he was having an affair with the girl. Calling her 'George' was a little too chummy. But, they did work together, after all. Katherine could be making something of nothing. It wasn't the first time. She'd done it before.

Should she send Jared a text? If something serious happened, would he even be able to respond?

~ 25 ~

19th March, 2011

Pilot, Dominic Ballesteros and his co-pilot, Edward Trowbridge completed their pre-flight checklist, in preparation for their trip back to Aberdeen.

Before departing from the helipad, he had done a thorough inspection of the Super Puma AS332 L2 bearing the call letters T-BLUE. Maintenance records were requested from its last service to ensure everything was as it should be. He went above and beyond when it came to the 'copters he flew.

The trip to the rig was uneventful aside from being one passenger short. With his thirty years' experience, Dominic knew someone would not be coming with them – at least not today. While he waited for his passengers to arrive, he exited the cockpit and did another walk around looking at everything. Assured all was in order, he climbed back in and secured his harness.

This was his last journey of the day ferrying people on and offshore. He couldn't wait to get home to his wife, Helen, when he arrived in Edinburgh later in the evening. Years ago, Dominic lost control of their 4x4 when a front tyre burst and the vehicle rolled several times, leaving her with severe detriments to her body. She still walked with a cane and the damp weather made her bones ache. He should retire and take her to a drier climate where she would have less discomfort from the injuries he inflicted on her that day.

Soon the parade of workers dressed in blaze orange, neoprene survival suits marched across the helipad, carrying duffel bags of assorted sizes.

"Good morning gentlemen," Dominic announced over the radio as the passengers took their seats and strapped in.

"What am I, chopped liver?" Georgia Wescome asked and laughed.

"Sorry George. I didn't know you were on this flight. Let me rephrase that. Good morning lady and gents. Better?"

"Much," she replied.

"It looks like a great day for flying and we'll have you back on land in about three hours. So sit back and enjoy the ride."

"She got you good on that one, Dominic," Steve Norton called through to the cockpit getting a laugh from those onboard.

Jared detested air travel. He hated disappointing Kat when she suggested an all-inclusive trip to a resort on a tropical beach, but having to for his job was one thing – for pleasure something else. Besides, a flight to the Caribbean or the Mediterranean were both longer than he was comfortable spending in a cigar tube with wings at over thirty thousand feet. At least the flights to and from the oilfield were only about two hours.

T-BLUE was emblazoned on the fuselage. He crossed himself before boarding and chose one of the two single seats by the door on the left side. If this thing was going down, he wanted to be by an exit so he would stand a chance of getting out.

The only drawback to this seat was the sliding door moved forward to the cockpit and blocked the window next to him. Still, near enough to the door, as long as it opened, escape was possible. Seatbelt fastened, he leaned back and tried to get comfortable. Would Kat be waiting for him at the terminal building at the Aberdeen Airport? She surprised him by coming out to meet him on other trips to the mainland.

The familiar call letters and memories of that awful journey niggled at him even before they soared off. He was less comfortable on the Super Puma today than on previous flights. The safety video, mandatory viewing prior to takeoff, indicated they would be taking this particular aircraft. The room turned noisy with sighs and groans upon discovering the information. Was that the reason behind Jared's unease.

By now some of the men snored, bored with the usual commute. Out over the water, there was nothing to see. The occasional oil or gas platform, a fishing trawler, supply vessel, but mostly water. Lots of water.

When they were about fifteen miles from land, the helicopter shuddered. Dominic checked the instrument panel. No alarms sounded. Everything was normal. "What was that?"

Edward Trowbridge wore a puzzled expression on his face and shook his head. "Damned if I know."

After a deafening bang, the bird pitched right yanking the joystick out of Dominic's hand. He and his co-pilot struggled to regain control but to no avail.

The rhythmic thwunk, thwunk of the blades disappeared replaced with an eerie quiet. The Super Puma nosedived.

"Mayday, mayday, oh fuck…"

The force of the collision with the water knocked Jared into the fuselage wall. The bones in his forearm cracked from the impact sending an excruciating pain through his entire body. His ankle crashed against the metal frame and it, too, shattered. His head struck the casing surrounding the window. Blood poured from the gash on his forehead into his right eye, blinding him on that side.

Determined not to die out here, he unfastened his seatbelt with his good hand. The helicopter was sinking fast. Jared wrenched the door on the opposite side open. The life raft deployed. He had to move quickly because the chopper had begun to roll.

Adrenalin coursed through his system and with one hand, he managed to drag two of his badly wounded co-workers into the inflatable and activate their emergency locator beacons. "When this thing sinks, cut the rope," he yelled. Swiping the blood away from his face with his injured hand, he dug out his Swiss Army knife and tossed it into their raft.

"Come on, Andy. You got to get out of here." He reached for the buckle on the seatbelt harness.

"No. Can't go without George."

Jared turned Georgia Wescome's face to him. A jagged shard of moulding protruded from her neck. She had died in the crash. He knew the look of death well after finding his sister's lifeless body in the bathtub when he was a teenager.

"Too late for her. She's dead." He didn't like being so blunt with his co-worker, but if that was what he had to do to get him moving, he would. He yanked Andy up and pushed him out the door into the raft.

Chuck Adams, seated in front of Jared, bled from a gash in his cheek. His left arm dangled at an odd angle. "Where am I? What's going on?"

"We've crashed. I need to get you out."

Tristan McKnight, a giant of a man, struggled to extricate himself from his seat. By now, the frigid, North Sea drenched the interior waist high. No time to rescue anyone else. They would have to do it themselves. Jared opened the other door and with Tris's help, wrestled Chuck into the other boat. When they moved him, the man screamed in agony.

Then he shoved Tristan to safety before taking one last look to see if he could save any of the others.

"Come on, man. Get out of there. You can't do anymore," he called from the lifeboat.

The helicopter pitched right. "Sorry guys," he said to the ones being left, before diving into the life raft. He had given his cutting tool to the lads in the other inflatable. "Knife. We'll need to cut ourselves free when this thing goes down." He reached over and activated the emergency locator beacon on Chuck's suit before setting off his own.

Tristan, still lucid, pulled his cutter out and handed it over, then did the same.

The aircraft rolled left and sucked their oversized dinghy down. The flotation bags hadn't deployed and he didn't remember seeing them on the other side. Jared lunged for the knife and sawed through the rope tethering their boat to the fuselage before pushing them away from the stricken craft. A high-pitched whistling forced him to look up. The blades and part of the gearbox – detached from the chopper – plummeted towards the North Sea.

Seconds later, the falling debris splashed into the water thrusting them away on a gigantic wave.

Katherine flipped through a catalogue the builders left with her when they installed double-glazed windows the preceding summer. She wanted new doors at street level – matching French ones. They would make the store space and the foyer to the living accommodations above, much brighter. The heavy steel slabs the previous owners used suited the building's function then, but not now as a retail outlet.

It took a long time to snap out of her funk since Colin died, but now she was more like her old self. With Jared back in her life, her attitude had become much more positive. She was ready to take on the world.

The music on BBC Radio 1 stopped. Katherine turned to the shelf. The lights on the device's screen glowed so power still ran to the stereo. The cause of the sudden silence not an electrical fault.

"This just in. A Nexus-owned Super Puma, flight 63M, has ditched roughly sixteen miles off the Aberdeenshire coast. Initial reports claim it was en-route from the Alpha Ecosse platform in the Arbroath Oilfield. There are no known casualties at this time."

Katherine gripped the worktop to steady herself. That was the one Jared worked on. He came home today. She screamed then collapsed. Gut-wrenching sobs echoed. Not again. She couldn't lose him. Once had been bad enough. They only just found each other a few short months ago at Hogmanay.

Pains in her chest made it difficult to breathe. She needed help.

"Kat, you in here? You missed our lunch date. I thought I best come see what kept you," Stephanie called, stepping through the door. The place was in perfect order, just the way her friend maintained it. Still, if the shop was closed, the door would have been locked. It wasn't.

She wandered through the beaded curtain which separated the retail space from the small office at the back. When she turned around, Kat was on the floor behind the counter curled up in the fetal position. "Oh my God," Steph cried, "Are you all right? What's wrong?"

"N-n, J-Jared."

"What about him? Did you two have a fight?" Stephanie crouched beside her, examining her for signs of assault. The girl vibrated, she shook so much. "Who did this to you? Were you robbed?" That didn't fit with the state the store was in, or with the door being shut and latched. Burglars didn't close up after themselves. They were too busy trying to abscond with their haul to be concerned with social niceties.

Kat shook her head. That was a blessing. She didn't appear to be injured. Still, what caused her to meltdown like this?

The music stopped again, interrupted by another bulletin. "A Nexus-owned Super Puma has ditched approximately sixteen miles off the Aberdeenshire coast. We can now confirm the helicopter was en-route from the Alpha Ecosse platform in the Arbroath Oilfield. Search and rescue choppers and RNLI lifeboats have been scrambled and are on their way to the crash site.

Now, the gibberish coming from Kat made sense. "Jared's on it?" she asked, moving her friend into a sitting position, leaning against the wall.

"Wh-why?" the pale-faced, wide-eyed woman asked. "I lost him once. I can't go through it again," she said between ragged breaths. "Why am I being tortured like this?"

"No one is torturing you. I'm sure it's not his flight. There are dozens going back and forth every day." Stephanie hoped she convinced her since the two had been friends for so long, but she doubted she had. "I'm going to get my car and take you to the terminal. We'll find out what's going on."

"Th-thank you." She grasped her friend's hand.

All the way to the company's headquarters at Aberdeen International Airport, Kat chewed on her thumbnail. It couldn't be Jared's flight. It had to be one of the others. When they arrived, she spotted Cherie Young, sprinting to the door. Her heart sank at the sight. Cherie's partner Tristan worked the same shift rotation as Jared. Why else would she be there?

Before Stephanie shifted the car into park, Katherine was out and running for the door. A crowd of reporters and photographers hovered in the lobby, each asking questions over one another; their noise deafening. She sought out Cherie. "Tell me it's not them, please." Kat begged hoping the sinking feeling was wrong.

The moisture in the other woman's eyes, told her the truth she didn't want to hear.

"There had to be another crew flying back today. Must have been their flight that went down."

Tris's partner shook her head. Tears spilled down her cheeks.

So far, they had gone unnoticed by the press contingent. Reeling with the news, the last thing Katherine needed or wanted was to speak with reporters.

"Do you ladies have a connection to the men onboard?" one of the journalists asked.

"Leave them alone," Stephanie demanded as she walked into the room. "They got enough to deal with now without you insensitive lot harassing them." She wrapped her arms around both her friend and the other woman and directed them to a corner away from the curious horde. "I'll see if I can get any information."

Katherine clutched Cherie's hand and squeezed. She needed to hang on to every ounce of hope Jared would come back alive and well. The woman's hand tightened on hers.

When Stephanie came back, she shook her head. "They're not saying anything. Protecting their arses more like. Say we need to go to the Maritime and Coastguard Agency at the harbour. They'll be bringing the casualties there."

Jared fired a flare hoping the rescue operation would spot the glowing ball and look for them. So far, the personal locator beacons in their survival suits had not done any good. When he cut them free, he had no idea the falling debris would send them out into the current away from the sinking fuselage. Still, if he hadn't, they would have drowned.

"You okay, Tris? You don't look so good."

"Don't worry about me. I'll be fine. Not so sure about Chuck," he answered, grabbing his side. "I think my ribs are broken."

The third man's face had turned gray. Jared sidled over trying not to capsize the vessel. The sea was cold and if they ended up in the water, none of them would have a chance – survival suit or not. When he got a good look at his co-worker, he knew the man had died. His complexion wore the same ghostly pallor as Georgia and his sister. "Too late for him. He's gone," he said, his voice devoid of emotion.

Tristan leaned over the edge of the life raft and hurled blood. Bright, red.

Jared hoped the man had an ulcer, not more serious internal injuries. This was his worst nightmare come true, dying out here in the middle of the North Sea. Dwelling on the negative wouldn't help anyone. "How's Cherie?" He had to keep his lone surviving raft mate awake, afraid if the man slept, he wouldn't wake.

"Good," he grimaced and clutched his side again.

"When are you two going to tie the knot?"

"I could say the same about you and your bird. When is she going to make an honest man out of you?"

A wave struck the life raft and they had to grab the safety rope to prevent being tossed out. The survival kit had become detached at some point so they had no way of keeping dry when the water sprayed over the side.

Tristan screamed.

Jared's wrist and ankle throbbed. The pain apparent now the adrenalin pumping through his system from the moment the chopper crashed had worn off. Now, the agony took over.

Stephanie wrapped her arm around Kat and walked her and Cherie to the door. The other two women clung to each other. When they stepped out of the building, a swarm of television cameras and still more reporters waited. "Bugger off," Steph snapped, placing her hand up in front of the lens. "Friggin' vultures. Un-bloody believable."

When they reached her silver Volkswagen SUV, she bundled Katherine into the shotgun seat then helped Cherie into the back. "I'll get you two delivered to the coastguard building, and we'll take it from there."

Backing out of the parking bay, she almost knocked down a relentless cameraman. "Cover your faces, ladies. We're not giving them anything." Steph rammed the car into gear and stepped on the accelerator, squealing the tyres.

"Why are they harassing us like this? Can't they see we're upset?"

"I swear they live for other people's tragedies. Shoe would be on the other bloody foot, if they thought it was one of their own," Cherie said from the backseat.

"Unfortunately, there'll be a lot of this these next few days. At least until everyone is rescued and even after that." Stephanie tried to remain positive for the sake of her friend and the other woman in her vehicle. Underneath the tough façade, she was frightened – for herself and her passengers. How long she could maintain this demeanor, she didn't know. But, she would for as long as these two women needed her. They shared too much since they were kids to abandon her now. She reached over and squeezed her friend's hand.

When they arrived at the Coastguard base at Aberdeen harbour, two hearses and an ambulance waited. Kat climbed out of the car and stood, fingers entwined in the chain link fence. She began to shake, so violently, her teeth chattered.

The tang of salt mixed with diesel fuel and gasoline impregnated the air. A large lifeboat approached. Crew jumped off and secured the vessel to the dock cleats.

Soon after the Bon Accord docked, men carried two tarp-covered forms off and loaded them into the waiting vehicles. Paramedics ferried a stretcher and emergency equipment to the quayside then boarded the boat. Katherine was so wrapped up in the activity she didn't notice Steph and Cherie joined her.

The lengthy wait was agonizing, but a third person strapped to a backboard, was loaded on the gurney and bundled into the back of the emergency vehicle. Blue lights flashing and siren wailing, the rescue transport sped off to Aberdeen Royal Infirmary.

If any of those three were Jared, she hoped he was the one transported to hospital and not one of the two carted off to the mortuary. He had to survive.

"Let's go inside. You're freezing," Steph clucked as she prised Kat's fingers from the fence. Holding hands, the three women walked to the lobby of the building.

Kirstie Simmons, Pete O'Brien's partner, disappeared through the closing door. Now there were three. Three from the downed aircraft. She had only met this woman once but her flare for fashion and ability to wear vivid colours, stuck with her. Taking hold of Cherie's hand, the two took tentative steps to the door.

"Kirstie, isn't it?" Katherine asked.

"Yes. Do I know you?"

"Our partners work with Pete. Have they told you anything?"

"I only just got here." She threw the tail of her colourful scarf over her shoulder.

"I mean before," Kat said, grabbing the woman's hands. "Did someone from Nexus call you?"

Pete's partner shook her head. "I only know what I heard on the car radio. Oh God, I am so frightened."

"Us, too." Katherine wrapped one arm around Kirstie and the other around Cherie. They group hugged. "Please, let our men be safe." She looked skyward. Coincidence brought Jared back into her life. He couldn't vanish again.

Over the course of the afternoon, more women wandered in to the Coastguard headquarters. Kat remained in the corner separated from the others. Even Cherie and Steph sat and chatted with them.

A grey-haired woman arrived around six o'clock. Despite the worry etched on it, her face was kind. She guessed her age to be about the same as her mother's. A warm smile formed on her face and she approached. "I'm Beryl. Chuck Adams's wife. He works on the Alpha Ecosse, too. And you are?" She extended her hand.

"Katherine Murphy." After the fiasco of her emotional breakdown at the Burns Supper, she quit using her married name and reverted to her maiden one. She had started the legal process to remove Colin's surname from her identity and some of her documents were already changed. "My partner is missing, too." A tear ran down her cheek as she spoke.

Putting a motherly arm around her, the woman said, "They'll be found in no time, safe and sound. Let's find a place to sit. It will make the wait more comfortable."

How long before the first casualties were identified?

"Here drink this," Steph handed Katherine a cup of tea from the vending machine. "Probably not the greatest tasting but it's hot and sweet," she said before sitting in the unoccupied chair on her friend's left.

Aside from Cherie and her bestie, the only other person she knew in the group was Kirstie, and not all that well. The women talked in muted tones. She couldn't tell if they were just visiting amongst themselves or talking about her. One of them glared at her or was it her imagination playing up.

Kat rolled a tissue around in her hand. "It will work out, I'm sure," Beryl said patting her arm.

"I'm so afraid."

"I know. We all are." She pulled a crochet hook and yarn out of her bag. "Never go anywhere without it. Helps with the distraction."

About seven o'clock, another woman arrived. The lobby became stuffy from the number of people crammed in. "That's Marilyn Trowbridge," Mrs. Adams said. "She's the co-pilot's wife. I've only met her a few times, but she's a lovely woman."

Kat nodded then wandered to the far side of the room. The latest arrival spoke with the employee on duty then took over the chair she had vacated.

Two constables wearing yellow hi-vis jackets entered.

After casting their eyes around the gathering, they walked away from where she stood and stopped in front of the huddle of wives and partners. "Lesley Gilbertson? We're looking for Lesley Gilbertson."

A piercing shriek forced Kat to cover her ears. They had located the person they sought.

"Nooooooo," the woman wailed and clutched her stomach. "Please God, no. We just found out we're having a baby." Her cries of grief filled the room. Any attempts at comfort made the racket worse. With a cop on each side supporting her, they escorted her out of the building.

A woman dressed more like a footballer's wife than an offshore worker's swanned into the lobby. "What's going on? I demand to know. My husband was on that helicopter."

"Sit down with the others. When there's word, you'll be told."

"I better had." She plunked down in the seat vacated by Lesley. "Here's a photo of my Steve. Isn't he handsome?"

The display sent the other women rummaging through their handbags for pictures of their men, making Kat feel lonelier than she already did. She didn't have any photos of Jared – not even prior to her move to Canada. No photographic evidence of their relationship existed. She only had what was in her heart and in her mind, fueled by passion, both positive and negative.

It spoke volumes about their connection. If he died in this tragedy, all she would have were her memories.

~ 26 ~

20th March, 2011

The chair in the small office scraped against the floor, followed by footfalls. The doorknob clicked open. Everyone turned in that direction. The man who worked in the tiny space approached the women. "I'm sorry to say three more victims have been found. The pilot is alive and they're transporting him by helicopter directly to Aberdeen Royal Infirmary. If any of you are related, then we'll arrange to get you to him."

No sooner had the announcement finished, members of the force entered. One of the constables strode to Victoria. "No," she screamed. "He can't be. Why him?" Then, she turned to Dominic's wife, Helen. "It's all his fault. He kills my Steve and he lives? Where's the justice in that? The accident was down to your husband's mistake. Now, mine is dead thanks to him."

Katherine stormed from the corner she spent most of her time in at the Coastguard building while waiting for word and, risking being done for assault, slapped Victoria hard across the face. "This isn't all about you. We're in this together, whether you like it or not. At least you have closure. You know his fate. What about the rest of us? We don't know. We're still playing a waiting game. So don't turn this into your show."

Beryl helped Victoria back into a chair and attempted to comfort her which only made things worse. The woman's high-pitched, whiny cry grated on Katherine's nerves. She stepped outdoors to escape from the racket and met two more uniformed cops on their way in.

Following the constables, Kat needed to know the identity of the next unfortunate woman. Every time someone else received bad news, the hope Jared survived remained. This time, they stopped before Zoe Richmond. The colour drained out of the young woman's face, her eyes widened and her mouth gaped open. She slumped over in a faint.

Relief washed over Katherine. He might still be alive. It sounded selfish, but all she could think of was her rebuilding her life with him. She went back outside. The stink of raw diesel fuel lingered. Exhaling, a cloud of steam from her hot breath formed in front of her. She jammed her hands in her pockets and walked to the fence separating the roadway from the docks. Support ships and cargo vessels tied up along the pier.

Television trucks lined Blaikie's Quay. Cameramen filmed the newscasters standing with their backs to the barrier. The wind whipped Katherine's hair across her face. She tried, without success, to tuck the wayward strands behind her ear. Bloody hell. Hoping no one noticed her, she turned to cross over the road and return to the warmth of indoors. An ambulance rounded the corner by the ferry terminal and sped to the Maritime and Coastguard Agency building, blue lights flashing and siren wailing.

It pulled to a stop by the doors she exited from minutes before. Paramedics unloaded a stretcher and piled their equipment on the gurney. Kat rushed over and held the door open for them. Once they were inside, she followed. They came for Zoe Richmond. Cherie and one of the other women worked over her. The poor girl did more than faint. She had a seizure or heart attack or something.

Someone had turned on the television mounted on the wall near the ceiling. An STV North reporter stood outside Aberdeen Royal Infirmary. The ticker across the bottom of the screen mentioned the crash. "Turn the volume up." Kat slapped the counter under the window.

The official in the small office complied.

"Thank you."

"The Super Puma returning from the Alpha Ecosse platform in the Arbroath oilfield suffered a catastrophic failure about twenty miles off the coast of Aberdeenshire. An eye witness on a nearby supply ship reported hearing the 'copter overhead but being so used to the noise didn't think anything more until the sound vanished. That was when he saw the aircraft strike the water with the blades and gearbox detached from the fuselage. That section plummeted to the sea soon afterwards."

Katherine's knees weakened. She slumped into the chair behind her.

The report continued. "The first of the casualties have been ferried to shore. The bodies of Bradford Gilbertson and Fletcher Stockwell were recovered on 19th March, the same day as the crash. Another passenger, found in the life raft with them, survived and was rushed to Aberdeen Royal Infirmary. His condition isn't known at this time. Three more were transported ashore earlier today. Their identities won't be revealed until their next of kin have been notified."

Steve Norton and Nick Hudson were two of them. She didn't need to wait for the formalities of the families being told. Both Victoria and Zoe were made aware their men had been found dead.

"It's come to our attention as well," the reporter continued, "although fourteen members of the crew on the Alpha Ecosse were to fly home today, only thirteen got on the helicopter. Fate smiled down on the one who didn't board that flight."

Could it be Jared? Did he stay behind for some reason? Katherine rummaged in her handbag for her mobile.

U okay? Love you. xx

After pressing send, she held her BlackBerry in her hand. If he got back to her, she didn't want to miss it. Determined not to give up on him being found alive, this revelation raised her hopes. Staying behind because they needed him was something he would do. He went in to cover for one of the guys on the opposite rotation after they returned from London.

~ 27 ~

21st March, 2011

Jared woke with a start. The emergency locator beacon on his survival suit stopped working. The North Sea was void of ships of any kind. How far had they drifted since he cut their raft free from the sinking chopper? Would they be found? No food and water for who knew how long, took its toll on him. He nudged Tristan's foot. "You okay?"

The man groaned in response.

At least he wasn't adrift somewhere with two dead men. "I could murder a fuckin' pint about now. How about you?"

"No," he grunted.

Shifting to a less painful position, he rocked the inflatable boat. His good hand pushing down on the bottom elevated the side nearest Tristan. The man grimaced in pain. Guilty for the discomfort he caused, he stopped and the life raft bobbed up and down like the mattress in a waterbed.

Rescue couldn't happen soon enough. How many days now? He spent most of his time asleep, unconscious from the agony. He hadn't heard a helicopter, since … since the journey on that cursed T-BLUE. Should he have complained after the flight back to the depot at Aberdeen Airport?

Why didn't they red tag or whatever the fuck they do to the fucking chopper to remove it from service? Maybe they had. The trip from hell was … was a month ago. Maintenance and repairs should have been done in that length of time. Dizziness took over. Jared's vision blurred and he drifted into unconsciousness.

The ringtone from a mobile phone jolted Katherine awake. She reached for her purse and rummaged for her device. Not hers. No response from Jared to her message. Her heart sank.

One by one, the other women retrieved their mobiles. Disappointed sighs filled the room. Hopes dashed, some wept.

She blinked back tears, determined not to cry. Not here and not now. Taking a deep breath, she checked her texts again. The last one was the one she sent to Jared the previous night.

He was strong – a survivor. Growing up in an abusive home taught him how to manage. This was a different situation. Would those skills be of any good to him now?

A woman with short, streaked blonde hair, who Katherine assumed was in her mid-forties held a phone to her ear.

"Ian, why didn't you call me sooner? I've been going out of my mind with worry," Fiona Dunbar scolded.

"Been trying, love. Mobile networks have been overwhelmed since the crash. This is the first chance I've had."

Tears of joy streamed down her cheeks. She dashed out the door not feeling right about being happy in front of the other women and fist-pumped the air with both hands.

Microphones and television cameras were shoved at her face. Reporters surrounded her, asking questions at the same time.

"I take it from your reaction, your husband has been found alive," a man holding an STV mike said.

"Yes," she exclaimed. "He never left the rig."

"He was the fourteenth man. The one who should have been on flight 63M but wasn't. Have you spoken to him directly or from the company he works for on the Alpha Ecosse?"

Fiona dropped her husband in limbo when the reporters swarmed her. "Ian, honey, are you still there? Sorry. I came outside when I got your call and the next thing I knew I was surrounded by the media."

An alert flashed on the television screen. A representative from the Maritime and Coastguard Agency stepped forward to the microphone. "We resumed the search early this morning after expanding the area last night. We're now searching over thirty-five square nautical miles. That being said, with two days having lapsed since the Nexus Super Puma went down, the hope of finding survivors has been greatly reduced. We must face the grim reality the crew has been lost. We now must switch our efforts from rescue to recovery. We've been lucky the weather conditions have been favourable but that aside, the North Sea is a harsh environment. Temperatures hover about eight degrees at this time of year which reduces a person's ability to survive."

Cameras flashed and reporters scrambled for the best position to get their questions answered. The delegate spoke again. "Our thoughts are with the families of the lost and deceased crew. There will be a book of condolence opened at the Oil Chapel in The Kirk of St Nicholas."

The news hit Katherine like a punch in the stomach. They couldn't stop looking. She tapped a finger on her thigh for each member unaccounted for and hoped no one was watching. Besides Cherie, Beryl and her, Marilyn Trowbridge, the co-pilot's wife; Kirstie Simmons, Pete O'Brien's partner were the only ones there. No family, spouses, nor partners in attendance worrying about Georgia or Carter. Sad.

"We take you live now to Aberdeen harbour outside the Maritime and Coastguard headquarters," the anchorman said.

Kat sat in stunned silence. The television screen displayed the familiar waterfront lined with ships and a smiling Fiona talking with a reporter in the foreground.

"Mrs. Dunbar, you received the best possible tidings in this situation. Can you tell the viewers?"

"My husband is alive. He didn't get on the helicopter. He stayed behind." Her eyes sparkled as she spoke.

The woman beamed. Seeing her on the telly didn't help Katherine or the other women still waiting for word.

"The fourteenth man scheduled to return on flight 63M has

been identified as Ian Dunbar of Montrose. For one lucky family there is reason to rejoice. We can now name some of the victims of the air accident – Brad Gilbertson, 31, of Kirkintilloch; Fletcher Stockwell, 53, of Banff; Nick Hudson, 29, of Inverness; and Steve Norton, 33, of Norwich, England. Andy Pascoe, 34, of Dundee, rescued the day of the crash is recovering from his injuries at Aberdeen Royal Infirmary, as is captain Dominic Ballesteros, 51, of Edinburgh. Their conditions aren't known at this time. One of the deceased remains unnamed until his next of kin have been notified. According to the manifest, fourteen workers along with the pilot and co-pilot were to be on the ill-fated flight. As you heard, Mr. Dunbar remained behind. Still missing and unaccounted for are Chuck Adams, Carter Alexander, William Bateman, Jared Martin, Tristan McKnight, Pete O'Brien, co-pilot Edward Trowbridge, and the only female onboard, Georgia Wescome."

If not for the hordes of media surrounding the Coastguard headquarters, Katherine would have bolted from the building. Seeing another woman so happy because her husband didn't board that doomed passage, made her pain at Jared's loss even worse. She walked to the corner of the room and rested her head on the cement block wall.

A warm hand touched her shoulder. "Don't give up. They'll find them."

The gesture, meant to be comforting, was far from reassuring. She burst into tears and fled into the women's toilet.

When she failed to rejoin the others, Cherie volunteered to look for her. She discovered Kat in the ladies' bathroom, sitting on the floor sobbing, knees drawn up to her chest, arms folded around them, and her head bowed forward.

She plunked down beside her and took one of Katherine's hands. When she acknowledged another person's presence in the room, her eyes were red and puffy, and filled with tears.

"I've lost him again, haven't I?"

"You must remain positive. It's only been a couple of days

..."

"In harsh conditions. He could be injured – maybe even dead. I can't go through another senseless death. First, my husband in the London bombings back in 2005. Now this? I can't do it again." She stood and braced herself against the sink.

To support her friend and part-time employer, Cherie scrambled to Katherine's side. "I'm scared, too. I don't want Tris to die. He's my life. We have to be brave for them." She exhaled a ragged breath, herself on the verge of breaking down. Knowing as little as she did about Kat's life, she was gobsmacked the woman was widowed in the events of July 7, 2005.

Did she believe the words she spouted? Being strong for the men? Not for a second. Truth be told she was every bit as scared as the others who still hung in limbo. How had she maintained the charade this long.

The sooner they found the rest of the crew – whether deceased or living – their ordeal over, the better off she and the other women encamped at the Coastguard headquarters would be. They needed closure and until their men were brought back safe or the worst case scenario, dead, they didn't have it.

"Come on. Let's go back out there. Maybe they have more information." Tears pricked her eyes. There could be bad news. She couldn't bear it.

Cherie and her man were total opposites. She was short. He was tall. Her head reached no higher than his chest. She was a voracious reader. He read the sports section of the paper and ogled the photo of the topless model on page three of *The Sun.*

She liked to put on her glad rags and go out for a meal. He was happy with a takeaway. The one thing they had in common, well, it didn't bear thinking about at the moment because he wasn't there to scratch that itch.

When Tristan was home, their sex life was phenomenal. The fortnight at a time away from each other ensured it. She considered herself lucky her periods came soon after he went offshore leaving her primed and ready for his return. But, she was overdue.

Cherie turned her back to Katherine and counted on her fingers. Over six weeks. They had always been careful. She took birth control pills. Was it possible? People did get pregnant when on them. She rubbed her stomach.

Lesley Gilbertson – motherhood just confirmed and now the unborn baby's father was dead. The poor girl. Did she dare raise her hopes she and her partner were to become parents? A home pregnancy test would confirm it one way or the other. No. She couldn't do it now. She needed to wait. What if she was and Tristan didn't survive?

The live feed switched back to the studio. A map showed the location of the crash with a dotted circle indicating the search area. That image was replaced with the remains of the chopper being lifted to the deck of a salvage vessel. Kat gasped. "We now know divers recovered the wreckage on the sea floor overnight and have removed the bodies from within. Once the remnants of the helicopter are loaded on to the ship, the vessel will make its way to Aberdeen harbour with it, the 'black box' and the victims onboard."

The knowledge of the discovery was too much for her. She bolted from the room and past the swarm of reporters, waiting like vultures to pick the women's emotions clean.

When she escaped the vicinity, relief washed over her. It would be easy to run home and lock herself in, but that would be the coward's way out. She took a deep breath and walked up Market Street to Union. Something compelled her to visit the Oil Chapel located in The Kirk of St. Nicholas. She paused at the ornate gated wall of the churchyard before winding her way along the path of the ancient burial ground.

The thick, oak door was unlocked. Katherine pulled it open. It clattered shut behind her. Her plan to make a discreet entrance into the hallowed area shattered by the noise. The click of her stiletto heels echoed in the cavernous, granite structure. Finding the room, she stood in the entryway staring at the huge stained glass window before sitting in a nearby seat.

Squeezing her eyes shut in attempt to stem her tears, they

streamed down her cheeks anyway followed by agonizing sobs. Her nose ran and she sniffed while she dug for one of the tissues she always carried with her.

Before she managed to extract one, someone held out a handkerchief. A tall, bearded, grey-haired man stood facing her. He was attractive and his blue-green eyes appeared sympathetic.

"Take it," he offered.

"Th-thank you."

He sat beside her. "I'm Martin Grashoff, the new chaplain for the UK offshore oil and gas industry." He extended his right hand.

Katherine shook it. Her breaths were ragged, preventing her from speaking. She wiggled in the wooden chair trying to make herself comfortable. When she made the decision to come here, she wanted to be alone, but couldn't very well tell the minister to get lost. She smiled and dabbed her eyes with the hanky he provided, leaving the pristine, white cloth covered with streaks of black eyeliner and mascara. She ruined his monogrammed piece of cotton. As if she needed that on top of everything else. She didn't feel bad enough already.

"Terrible tragedy this helicopter crash. You had a loved one on it?"

Still unable to speak, she nodded.

"I'm so sorry for your loss." The reverend took her hand in his and placed his other one over hers.

Katherine didn't envy the man's job. Dealing with bereft people, counselling others. How did he cope? She wasn't.

"Whenever you're ready … if you want to talk. I'll spend as much time with you as you need."

"Th-thanks." Handkerchief already ruined by her makeup, she blew her nose. "M-my b-boy … partner was on that flight. He's still missing." No sooner had she uttered those words than she burst into tears. "A-and now things have changed from rescue to recovery. I-I'll never s-see J-Jared again," she bawled.

Reverend Grashoff let go of Katherine's hand, encircled her shoulders with his arm, and rubbed her back.

The comfort in his touch calmed her. "I'm sorry. I ruined your ...." She sniffed.

"Peril of the trade. Don't fret."

Smiling, she said, "I have to go. I need to get back. Been gone way too long. They may have found something." She sprang up from the chair and darted out of the chapel and into the adjacent aged churchyard.

~ 28 ~

22nd March, 2011

Katherine rummaged through her wardrobe for something to wear to Brad Gilbertson's funeral. It was the last place she wanted to be. She preferred to remain at Coastguard headquarters at the harbour waiting for word on Jared. Steph persuaded her to attend in a show of solidarity to the other wives and partners. After a great deal of deliberation, she selected her black trousers, and turquoise V-neck jumper. Tasteful, yet not out of keeping with the situation.

Someone, presumably Lesley, made the decision for just a simple graveside service at Trinity Cemetery rather than a funeral at the crematorium.

Ominous, black clouds hung in the sky. Anytime now the rain would pelt down. Steph pulled her silver Tiguan into one of the remaining parking bays on Errol Street and turned off the ignition. "You ready to do this?" she asked.

Kat nodded as she yanked a handful of tissues from the box between the vehicle's front seats. Her vision blurred from hot tears.

Steph exited the SUV. Before coming around to the passenger side, she pulled two umbrellas from the back.

By now, Katherine slipped into her wine coloured mac. The first drops of rain pelted the pavement. Brollies opened, the two walked with their arms linked through the gated entrance of the graveyard. Buds formed on the trees indicating the beginning of life – stark contrast to their purpose in the cemetery today. The sweet smell of the fresh cut grass mingled with the scents of turned earth, floral tributes, women's perfumes and men's colognes.

The paved entrance gave way to gravel which crunched under their feet with each step. Rows of granite, marble and sandstone headstones stood like silent sentries guarding the sombre scene. The hearse and the funeral director's limousine, headed a line of cars parked along the narrow, winding road. Mourners gathered a short distance away huddled together against the wind and rain.

***

Her red hair bounced on her shoulders as she walked. The area he chose was the perfect location. There were enough monuments and trees between him and where the service was being conducted, he wouldn't be seen, yet he could observe her every movement.

He longed to rush over and snatch her away from the mourners but he had to remain patient. She had to be alone, not with a crowd of people nearby. She was not his first execution in Aberdeen. He murdered the poor girl not far from here. Slit that one's throat and pushed her over a cliff. His mistake was staying to revel in the excitement. He couldn't perform with her, but once she was dead, his willie stiffened with desire.

When the authorities found her twisted body on the rocks, her pants were around her ankles. Like an idiot, he stayed atop the precipice. When the coppers nicked him, his cock was in his hand and he was wanking. The release he craved never came. They cuffed his hands behind his back before he finished. Charged as a youth offender, he served a custodial sentence for his deed.

Not long after his discharge, he killed again when in the company of a woman who mocked him for his lack of sexual prowess. This one he suffocated by shoving his flaccid member in her mouth and holding a pillow over the rest of her face.

With each kill, the violence escalated. But since his first, he never made the mistake of remaining at the scene. Stabbing, strangling and suffocating, he moved south and out of Scotland.

The one with the red hair – it all started with her. She was the one who turned him into a serial killer. She approached him. The voices chanted in his head; their cacophony deafening. Kill. Kill. Kill. Make her pay. She did this to you. He clamped his palms over his ears but couldn't shut them out. It only made them louder.

The further into the graveyard they walked, the more Kat resisted. She found a place beyond the curve in the avenue and stopped behind one of the large headstones on her left. What started out as a light shower turned into a torrential downpour. The rain lashed against the nylon canopies of the mourners' umbrellas in a furious staccato like machine gun fire. "Let's go over," Steph said, reaching for Kat's arm.

She recoiled. "No." It came out firmer than intended. Still, not bad enough to approach the graveside. She would stay right there.

"Suit yourself."

Watching her friend walk away, she blinked back tears. The wind picked up and tugged at her brolly threatening to yank it out of her hands. Kat tightened her grip on the handle.

The minister started the Sacrament. Muffled sniffing and crying floated on the breeze. Kat's heels sunk into the soft ground and she repositioned herself many times only to sink again. She inched forward until she stood on the gravel surface of the road. Her logic remained if she avoided the burial place, Jared would still be alive.

Pallbearers lowered Brad's casket into its final resting place. Katherine didn't recognize any of them. They may have been from one of the other rigs. The men and women were a close-knit group. Family. One by one, the mourners filed by the grave and dropped long-stemmed roses into the cavity. They landed on the coffin's wooden surface with a soft thud. Lesley had to be helped forward to drop hers in by an older couple, likely her parents. The young woman's gut wrenching sobs brought more tears to Katherine's already watery eyes.

When the service ended, instead of returning to the SUV, she walked in the opposite direction through the cemetery. By now, the rain had stopped and the sun tried to peek out from behind the clouds, making them appear blacker than before. These few minutes of solitude calmed her.

When Stephanie noticed Kat walking away from the location of the car, she called, "Where are you going?"

She didn't receive an answer. Instead, the woman ran faster. A glint of once neutral coloured fabric flashed between two of the tall headstones in the middle section. Him. The creep who had been spending so much time around Katherine's place. Hell, he even had the bollocks to go in the shop. He followed them into the pub the day Jared gave Kat that expensive diamond engagement ring.

Breaking into a run, she tore off down the hill, all the while watching this strange man loping through the burial ground, vaulting over shorter stones, zigzagging between others. His overcoat trailed behind him. He kept one hand to his head, holding his black Fedora in place.

By now, Kat had reached the far end of the cemetery. Stephanie quickened her pace. She had to reach her before this man, whoever he was, did. Soon, she found herself at Park Road which bisected the graveyard. Her chest heaved as she tried to catch her breath. She clutched her side trying to numb the pain.

If he remained in this section, he concealed himself behind the stone markers laid out in continuous, undeviating rows, some perpendicular to the street she stood near, others parallel to it.

Where were they? People didn't just vanish. She turned in the direction she came from but no sign of Katherine or whoever this guy was. Scared for her friend, she pulled her mobile out of her bag. The battery was flat. Of all times for it to happen.

About to give up, she shoved her phone in to her pocket. At that instant, she spotted Kat near the crest of the hill. Stepping into traffic without looking, she drew the ire of a motorist who leaned on the horn, jammed on the brakes and shook his fist at her. Stephanie nodded an apology and carried on.

Katherine continued to a crag where she looked out over the North Sea. An icy wind whipped her hair. She folded up her collar to cover the back of her neck and shivered – her mac not warm enough for the miserable conditions. Why hadn't she gone back to the car with Stephanie to escape the inclement weather? Instead, she chose to run away.

Monstrous whitecaps smashed against the rocks below. This cold, uninviting body of water could be where Jared lie dead. Three full days had elapsed from the time the helicopter ditched. Now, day four was more than half over. Could he survive the ordeal? The clouds swirled thanks to the gale. For a brief moment, they formed a man's face. She rubbed her upper arms in an attempt to generate some heat. It worked as long as she did it, but when she stopped the chill returned.

The skies had been void of choppers, other than search and rescue flights, since the crash. Their sounds, mere background noise in the city centre, missing. While Kat stood on the cliff, the familiar clatter in the air intensified. One, belonging to one of the other companies that shuttled the men and women to and from the rigs flew overhead. The setting sun glowed red in the sky. Maybe, Jared would be found later tonight or tomorrow.

She must not interfere with his plan. He bent down and picked up a rock about the size of a cricket ball. This would stop that meddling woman. He hid behind a tree and waited for her. The voices egged him on. Do it. Do it now.

The red-haired woman must pay for her sins with her life. How he murdered her was up to him. Mr. Cocksure was out of the picture … dead somewhere in the North Sea thanks to a helicopter crash. One less person to contend with. For now, this friend of the ginger 'hoor' had to be eliminated.

When she drew parallel with the tree, he stepped out. "Hello Steph …." Before he finished his greeting, he swung the rock hitting her temple with a sickening thud mingled with the crunch of shattering bone. She dropped to the ground, the injured side of her face pointed skyward. Her blood spattered on his face and dribbled to the corner of his mouth. He captured the drop with his tongue – its copper tang, tasty.

Swiping his sleeve across his face, he marvelled at how fragile life was. How powerful the weapon he held proved to be. He contemplated discarding the chunk of granite beside Stephanie's still body. He juggled the thing a few times getting acquainted with the stone then shoved the small boulder in his topcoat. It could still be useful.

Leaving Stephanie for dead, he started after the ginger-haired woman. He relished this one more than the others. He waited a long time to exact his revenge. He would ruin her just like she ruined him, but he would live. As he followed, he played over her death in his mind. It would be his most depraved act yet. His lips curled into a smile.

No, this time, there would be foreplay. Bloody and painful. Then strangulation. Maybe even conflagration, but he had to be more careful. When he attempted to set fire to one of his victim's before, the petrol spilled on him and he was the one who ended up suffering third degree burns to most of his body.

Her flawless complexion would be no more. She'd be scarred and ugly. The ideas swirled in his head aroused him, and made him hard with excitement.

She stood on the periphery of the cliff, her red tresses blowing in the wind. He could rush up behind her and rugby tackle her over the edge. She would never know what hit her. But it would be too quick, not to mention he might go right along with her if he built up that much momentum. No, he wanted her to suffer instead. He put his hand in his pocket and grappled for the flick-knife, familiarizing himself with its position so he could extract the blade with ease when the time was right.

His shadow darkened the ground in front of him making it impossible to sneak up on her from behind. So close. She would soon die. The more he thought about killing her, the hornier he got. He could wait. As a final parting gesture, he would wank on her dead body, preferably her ruined face. Once she died, he didn't care if he were caught. His mission would be complete.

If he skirted off to the right by about ten to fifteen yards, he could backtrack and come face to face with her. He increased his pace and worked his way up the hill and back across near the precipice. "Hello, Katie."

No one ever referred to her in that manner except Graeme Ross, her first boyfriend, if he could be called that. He was the first boy with whom she ever had sex.

"Haven't thought of you in ages."

"No doubt." He seized her by the throat with a gloved hand and shoved her backwards into the trunk of a nearby tree. "You were a wee hoor then and you're still one now." He leaned into her face.

She twisted her head away, unable to look at him.

His grip on her neck tightened.

"I-I can't breathe you daft ape."

"All part of the plan."

Before she had the chance to speak, he drew his other hand back, balled it into a fist, and punched her in the stomach doubling her over, never letting go of her throat.

Breathless and in pain, she folded her arms over her torso to protect herself from the next blow. Why had he come back after all these years? She regretted their intimate encounter. Told him back then – many times. But he pursued her. He didn't take the hint. Even after she and Jared started seeing each other. He was a control freak then.

If anything good came out of the family move to Canada, it was getting away from Graeme. Now he was back and the harassment would start all over. Except it already had. The pieces fell into place. He was the homeless person who turned up in late December and lurked about the streets near her home and business. "What are you doing back here?"

His grip loosened. "I came for you."

The sentence terrified her. "But, I'm engaged."

"To him, Mr. Cocksure? I shouldn't think so. Besides, he's dead. Feeding the fish by now, I expect."

No one knew for sure if Jared perished in the crash. All anyone knew was he was one of the unaccounted for

243

passengers on the flight. She wouldn't stop believing he survived until his body was brought ashore. Kat spat in Graeme's face.

His free hand reached into his topcoat and pulled out a knife. At a press of a button, the business end snapped out. He leaned closer to her and held the stainless steel cutting edge on her cheek. "I could use this on you now. Cut that perfect face of yours. Slit your throat, but I'm not going to. You know why?"

Kat shook her head. Tears formed burning her eyes. She tried to blink them back. She couldn't cry. Not now. Not in front of Graeme.

"You ruined it for me. After you, I could never shag another girl. I would get all horny and ready for action, then my willie would let me down. All because of the way you treated me after we did it." He ran the blade down the side of her face.

She cringed and shrank back into the tree trunk. Beads of sweat formed at the base of Kat's skull dampening her hair. Unable to look him in the eye because just being with him repulsed her, she turned her head but remained focused on the cold metal pressed against her face.

"God, we were only fourteen. We didn't know what we were doing. You hurt me. I'm glad we only ever shagged once. I wasn't prepared. You weren't ready. Your willie let you down then, too. Was nothing to do with me." Thinking back to that awful experience, she shivered.

When they messed about before the disastrous encounter, he was clumsy and awkward. She didn't know any different at the time, though. Not until Jared took her the first time, she knew.

By now, Graeme traced the tip of the blade down her neck to the collar of her mac. "Unbutton it," he ordered.

What was he going to do to her? Her fingers trembled so hard she had difficulty unfastening the toggles.

He pushed the jacket open, keeping hold of the bladed weapon the entire time. Sun glinted off the steel and reflected in her eyes. Her eyelids flickered preventing her from being blinded by the brilliant light.

"You tortured me, Katie. Prancing around in your airplane skirts."

What was he talking about? She never had anything which remotely resembled that.

"Your school uniform kilt – rolled up at the waist so many times that your cockpit showed."

She and every other girl did that with their clothes. Leave the house with their skirt at the proper length and once out of sight of home, hike it up short.

"You ruined me. Now I'm going to ruin you. If you survive this, you'll never want to have sex with a man again. Be too painful for you. I'm going to shag you with this," he said, waving the weapon back and forth in front of her face. "Cut you up so bad, you'll beg for me to murder you. Put you out of your misery."

Graeme spun her around so he stood behind her. His hand encircled her neck tipping her head back. Her bones cracked from the force. The cold metal of the knife chilled her flesh. Don't hurt me she repeated in her mind.

There had to be something she could do but with a six-inch blade capable of slitting her throat in an instant, she was stymied. The point pierced her skin. She winced. Something warm trickled down from the spot. Hot, moist breath puffed on her injury followed by a rough tongue. The sick bugger licked her wound.

They stood about ten feet from the edge of the cliff. Could she lead him that way and escape? Not likely. The tree he pushed her against earlier was closer. The decision was made for her.

He shoved her headlong into the trunk. The rough bark cut into her forehead and cheek. She was going to die out here. A horrible death and she was at a loss as to how to prevent being murdered. Not many people came up here because the cliffs were dangerous. Kat regretted her choice of places to spend her alone time. Now Graeme made her pay for her decision. He twisted her arm up her back and forced his knee between her legs.

"Did you know you paid for this knife, Katie? I found a stash of money under a false bottom in the desk drawer in the room you use as an office. I took it. Bought this with your dosh." Graeme pressed the flat side of the blade against her cheek again. "Been in your place more than one time. I would have thought your underwear would have been more organized. Not just everything shoved in willy-nilly."

The idea of him being in her home and rummaging through her things sickened Kat. "H-how?" Filled with fear, her body trembled. She had been careful. Always locked the front and back doors downstairs. No way from the retail space into the office without being captured by the security camera. How did he get in?

"You really should have come up with a better combination for your lock box on the backdoor. Took me a few tries, but I figured it out. And you made things so easy for me by not locking your upstairs door. Once I gained access to the building, I had free range."

Never again, if she survived this ordeal, would she leave the apartment door unlocked when she was away from home. Even if she was in the store or office. There were times things were a bit off but couldn't place what seemed different – out of place.

Graeme put his mouth next to her ear. "You're not getting away, Katie. Not this time. Not any time. You're mine to do with what I please." He gripped the handle in his teeth and pulled out the rock. Once he extracted it, he returned the switchblade to its position against Kat's neck.

"See this?" He held the round piece of granite in front of her face. "I used it on your meddling friend. I killed her. Stephanie's dead. This is her blood." He licked a stained patch on the mass. "Mmm, she tastes good. Better fresh, though, like when she splattered on my face." He smiled and ran his tongue up her cheek.

Katherine squirmed. She couldn't escape. He wouldn't allow her. He wrenched her arm further up her back. She cried out. He relished her anguish. He wanted to bash her in the face but the voices told him it was too soon. She needed to suffer more, first.

He flung the knife. When the blade pierced the dirt, the weapon vibrated. Now he had a hand free. He snatched Kat's hair and threw her to the ground. Grabbing her shoulder, he rolled her to her back and sat on her stomach pinching her arms to her sides. She kicked and flailed. He covered her mouth and pinched her nostrils so she couldn't breathe.

Graeme held her in that position, rock above his head ready to bring it down on her if she refused to cooperate. When her struggles slowed, he released his grip on her face. Her chest heaved as she swallowed in air. This was fun. He could do this to her all day. She fought against him again. Her fingers clawed the earth near his knife. No, she must not have it. He swung the stone but stopped less than an inch away from her head. She couldn't die that way. Still, the threat quieted her.

With only one free hand, he would accomplish nothing. He dropped the granite weapon behind him well out of her reach. He patted the overcoat. Her black, satin pants he stole and wanked in. He yanked them out, forced her lips open, and shoved them into her mouth. She gagged. "Yes, these are yours, Katie. Another thing I took from you on one of my visits to your flat."

He plucked his weapon of choice out of the soil. Dirt adhered to the blade. In one swift movement, he sliced through the front of her jumper. She wriggled below him. He spread the fabric wide, exposing her bare flesh. Next, he cut her bra. When he freed her breasts from the lacy garment, he groped them with his gloved hands. He took one into his mouth, swirled his tongue around her nipple. It tightened at his contact. He wanted to bite it. Chomp the hardened bullet from her chest, but not yet.

His touch nauseated Kat. How could she escape this evil person? Despite his thinness, he was heavy. Writhing beneath him, she managed to free her left hand. She needed to remove her underwear he used as a gag. Turning her head to the side, she reached in and plucked them out.

"You shouldn't have done it, Katie. You've made me angry. You don't want me in that state."

Kat didn't care what frame of mind he was in. She only wanted to escape from him. She raised her hand intent on clouting him but only knocked his Fedora off his head before he snatched hold of her wrist, and pinned her arm to the ground above her head. He squeezed hard and her grip on the underwear loosened. She clenched her jaw. If he was going to shove those things back in her mouth, she was going to make it as difficult as possible.

When he lowered his hand to her lips, she lunged and bit him. Sunk her teeth in and didn't release him.

"Ow, you cow." Graeme slapped her hard with his other hand.

Unable to prevent it, she let go. Her head spun and her vision blurred then everything went black.

Serves her right. She deserved that and more, the biting bitch. He took the glove off his injured hand. She didn't draw blood, but bruises formed around the indentations from her teeth. If not for the protective covering, she would have torn the flesh away from the bone.

With his knife, he traced the point across her throat, down her neck beneath her ear. This time he exerted more pressure. Still not sufficient to break the skin but enough to leave marks everywhere he drew the weapon.

He paused when he reached her torso. He pushed the tip against her breastbone. The flick-knife would never penetrate here. He would have to shove the dagger through the gaps between her ribs. With any luck her lung would be punctured or better still, her heart. Why didn't he think of it before now? Use 'Cricket' as a hammer and pound the blade through her bones. That would cause maximum pain and result in a slow, excruciating death. Still, not as good as raping her with the dirty, Sheffield stainless steel.

Graeme remained on her with the switchblade poised to kill her. He hated her since their failed sexual encounter as teenagers and more now she lay unconscious and vulnerable under him. The longer he sat on her, the harder he became. That was it. Necrophilia. Dead women's corpses turned him on and he stayed erect, but Katie wasn't dead, yet. Her chest rose and fell with each shallow breath. She could be. He was in control. He had the power, the knife, and the rock.

She stirred and her eyes flickered open.

"Welcome back. While you lay there lifeless, I thought of things I can do after I annihilate you."

Now what sick, twisted plans did Graeme have for her? She didn't have to wait long to find out.

"I'm going to shag your dead body and if you're not already, you'll be so close to death, it won't matter. You won't put up a fight. Hell, you might even like it. I know I will." He winked at her. "Then when I'm finished, I'll cut you up inside like I promised."

What a sick bastard. Things he said when they were kids made sense now. He was a sadistic so and so then. He bragged of what he did to insects, then frogs and toads. Would have tortured their cat save for his mother interrupting.

But the woman protected him. Why? He needed help not her covering up his deeds. In her head, Kat kicked herself many times for getting involved with him. Now, she would be his next victim. How many women had he killed? Did he murder Stephanie or tell her he did to force her to submit to him?

"You did this to me, Katie. It's because of you I'm the way I am." Graeme yanked the compression bandage off his head and tossed the mask aside. "This is me for the rest of my life."

"I wasn't even there. Me? How?" His scarred face and ears burned to the point they melted into his scalp revolted her. A few fine wisps of dark brown, almost black hair stuck out from various places on his head. This disfigured man who sat on her looked nothing like the gawky, fourteen year-old boy she had her first sexual encounter with. She turned away from him and vomited.

He squeezed her neck. "Look at me," he growled and

twisted her head back so she faced him.

"Wh-what happened to you?" she gasped.

"One of my conquests – she wouldn't give up. Fought like a tiger. I grabbed a petrol can. When I poured some on her, she kicked the fucking thing out of my hands. Before you could say Bob's your Uncle, she doused me in the fuel and lit the match. It wasn't supposed to happen that way. I was to set her alight."

"H-how many women have you murdered?"

He shifted his weight on her stomach and she grimaced. Graeme was downright skinny, not just thin, and his bones dug into her.

"Most recently, Stephanie. At least I think she's dead. Bashed her hard enough with 'Cricket' here ...." He juggled the rock in her face. "Let's see, my first kill. Brought a girl up to these parts for a shag. I mean the cliffs are fenced off from the cemetery. What better place to be alone? When the old boy didn't cooperate, I slit her throat and pushed her off the cliff. Her pants were down around her ankles. Big mistake on that one. Stuck around wanking because the whole thing turned me on. Spent time as a guest of Her Majesty after that wee madam. After my release, I got another in Dundee, then Queensferry, Peebles, then over the border. Worked my way to London killing as I went. But after getting nicked the first time, I was a lot more careful. No wanking on corpses. Even before the bitch set me on fire, I started wearing leather gloves. Didn't get caught again until after then. And only because she ran off with her legs flaming and screeching like a banshee."

He picked up the round piece of stone in both hands and held it in the air ready to smash her in the head. Kill the red-headed bitch once and for all. They only did him for one murder but he confessed to more. She had to die if only to keep her from spilling her guts about the others.

"DI Robertson, Grampian Police. Put the weapon down."

Fucking hell. Who called the cops? He ignored the man. Hoisted the stone higher, instead.

"I wouldn't do that if I were you."

He released one hand from the rock and covered her

mouth. "Don't you even think of it," he warned.

She bit him again. Same hand. He pulled back, shaking his injured appendage. He swung the miniature boulder at her but she put her arm up to protect her head.

"Graeme Ross, I'm arresting you for the murder of Stephanie Lindsay. You are not obliged to say anything, but anything you do say will be noted and may be used in evidence. Do you understand?" As the Detective Inspector spoke, he latched handcuffs around Graeme's wrists behind his back.

"Ouch. You don't have to be quite so rough," he snapped. As the plainclothes officer yanked him to his feet, he continued his tirade. "You don't get it. This woman has made me what I am today. She's the one what needs arresting. Not me."

Another cop, this one a woman assisted Kat to a nearby park bench. "I'm DS Angel Thompson. And you are?"

"Katherine Murphy ..." she trailed off, "... Whithorn." With the revelations which came to light about her dead husband saying the name offended her. If only she could introduce herself as Katherine Martin. She would drop her maiden name in a heartbeat if she married him. But it wouldn't take place now. Even though he bought her the expensive engagement ring and told her he would wait for her, it would never happen. Not now after what Graeme did. And that was if Jared survived the crash.

"In addition to the visible physical evidence, did he do anything else to you?"

When Kat wrapped her mac around her and cinched the belt to cover her nakedness, she turned away. Every bone in her body ached. "No. What you see is it."

"He didn't rape you."

She touched her left forearm where the rock made contact and winced. "No."

"What's wrong with your arm?"

"I tried to protect myself from being hit in the head with the chunk of stone he had. The one he said he used to kill Stephanie. She's really dead?"

"Friend of yours, was she?" The female officer leaned forward and held Kat's hand.

"Besties since we went to primary school together."

"I'm sorry for your loss. Does she have any family? They'll have to be notified."

"Just her cat. Her parents were killed in a car accident 'bout ten years ago, outside of Huntly. Glens of Foudland, I think. She had a brother. Not sure what became of him."

"That's fine."

Stephanie dead. Did she see Graeme and come to warn her? Protect her? And that creep got to her first? Did she even recognize him and know he was not some random person? A tear escaped from her eye and ran down her cheek. The two most important people in Kat's life – gone. One murdered and the other missing, and in all likelihood, dead.

"You must come to police HQ on Queen Street and make a statement. And your injuries need to be documented, not to mention require medical treatment."

"I can't. My husband-to-be was on the helicopter that went down. He's still unaccounted for. I have to get back to the Maritime and Coastguard Agency."

"Without your side of the story, we can't charge Graeme with anything else."

"Isn't my friend's murder enough?" Kat balled her hands into fists.

The woman stood and turned her back to Katherine. She talked into her mobile device set on speaker, and said, "She refuses to come to the station. Says her fiancé is one of the men missing in the Nexus crash. Insists on going back to the coastguard headquarters for news."

"Then take her statement – you do carry a recorder with you."

"Not an official one, but my phone."

"Use it. Have someone from the forensics team bring a camera and do it here. The murder victim isn't going anywhere. Irregular, yes, but will do for now. At some point, she'll still have to come to the office on Queen Street so we can conduct a formal interview."

DI Robertson's comment about Stephanie was cold and insensitive. Her friend deserved more dignity than that.

"Thompson here. Hate to interrupt your investigation but we need the photographer up to the area above the cemetery."

"You know the rules. Once scene at a time."

"With all due respect, sir, put another card in the camera for this." The woman turned around a few minutes later. Now, she pressed buttons on her device.

"DS Angel Thompson interviewing Katherine Murphy-Whithorn. Interview commenced at sixteen hundred hours."

The sun had disappeared below the horizon but the sky remained light. Not much longer now until darkness closed in to the point of being pitch-black up here on the hill. It took forever to get through the ordeal. Kat, forced to relive every detail of Graeme's attack on her, stopped numerous times.

The official photographer arrived carrying an SLR camera with a huge lens and flash unit affixed to the accessory shoe. He photographed the injuries on her face, her neck, her arm. Every time the light went off, Kat was blinded and she blinked. After each burst, spots danced before her eyes. The most humiliating was when she had to stand with her coat and ripped jumper open in order for the ruined clothing and scratches on her breasts and torso to be captured.

"That's him off to the nick," Detective Inspector Robertson said when he returned to the scene. "You got a statement from the victim? Photographs?"

"Yes, sir."

"Come on then young lady. We'll take you back to Coastguard HQ."

Out of habit, Kat reached for her handbag. It contained her life. Driving licence, credit cards, cosmetics – everything. Missing. When she came up the hill, she carried it slung over her shoulder. She must have dropped her leather carryall or Graeme wrenched the thing off her when he first assaulted her.

Shuffling in the direction of the tree, she stubbed her toe. When she bent down and ran her hands over the ground, she found the strap. Katherine patted the bag and breathed a sigh of relief to find the zipper remained shut. Her engagement ring from Jared was inside. She couldn't lose it. It might be the only part of him she would ever have.

"You should go to the hospital and have those head wounds treated. You could be concussed. We can take you there first. Coming in with us, you'll be seen quicker," said DS Thompson.

"No. Coastguard headquarters. I need to know if there's any more news."

Huge black clouds formed and the wind increased. Heavy waves rocked the life raft. Jared gripped the rope with his good hand. The cold, wet nylon was slippery and he couldn't maintain a strong grip. Tristan's colour had greyed in the last two hours. He groaned. He was still alive. The end was near for his bunk mate and friend. With the way the man hurled blood before, by now he was close to bleeding out.

Weak and in pain from his injuries, Jared struggled to open the pouch for the buddy line on the upper left arm of his survival suit. If he only tied them off in the beginning, but the sea was calm and their bright yellow raft, and orange protective gear should have been spotted by now. He eased his way around the lifeboat and extracted the lines from Chuck's and Tristan's suits and clipped the carabiners to the boat's safety cord. If the craft flipped over, at least they'd remain with it.

The North Sea calmed and the dark clouds overhead broke up, but the storm was far from over. A brilliant bolt of lightning streaked across the sky followed by a pause and the low rumble of thunder. Jared relaxed, leaned back, and rested his head on the wall of the craft as the first drops of rain spattered against his face.

Whitecaps formed on the crests. The boat rocked. An enormous breaker lifted their vessel and flipped it upside down, sending him and his co-workers into the frigid water. This was it. He was going to die out here in the middle of an angry body of water. Fuck. Not the way he envisioned his death.

They – he – wouldn't survive long now. Chuck died soon after exiting the chopper. Tristan less than thirty minutes ago. An air pocket existed under the inflatable in addition to protection from the icy gale. Did he separate himself from his dead companions? He couldn't leave them to the elements.

One by one, he wrestled their corpses beneath the lifeboat and followed. He would find out how well the neoprene immersion suit worked at keeping him dry. Its bright orange colour and the brilliant yellow of the raft hadn't helped their visibility. Fucking thing was useless. How far had they drifted after Jared cut them free from the helicopter to prevent them from sinking when it went down? Did he kill his workmates with his actions?

When Katherine entered the Coastguard building, supported on both sides by members of law enforcement, the enormity of what she went through hit her. She trembled and folded her arms in front of her pulling her mac tight around her. She shook.

Cherie and Beryl rushed to her. "Where have you been? We've been worried sick when you didn't return after the funeral," the older woman said as she hugged her.

"St-Stephanie is dead." The words came out flat, matter-of-fact, drained of all emotion.

"What?" the women asked in unison.

When she burst into tears, her body convulsed with every sob. The feelings of grief and fear that didn't come out before spilled from her. "Gr-Graeme, ol-old boy-boyfriend."

Cherie retrieved her handbag and they bundled her into the women's toilet. Once in the relative privacy the room offered, the questions began. "What are you talking about?" she asked as she rummaged through it for something to clean the wounds. When she couldn't find anything, she opened the door and yelled, "First aid kit. You got one? We need it." She returned her attention to the traumatized woman.

Kat slumped against the wall and held herself tighter, unable to look in the mirror for fear of what would stare back at her.

Beryl stroked her arm as she cried. "It's all right, sweetie. Let it out."

First-aid kit in hand, Cherie cleaned Kat's wounds. "These

are nasty. What happened? Did you fall?"

"N-no. Gr-Graeme. T-tree. Kn-knife," she said, her words incoherent. When the alcohol swab touched the cut and bump on her forehead, she winced and reached for Cherie's hand. Her mac fell open. Embarrassed, she fumbled to pull her coat around her.

"My God, what else did he do to you?"

She hadn't been exposed long, but more than enough time for Cherie to glimpse the scratches from the knife and her ruined clothing. Kat relayed the sordid details of the attack - the humiliation of having her injuries recorded by the forensics photographer. "He would have killed me, too, if not for the police. H-How did they know?"

"When you didn't come back with, or a bit later than the others, we got worried. I called them. I knew you'd want to be back here straight away in case there was news. I didn't know if the weird guy who'd been hanging about had anything to do with your being late back, but I mentioned him, too."

Kat nodded in gratitude. "You saved my life. Not that it's worth much without Jared."

Cherie pulled a jumper out of her bag. "Here, slip into the cubicle and put this on. Should fit. But don't throw the other one away. The lab people will likely want it. Evidence and all that."

Always the logical one, or read too many crime novels. That was how the two women met in the first place.

Kat exited holding her ruined top in one hand and bra in the other wearing the garment from Cherie.

"I don't know how to tell you this," Beryl said, "But I'm afraid I have bad news. The search has been called off. Say there's no chance of finding them alive. It's cold, a storm is blowing a gale and the swells on the North Sea are enormous. No one could survive those conditions."

Katherine removed the woman's hands from her arms and stormed to the office window. "What do you mean it's been stood down? You can't do that," she cried. She put her hands on the counter and leaned over its surface.

"Sorry, but we've thoroughly searched the entire area. No

sign of bodies or debris from the crash."

"Obviously, not painstakingly enough." Katherine broke out in a cold sweat. Her forehead dampened as did her armpits. This couldn't be the end. She only had Jared back in her life for three months – not even – she couldn't lose him now.

The strain of the unknown played heavily on the women. At least for some there was closure. And for others, they got their men back alive.

"Calm down now." Beryl's voice offered no reassurance.

"My fiancé is still out there. You've got to find him." Finally ready to accept his proposal if he survived, she collapsed against the older woman.

Katherine hated having to go home this way. She did not know if Jared was dead or alive and quite possibly never would. She dropped into the seat and wished he would walk in through that door and flash his brilliant smile in her direction.

A glint of light sparkled before her eyes. A closer inspection revealed the engagement ring and wedding band from Colin occupied her finger. Why had she not taken them off when she stripped the chain from around her neck? She rummaged through her handbag. Panic ensued when, at first, she could not find the small package from Jared.

Once she did, she opened the box. His voice whispered to her telling her to wear the piece when she was ready. She was, but was he still alive? She removed the jewellery from her late husband, dropped the gold bands into her bag, and replaced them with Jared's promise of forever.

Beryl and Cherie came over, bags in hand, to say their goodbyes. She stood and hugged them both, not wanting to let go. The three shared a bond. They might never see each other again but the fact they would never fathom what happened to their men linked them for eternity. Slowly, with slumped shoulders and heavy hearts they headed for the exit.

"Ten-four. I copy. Something, possibly debris, has been spotted beyond the examination area," the radio operator spoke into his microphone. "Search and Rescue being dispatched to your location now."

Had she heard correctly? "Where?" She barged into the

control room. "What?"

"I don't know anymore, ma'am. Sorry."

"Can you find out? Please."

"Wait out there with the others whilst I check."

Katherine rushed back to the women. "They've found something." She tried not to raise her hopes, but this news could be what they've been waiting for.

They took each other's hands and anticipated – expecting the worst, hoping for the best.

"A life raft from the downed Super Puma. They're salvaging it now," the man said when he finally came out to speak with them. "A fishing trawler blown off course by the gale spotted something in the water. They've kept their search light trained on it. Make it easier for the salvage crew."

"And?" Katherine asked. "What about the men? There are still three unaccounted for. Were they in that raft?"

"Three casualties discovered under the lifeboat, ma'am. They're being airlifted to the airport as we speak."

"Well? Are they …?" Cherie asked.

"No word on their condition," he said.

Katherine was frantic. They found the remaining men, but were they dead? She wasn't one to pray, nor was she religious but at that moment, it was the thing to do. If a powerful being existed that could bring Jared back to her alive, she'd do anything and everything to save his life.

Beryl and Cherie joined her. They embraced in a group hug. They were each the others' anchors.

"Excuse me, ladies. Grampian Police will transport you to the helipad if you'd like to come with me," a uniformed constable said as he entered the building.

Outside, an unmarked vehicle waited. The PC who met them inside, escorted them to the car. When DI Robertson and DS Thompson exited, Katherine breathed a sigh of relief, thankful they stayed after bringing her here earlier. Their familiarity gave her comfort. Tears blurred her vision. One escaped down her cheek and she dashed it away with her hand. The two other women piled into the back with her.

Once everyone was buckled in, the constable nodded to

the detective inspector. Seconds later they careered through the streets of the city, blues and twos activated, en-route to Aberdeen Airport. If they were going to hit something, she didn't want to see so clamped her eyes shut.

~ 29 ~

23rd March, 2011

The moment the vehicle came to a stop, Katherine unbuckled herself and scampered to the barrier separating them from the helipad. An ambulance waited by the corner of the terminal. She reached out with her right hand for Beryl. Cherie was on the woman's other side, her fingers entwined in the chain link.

The sky lightened bringing about a new dawn. Day five since the Super Puma ditched. Had they not learned anything from previous incidents? Would the men have survived that long? A tortuous delay occurred before the distinct sound of a helicopter became louder. Kat squeezed Beryl's hand. At almost the same instant, two hearses pulled out from behind the Nexus terminal building and joined the ambulance. Hope drained from her. Overwhelmed by nausea, her knees weakened. To keep upright, she latched hold of the fence.

With its bright landing lights illuminated, she followed the helicopter's approach to the airport. It finally landed and taxied to its bay on the tarmac. Once the rotors stopped turning, the emergency personnel approached it. One man was alive. But who? One after the other, two bodies covered in yellow vinyl sheets were unloaded and installed in the waiting hearses.

She stood by helplessly as the paramedics disappeared into the fuselage. She chewed on her bottom lip, a nervous habit she acquired years ago. An EMT emerged assisting the lone survivor of the crash. She couldn't determine the person's identity. The man had a blanket, like the ones draped over the bodies, around his shoulders, his left arm around the neck of the other paramedic. He stumbled, his weakened legs unable to support his weight, even with the aid on each side of him. Finally, the wounded man raised his head. Jared.

Katherine dashed to the gate. "Hurry up. Open the bloody thing." She urged the security guard to move faster, dancing from one foot to the other in anticipation. She glanced over at Cherie and Beryl huddled together, their faces buried.

She knew they were devastated at the outcome but was wrapped up in her own joy and relief. "Come on." Katherine couldn't wait any longer. Once the passage opened wide enough for her to fit through, she sprinted across the tarmac with her arms outstretched. When she reached him, she crashed into him with such force, she almost knocked him over. "Jared," she cried. "Yes, I'll marry you."

Also by Melanie Robertson-King

The Consequences Collection
Tim's Magic Christmas
The Secret of Hillcrest House
A Shadow in the Past (second edition)
Shadows From Her Past
Cole's Notes (Revised version)
It Happened on Dufferin Terrace
All Aboard the Canadian with Buddy and his Four Fantastic
Furry Friends!
It Happened in Gastown
(King Park Press)

Cole's Notes (A Short Story)
EFD1: Starship Goodwords – a cross genre anthology
(CARRICK PUBLISHING, 2012)

MELANIE ROBERTSON-KING

www.melanierobertson-king.com
www.melanierobertson-king.ca

Melanie Robertson-King has always been a fan of the written word. Growing up as an only child, her face was almost always buried in a book from the time she could read. Her father was one of the thousands of Home Children sent to Canada through the auspices of The Orphan Homes of Scotland, and she has been fortunate to be able to visit her father's homeland many times and even met the Princess Royal (Princess Anne) at the orphanage where he was raised.

www.ingramcontent.com/pod-product-compliance
Lightning Source LLC
Chambersburg PA
CBHW031105260626
47172CB00001B/230